"Ophelia," Abby said, "I have something to give you."

She placed a small leather pouch on the table beside me.

"What's this?"

"Runes," she said. "They belonged to my grandmother. I think they will help you focus."

I picked up the pouch and drew out the small stones. Each was white and round and had a symbol painted on it. My hand grew warm and it tingled while I held them. When their energy snaked up my arm, I quickly placed them back in the pouch."

"I want you to keep them with you at all times," Abby said, "even sleep with them under your pillow. You need to get to know them, understand their meanings."

"Are you crazy? I'm not sleeping with a bag of rocks under my pillow. That's nuts."

Abby's hands clenched. "I'm serious about this. I thought we'd have more time, but we don't. Trouble's coming and you need to be prepared."

My stomach did a slow slide to my toes at Abby's words.

"Not again," I moaned.

"Yes again," she said.

Ophelia and Abby Mysteries
by Shirley Damsgaard

CHARMED TO DEATH
WITCH WAY TO MURDER

SHIRLEY DAMSGAARD

CHARMED TO DEATH

AN OPHELIA AND ABBY MYSTERY

AVON BOOKS

An Imprint of HarperCollinsPublishers

This is a work of fiction. Names, characters, places, and incidents are products of the author's imagination or are used fictitiously and are not to be construed as real. Any resemblance to actual events, locales, organizations, or persons, living or dead, is entirely coincidental.

AVON BOOKS
An Imprint of HarperCollins*Publishers*
10 East 53rd Street
New York, New York 10022-5299

Copyright © 2006 by Shirley Damsgaard
ISBN-13: 978-0-06-079353-1
ISBN-10: 0-06-079353-8
www.avonmystery.com

First Avon Books paperback printing: April 2006

Avon Trademark Reg. U.S. Pat. Off. and in other Countries, Marca Registrada, Hecho en U.S.A.
HarperCollins® is a registered trademark of HarperCollins Publishers Inc.

Printed in the U.S.A.

10 9 8 7 6 5 4 3 2 1

To my own personal cheering section—
Eric, Christine, Scott, and Sara.
I love you.

Mom

Acknowledgments

The success of a novel truly is a team effort, and I'd like to thank "my" team:

Stacey Glick of Dystel and Goderich Literary Management, for finding Avon Books as a home for Ophelia and Abby.

Sarah Durand, Senior Editor at Morrow/Avon, and her assistant, Jeremy Cesarec. You've guided me, held my hand when necessary, and been unbelievably patient with me. Your input and ideas were invaluable to me in the writing of this novel.

Nadine Badalaty and Tristan Elwell, for designing such eye-catching covers for the series.

Danielle Bartlett, for steering a new author through the shoals of promotion.

All the copyeditors, proofreaders, sales reps, and other staff members at Avon who've worked so hard behind the scenes to make this series a success.

Pat and Gary (Hey, Michael), Sheila, Amy, Beth, Diana, Kate, Karen, Ursula, and all the booksellers I've met over the past few months. You've gone above and beyond to help promote this series.

Dr. Jerri McLemore and Paul Steinbach of the Iowa State Medical Examiners Office, for their expertise on how poor victims might meet their untimely end.

Sharon Jurgensen, Autumn Dean, and Bob Cook, for sharing all their research and answering my questions concerning hog confinement facilities and their impact on the environment.

Theresa Powell and Donna Reynolds, for covering all the bases in my absence.

My friends—Bea Coe, Kristi Elick, Linda Eckles, Cheryl Powell, and Cindy Vokes—for their support and their willingness to cajole everyone they know into reading this series. (And to Cheryl and Cindy—only you could've come up with the idea that a book about witches would make a good Christmas present!)

R.J., for insight into the Latino culture.

My family—my children, Ellen, Aunt Betty, and Uncle Arnie. You're always there to encourage me when I need it.

And last, but certainly not least, all the readers who've taken the time to express their interest in this series. You've paid me the highest compliment one can pay to a writer—you've enjoyed my stories. It doesn't get any better than that!

CHARMED TO DEATH

Prologue

While I stood in the clearing, the soft wind ruffled the strands of my hair that peeked out from beneath my hood. Overhead the branches swayed gently to the rhythm of the wind. The fennel seeds I held tightly in one hand stuck to my palm. In the other hand, I held a small polished tiger-eye crystal.

"You know, Abby, this is dumb. I don't know why we couldn't have done this at home, inside. What if somebody comes by?"

"Nobody's out this time of night. Be quiet, Ophelia, and concentrate," Abby said.

"But it's cold out here."

"Shh. Quit whining."

I turned to look at Abby. A thin sliver of light from the waning moon marked where she stood. I could make out the shadowy shape of her figure—head down, the cowl of her long white robe covering her silver hair, a robe like the one I wore. If someone had told me six months ago I would be standing in the woods in the dead of the night with my seventy-four year-old grandmother, dressed in something out of Witches "Я" Us, I'd have told them they were crazy. The snort escaped before I could stop it.

"I heard that. Quit snorting and quit resisting. It's three days before the dark planting moon and a powerful time. A time for sowing the seeds of growth. And trust me, you need to grow. The time is at hand when it will be necessary to draw on all your powers."

Closing my eyes, I shook my head in frustration. "Ahh, jeez, Abby. Not more of 'the evil is coming and circles to be closed' crap. We went through all of that last fall."

"Yes, and I was right, wasn't I?"

I felt the weight of her stare in the darkness. She did have a point. She'd been right about the evil in the small town of Summerset, the drugs and the murder. Abby's magick had saved me. And Rick Delaney.

"Quit thinking about Rick," she scolded.

Whoops. One of the dangers of having a grandmother who's psychic.

"I wasn't really 'thinking' about him. He sort of popped into my mind."

"He pops in way too often if you ask me. You can't let thoughts of that young man distract you. You knew he wasn't the one when you two first met. It wasn't your time." Abby stood straight and tipped her head back, letting the cowl fall away from her head. "Now, let's get down to business."

"Yes, ma'am." I stood like Abby, head back, arms hanging loosely at my side.

"Hold the tiger-eye firmly in your palm. Empty your mind of all except the energy of the stone. Do you feel it?"

Closing my eyes, I banished rogue thoughts of Rick Delaney and concentrated on the smooth cool stone I held. While I stroked its glassy surface with my thumb, I felt the stone grow warm. Its heat vibrated through my thumb, up my wrist, along my arm. And with the vibration came a deep sense of calm. The turmoil I felt over Rick, over who and what I was, dissipated and was replaced by peace. My breathing slowed to a whisper while the wind sighed around me.

"Think of what you wish. Say it over and over in your mind," Abby said quietly.

What did I wish? For Rick to come back to Summerset? For the path I walked to be easy? My breath caught in my lungs. No, I wished to become the person I was meant to be. To accept all my gifts and talents and use them to the best of my ability. In my mind, I repeated the same words over and over: *Give me the strength to face my destiny.*

With each thought, my breath came faster and the wind grew in intensity. I heard the sound of it whip through the tall weeds in the clearing, rustling them till they rattled. The strong gusts lifted my hair and tossed it about my shoulders. It made the hem of my robe dance around my ankles. My thoughts filled my soul and I felt as if I could burst.

"Quickly, throw the fennel seeds," Abby urged.

I opened my palm and cast the seeds to the wind. I couldn't see the wind scattering them, but I knew it did. My palm was empty, but my soul wasn't. The peace I felt remained. I stood silently and let it flow through me. Finally, lowering my head, I noticed a soft breeze once again rustling the weeds.

Opening my eyes, I watched Abby close the circle. She moved to the north, the east, the south, and, finally, the west. Walking clockwise around the clearing, she drew in the remaining energy. I felt it fade, like air slowly escaping from a balloon. When she finished, she took my hand and we started the long walk home through the woods.

"Abby, I understand the energy of the tiger-eye is for clarity and to help with my psychic abilities, but why the fennel seeds?"

In the darkness I sensed Abby's frown.

"For protection, my dear. You're going to need quite a bit this time."

One

The voices drifted through the open window at the library.

"Everyone needs to disperse right now. I'm sorry, but you can't block traffic."

"What traffic, Brett? I don't see no cars comin'."

I recognized the deep baritone voice of Stumpy Murdock, proud owner of Stumpy's Bar and Billiards.

"C'mon, Stumpy, you know I can't let you have a sit-in smack in the middle of the four-way stop. Take the demonstration someplace else."

"We're exercisin' the right to peaceful assembly."

"Yeah." Several voices cried out—one of them, the voice of my sweet grandmother.

Crap. Abby was with them. I needed to get out there before poor Brett was forced to arrest all those subversive characters.

When I rounded the corner of the library, I saw the sit-in. Several of the town's senior citizens had planted themselves in the center of the four-way. How Edna Walters ever managed to make it to a sitting position in the middle of the intersection, I'll never know. But there she was, dressed in her pink nylon jogging suit and orthopedic shoes, holding a sign that said DOWN WITH FACTORY FARMS. The sun glinted on her blue-tinted hair, while her walker stood like a silent companion by her side.

Oh Lord.

"Hey, Brett. How's it going?" I called out.

Brett turned. Two blotches, one on each cheekbone and as red as fresh strawberries, stood out on his young face. Poor guy. Brand-new police officer dressed in his blue uniform, with its sharp creases, and wearing his shiny new badge being hassled by people old enough to be his grandparents. I bet the Academy never taught him how to deal with little old ladies. Definitely in over his head.

"Ophelia, maybe you can talk some sense into these folks. If they don't move, I'm going to have to arrest them for being a public nuisance."

"Oh, you wouldn't want to do that, Brett," I said and tugged on my jacket.

"That's right, young man. If you do, I'll never bring cookies to the station again," Mrs. Walters said, shaking her finger at Brett.

"Mrs. Walters, please. Get up. I'll help you." Brett reached down and offered his hand, but Mrs. Walters swatted it away, her pink jacket crackling.

"No." Her double chin trembled with indignation. "I'm staying until Ned gets here to take our picture."

The blotches on Brett's face spread. If Ned didn't hurry, the only picture he'd get would be Brett tucking Mrs. Walters, walker and all, into the back of his patrol car. I walked over to where Abby sat next to Stumpy.

She had evidently worked in her greenhouse before organizing her seditious demonstration. She still wore her work clothes—denim jeans, a flannel work shirt, and clogs.

I took a quick look at Stumpy. Was he her coconspirator

in this? He looked back at me through his thick glasses. The lenses magnified his eyes and he reminded me of a befuddled owl sitting there. But Stumpy wasn't befuddled. He was a sharp businessman and didn't tolerate any Saturday-night drunks causing trouble. If they tried, they'd find themselves staring at the business end of Stumpy's Louisville Slugger while he escorted them out the door. Shaking my head to clear the image of Stumpy as an owl, I bent down toward Abby and lowered my voice.

"You have to do something. Brett is losing his patience."

Abby stared at me, her green eyes flashing. "Edna is right. We need Ned," she said, her voice still carrying the cadence of the mountains in Appalachia where she was raised. "He's the editor and the main reporter for *The Courier*. He might give us the publicity we need. Who knows, *The Des Moines Register* could even pick up the story Ned writes? It's too good a chance to miss."

"Do you want to go to jail for trespassing and unlawful assembly?" I asked through clenched teeth.

"Maybe," she said, cocking her head to one side. "It would make a good story."

"Abby—"

A sudden cheer stopped me. Ned Thomas had appeared down the street. He walked confidently down the wide sidewalk of the business section, past the limestone buildings that had held local entrepreneurs since the turn of the century. His camera swung from the strap around his neck and a notebook stuck out of his shirt pocket.

Relieved, I watched while Ned approached the group. He stopped at the corner and started shooting pictures. The happy group waved their signs at him in response.

I stepped back to get out of the shot. Didn't need my picture on the front page of *The Courier.*

I walked over to where Brett stood, watching Ned.

"Gosh, I'm glad he finally showed up. Last thing I wanted to do was arrest all of them," Brett said.

Feeling his distress float around him, I patted his shoulder. "Don't worry. Everyone knows you're trying to do your job."

"Yeah, but I never thought it would include arresting senior citizens." Brett shook his head. "This hog confinement thing, it's not good. People are sure steamed up about it."

I tugged at my lip. "I know. It was bad enough eight years ago when they built the farrowing site across the county line. But now they're trying to expand into this county. No one wants a facility housing eight thousand hogs built next to their place. Abby says the amount of manure they'll produce will be monumental."

Brett nodded. "We were thinking about buying a house here in Summerset, what with the new job and all, but now I don't know. My wife doesn't care for the idea of living close to a place like that. Even if it is ten miles from town, she's afraid we'll be able to smell the stink."

The waste from eight thousand hogs and a humid summer's day in Iowa was not a good combination. The stench would drift for miles on the hot breezes. And Abby's farm was only two miles from the proposed site.

"Maybe this coalition will be able to stop it," I said, waving my hand toward the group in the middle of the street.

"I don't know. From what I've read in *The Courier,* there's a lot of money behind that corporation, PP International. And the head of it, Dudley Kyle, is a smart man. A real smooth operator. It's going to be hard for a small group like this to fight something that big. Plus, the politicians aren't much help. They want the campaign contributions the corporation gives them."

"Well, knowing Abby, the group will go down fighting."

"That's what I'm afraid of. I'm worried some hotheads will take matters into their own hands. Things might get violent. It's happened before, in other towns."

I looked at Mrs. Walters, sitting by her walker, a happy smile on her face, while Ned snapped her picture. Mrs. Walters, violent? No way. The worst she could do would be to put someone in a sugar coma by feeding them too many cookies.

My eyes moved to Abby. She had other tools at her disposal. Much more effective tools than a pan full of brownies. Would she use them? No. I had never known Abby to use her magick against anyone. She was too ethical to manipulate people against their will. *Wasn't she?* She did have definite opinions about the factory farm concept. Maybe Abby and I should have a talk.

Ned finished taking his pictures and walked over to where we stood.

"Hi, Brett, Ophelia. Brett, care to make a comment on today's little demonstration?"

"I don't think so, Ned," Brett answered, watching the group as they began to struggle to their feet. "I'd better go help. Looks like some of them are having trouble getting up."

"Do you have a comment, Ophelia?" Ned asked, stepping closer to me.

"Nope," I replied and held my ground.

Ned grinned. "Okay, how about dinner tonight instead?"

I returned his grin. "We had dinner two nights ago.

And I'm leaving in a couple of days for the librarians' convention in Iowa City, so I'm having dinner with Abby. But thanks for asking."

"That's right. I forgot. Darci's going with you, isn't she?"

"Yeah. It should be an interesting trip." I thought of my assistant, Darci—big hair, tight sweaters—at the librarians' convention. It would be like a peacock loose among a bunch of chickens. I chuckled.

"Think Darci will have a good time?" Ned asked.

I snorted. "Are you kidding? Darci always has a good time. She's already been asking about the nightlife."

"Oh yeah," Ned said, snapping his fingers. "I remember. You lived in Iowa City, didn't you? Got any special places to show her?"

Memories of my life five years ago crowded my mind and the smile slipped from my face. The library at the university where I'd spent my days surrounded by the smell of old books and young bodies. Picnics at Coralville Lake. The way my friend Brian had laughed and joked around at those picnics. Always the life of the party.

I shut my eyes against the sudden jab of pain in my heart when the last memory of Brian rocked before my eyes—Brian lying dead in a Dumpster, placed there by the killer who'd butchered him.

"No. No, there aren't any special places," I replied, my steps heavy as I walked away. "Not any more."

I saw the windows of Abby's farmhouse glowing warmly in the spring twilight while I drove up her winding driveway. As I parked the car and got out, I stopped, pulling my lightweight jacket around me, and stared at the house.

White with dark green shutters, a wide porch wrapped around three sides and I knew the third board near the door would creak when I stepped on it. Near the porch stood the old maple where Grandpa had hung my tire swing for me as a child. Inside, Abby's kitchen would be warm with the heat from Abby's old-fashioned cookstove and the light from the kerosene lamps would be reflected on the steam-covered windows. Though the rest of the house had modern conveniences, Abby preferred keeping her kitchen similar to the one in the cabin she'd lived in growing up.

Abby really believed in old ways, I thought, smiling to myself—and not only when it came to the style of her kitchen.

While I stood there, a sense of peace settled over me. Abby would be in the kitchen now, mashing the potatoes and making the gravy. The food for tonight's dinner would be my favorites. It was a ritual. When I was a child, I spent my summers with her and Grandpa. And on the last night before I went home she would make a special dinner for me. We'd sit around her big kitchen table, eating and laughing at Grandpa's gentle teasing. The love I knew they shared surrounded us.

But like Brian, Grandpa wasn't here any more. He had died of a sudden heart attack when I was fifteen. Abby's magick hadn't saved him, just as mine hadn't saved Brian. Regret tugged at my heart and some of the peace I felt dissolved. So many losses, so many people I loved—gone. It wasn't fair.

The door swung wide suddenly and Abby stood in its portal, wiping hands on the apron tied around her waist. The light from inside the house shone around her till it seemed to be a part of her. The light reached out to me, pulling me up the walk and into Abby's waiting arms.

"Hi, sweetie. How are you tonight?" Abby whispered.

The faint smell of wood-smoke, mixed with the scent of her favorite perfume, Lily of the Valley, tickled my nose. And the warmth of her body seeped into mine, restoring the peace I'd felt earlier.

"Fine, now. I was standing on the walk remembering. You, Grandpa, the dinners you always made on my last night. The memories made me sad."

Abby's arms tightened around me. "It's okay, honey. Sad is good sometimes. It means we haven't forgotten," she said, stepping back and placing her arm around my shoulder. "And as long as we remember, they're really not gone, you know."

"Yeah, I know, but sometimes it's hard. The remembering."

With her arm still draped around my shoulder, Abby shut the door. "Let's go eat, but before you leave tonight, I have something I want to give you." She gave me a light squeeze.

When I entered the kitchen, the aroma of Abby's dinner once again transported me back to my childhood. All I had to do was close my eyes and the images would materialize. Abby was right. Someone you have loved is never gone as long as you remember. The thought eased my spirits.

"This smells wonderful. What can I do to help?"

"Nothing," Abby said, waving me to the table. She went to the oven and began taking out plates full of food.

"What are we having?" I asked, pulling out a chair and sitting.

The steam in the kitchen had caused little silver tendrils of hair to escape the braid she wore wrapped around the top of her head. She swiped one away from her face with the back of her hand and peeked at me over her shoulder.

"Your favorites, of course," she said with a quick grin. "Roast beef, carrots, potatoes and gravy. And cherry pie with ice cream for dessert."

"Wow," I said, feeling my appetite jump. "I need to go away more often."

"Oh, by the way, your mother called," Abby said in an even voice and set my plate in front of me.

A groan slipped out. My mother, Margaret Mary McDonald Jensen, a former English professor, had retired several years ago and was living in Florida with my father, a retired history professor. A small, fine-boned, almost frail-looking woman. But looks are deceiving. I ought to know; I lived with the woman for eighteen years. She had the energy of a small tornado and the subtlety of a ball-peen hammer. When you'd least expect it, she'd hit you with some remark, some observation. *Boing,* right between the eyes. She was a force not to be ignored and one that often overwhelmed me.

"Everything okay?" I asked cautiously.

"Yes," she said, removing her apron and hanging it on a hook by the back door.

"Umm—she's not coming for a visit, is she?" I watched Abby carefully.

"No, she's not coming for a visit. She hadn't been able to reach you and she wanted to know how you were. You should call her."

I winced. My phone conversations with my mother usually involved a lot of questions—hers—and a lot of mumbled, semicoherent responses—mine. There wasn't a single aspect of my life she wasn't interested in and the idea of personal boundaries did not exist for Margaret Mary Jensen when it came to her only child. It wasn't that we didn't get along, we did, but I had always related better to Abby and my father than to my mother.

Abby saw my expression and gave me an amused look. "Come on, you know your mother loves you and wants what's best for you."

"Yeah, well, I love her too," I said as my finger traced the pattern on Abby's tablecloth. "It's just easier to love her when she's in another state."

She laughed. "Don't worry. She and your father are staying in Florida for now. They're both busy, but they might come to Iowa later on this summer."

Oh, goody. At least I'd have a couple months to prepare, to build my stamina so I could keep up with my mother. Forget it. If I wasn't able to stay ahead of her when I was a teenager, I doubt, now that I'm in my thirties, I'd be able to now.

Abby took a seat across from me at the table. "Quit worrying and eat. Your dinner will get cold."

Everything tasted as good as it smelled, and I ate as if it were my last meal. Abby watched me while she ate, with a benign look on her face. Finally finished, I pushed my plate away, only to have it replaced with another plate filled with pie and ice cream.

I held my stomach and tipped back in my chair. "Jeez, Abby, I don't know if I can eat any more."

"Sure you can." She stopped and watched me scoop up a large bite of pie and ice cream.

A small smile crossed her face before she continued. "Ophelia, I want to talk to you about something."

"Okay. Shoot," I mumbled, my mouth full.

"It's about your training. I have something to give you."

The fork hesitated between the plate and my mouth. "What?"

Abby stood and crossed to the kitchen cupboard. Opening the door, she removed a small leather pouch from the shelf. She placed it by my plate and then took her seat again.

My eyes narrowed while I focused on the worn pouch. "What's this?"

"Runes," she said with a slight shrug.

"What?"

"Runes. They belonged to my grandmother. I think they will help you focus," she said, sliding her own plate to the side and calmly folding her hands.

I picked up the pouch and drew out the small stones. Each was white and round and each had a symbol painted on it. My hand grew warm and it tingled while I held them. When their energy snaked up my arm, I quickly placed them back in their pouch.

"Abby, I don't know about this," I said, pushing the plate with the half-eaten pie away. "They make me nervous."

"Oh, don't be silly," she chided. "They're only rocks with symbols painted on them. It's how you use them that matters. And these stones will help you channel your intuitive abilities. I want you to keep them with you at all times, even sleep with them under your pillow. You need to get to know them, understand their meanings."

"Are you crazy?" I leaned back in my chair and folded my arms across my chest. "I'm not sleeping with a bag of rocks under my pillow. That's nuts."

Abby's folded hands clenched. "I'm serious about this. I thought we'd have more time, but we don't. Trouble's coming and you need to be prepared."

My stomach did a slow slide to my toes at Abby's words.

"Not again," I said, leaning back in my chair.

"Yes, again," she said slowly. "I told you last fall that there were circles in your life that needed to be closed. The runes will help you do that."

"Look, what happened last fall is over," I said, shaking my head. "Adam Hoffman, Benny, Jake—they're all in prison. Adam was convicted of murder and manufacturing drugs. Benny and Jake were found guilty of conspiracy for helping him. None of them is getting out anytime soon. Rick won an award for his story about the bust and went back to Minnesota. Everything got tied up with a neat little bow, so there's nothing left to close."

Abby stared at me intently, not giving in even a millimeter.

"Oh no," I gasped, suddenly understanding what she meant. "Not Brian's murder. That's over and done with too."

"It was never solved," she insisted. "And you are going back to Iowa City the day after tomorrow. While you're there, you could go talk to the police and see if they've had any more leads."

"It's been almost five years since it happened. I'm sure whatever leads they had are cold. The case is probably buried in their files by now."

Did my voice sound too desperate?

"Maybe, maybe not. You won't know if you don't talk to them."

"Well, I'm not going to do it," I declared and gave Abby a determined look. "At first they thought I was involved with his murder and their investigation made my life a living hell. That one detective, Comacho, was such a"—a quick look at Abby's face stopped me from saying the first word that sprang to mind—"a jerk," I amended, finishing the sentence.

Abby's eyebrows shot up anyway.

"Sorry, but he was," I said, looking away. Staring at the flickering light of the kerosene lamp, I took a deep breath and let it out slowly. "They were right. I was involved, but not the way they thought. I'd seen it all in a premonition. Couldn't tell them that, though, could I? Do you remember the guilt I felt because I wasn't able to stop the murderer? The breakdown I had because of it?" I looked back at Abby. "No. I'm not opening old wounds."

Abby's face was full of compassion. "Sometimes we have to open them in order for them to heal properly."

"I'm not," I said stubbornly. "My life is getting better. I'm no longer living behind the emotional wall I put up after Brian's death. *I* have opened up. I have friends again. I've found some peace in my life. I'm not going to risk what I've gained over something I can't change. I've even accepted that I'm psychic, that it's my heritage, my path."

"Ophelia, this *is* your path."

"My path is to relive the worst time of my life?" I asked, crossing my arms.

"No, your path is to find justice for Brian. To find the truth," Abby said quietly. "It's your gift."

"Well," I said and frowned. "That gift sucks."

The discussion was over as far as I was concerned. I reached out and pulled the plate with the unfinished pie toward me. Picking up my fork, I gazed down at the pie. My fork stopped midswoop.

The juice from the cherries had mingled with the melted ice cream, turning it a sickly red. Thick, congealed, it reminded me of blood.

Two

I pushed back my chair again, stood, and walked to the window. Through the steamy window and past my shadowy reflection, I saw the crescent moon hanging over the treetops, waxing. The dark of the moon—the Planting Moon—had passed. I had planted the seeds for my soul's growth that night in the woods, but I didn't like the direction it was taking me. I turned around and looked at Abby, sitting patiently at the table.

"Abby, I want a nice simple life." I shook my head. "I don't want the responsibility."

"With every gift comes responsibility, Ophelia. You do have a choice. You can accept your gift and everything that goes with it or you can deny it. But if you deny it, you will never be the person you were truly meant to be."

"And my responsibility is to solve a five-year-old murder?" I asked, my tone bleak.

"Possibly."

I turned back to the window. My shadowy reflection was still there, staring back at me. The same reflection I saw every day, same brown hair pulled up in a twist, same brown eyes, same mouth. Yup, it was still me. But it was a *me* who was changing, going through a transformation, whether I liked it or not. Would I still be me when it was finished? The thought frightened me.

Abby's reflection joined mine in the window. Through the thin material of my shirt, I felt her warm hands on my arms.

She gave them a slight squeeze before dropping her hands to her side. "I know. You're afraid. That's all right. Your spirit guides will help you."

Puffing out my cheeks, I exhaled. "Okay, run this spirit guide thing by me again."

I watched her reflection in the window while she answered me.

"Your spirit guides are those who have chosen to help you, to guide you on your path. We all have them. They're the little voices in our ears, the thoughts that pop unbidden into our minds, our sudden inspirations. They won't tell you what to do. There are lessons you must learn on your own, but they will be there to help."

"Hey, I'm not going to start seeing dead people like that kid in *Sixth Sense,* am I?" I spun around. "I really, *really,* would not want that."

Chuckling, Abby crossed to the table and sat. "No, you're not going to start seeing dead people. At least, I don't think so."

"That's it? You don't think so?" I asked as I joined her.

She shook her head while she hunched forward and placed arms on the table. "You've never shown any talent for it."

I rolled my eyes. "Well, thank God for small favors."

"I'm told it's not that bad. Your great aunt Mary saw souls who had 'crossed over.' It never bothered her much. She always said it was a comfort."

"Ha," I scoffed. "Wasn't she the one you said did astral projection?"

"Yes."

"Peachy—seeing dead people and floating around. As if I want to do either one," I said in a derisive voice.

"Oh," she said, waving a hand as if to shoo away my remark. "Quit worrying about it. You have enough on your mind without worrying about abilities you may or may not have. Concentrate on those we know you do have."

"That's what I've been trying to do, but I don't seem to be getting anywhere," I huffed. "I think Darci's more perceptive than I am. And she's not the one who's supposed to be psychic."

"You're trying too hard. Relax and it will come. The runes will help."

My look flickered to the bag lying on the table. "Why runes?"

Abby smiled. "They're part of your heritage. You should have an affinity for them. It's believed your ancestors, the Vikings, not only used them as their alphabet, but also for magick. And the mysticism of the runes is steeped with the legends of the old gods—Thor, Freya, and Tyr. The Viking shaman, or *vitki,* would cast the runes, either on a cloth or the ground. He would interpret what they meant."

"But aren't the stones evil?"

"Humph." Abby frowned. "I told you, they're rocks with symbols painted on them. And the symbols represent that which the universe is made of. Is the universe all good or all bad?"

"Of course not."

"Neither are the runes. They can be used for good or bad. It's what's in the heart and mind of the person using them that make the difference. If you want to use them to curse someone, you can. But remember," she said and gave me a stern look, "whatever energy you send out into the world will come back to you three times over."

Abby lifted the bag and shifted it from one hand to the other. I heard the stones rattling back and forth in the pouch. Reaching out, I took it from her. The bag felt heavy and I felt the hum of their energy through the worn leather. I looked up to see Abby watching me.

"Ophelia, *these* are for you. You're one who's tied to the earth. You have the ability, through touch, to feel the earth's energy."

"You mean like what happened the night in the machine shed, after Jake, Benny, and Adam Hoffman caught Rick and me snooping around Adam's meth lab? When Jake and Adam were going to kill us?"

"That's right. The shed was built on top of a special place, a place of magick. You felt it moving beneath the surface and you were able to harness the energy and use the magick to distract the three of them long enough for you and Rick to escape."

A slow shiver ran up my spine remembering that night, the *thrum* of the energy I had felt moving beneath me, through me. The shed had exploded in sound when I forced that energy up and away from me. The wind howled, pigeons flew wildly around the rafters, rats rushed from the darkened corners. Jake and Adam began to shoot at anything that moved, while Benny, Jake's brother, knelt on his knees, sobbing his fear. All the confusion had allowed Rick and me to escape into the night. Unfortunately, Adam followed us.

Looking at the bag cradled in my hand, I thought of how we had stumbled across the rough fields in the blinding snowstorm—with Adam right behind us. I shuddered at the memory.

"Never mind that I still managed to get shot when Adam caught up with us at the old cemetery," I said and put the bag down, rubbing the healed wound in my side.

Abby reached across the table and stroked my other hand. "There's something else I want to give you."

What now?

She stood and walked to the cupboard, opened it, and removed a book. She placed it in front of me, its cover stained and faded. It was an old-fashioned ledger.

"This is the journal my grandmother used. It contains all her notes, her observations, descriptions of her work with the runes. It would be helpful for you to read it."

Opening the cover, I read the faint spidery handwriting.

Thurisaz—giant, troll, demon...

I slammed the cover shut and my eyes locked on Abby. "Why? Why are you giving me these things now?"

Abby took my hands in hers. I felt the warmth, but it was more than simple body heat. Deeper, hotter, and the heat throbbed in my palms.

"Feel it?"

I nodded.

"It's the power, the gift you possess. Because of this gift, the stones will sing to you. And you will hear their song."

I smiled. "That's almost poetic."

Abby smiled back. "It can be, but the song won't always be a pretty one. Runes don't lie and the things shown might not be pleasant."

I released Abby's hands. "That's the part that scares me."

"I know, but true courage means facing the unpleasant in spite of the fear."

"Will the runes tell me what I'm to do?"

"No."

I scooted my chair back. "Well, that stinks."

Abby grinned. "What do you want? The runes or your spirit guides to tell you, 'Go to the corner of Fifth and Madison at two o'clock on Thursday and you'll meet your soulmate. He'll be wearing a red carnation'?"

"That would be nice."

She shook her head and her grin widened. "Honey, your gift will help you, allow you to help others. But in the end, it's your life, and you're the one who must live it. You can hear the song, but it's up to you to listen, to choose whether or not to follow it."

"And if I don't follow?"

"Like I said, your choice. Free will overrides all, even a gift as great as yours."

"If I don't listen, I won't be fulfilling my destiny. Right?"

Abby watched me steadily.

"Okay, I know when I'm beat. Other than sleep with a bag of rocks under my pillow, what else do I do?"

"Grandma's journal will explain. When I was a child, I watched her work with the runes. Sometimes she would cast all the stones and read them. Sometimes she would draw one at a time and place them in a specific position. Each position meant something and the meaning was affected by the rune next to it. It's all in her journal."

"Great. Sleep with the rocks and read the journal, then all will become clear," I said with no small dose of sarcasm.

Abby laughed. "Not exactly. Once you become familiar with the runes and their traditional meanings, you'll need to start thinking outside the box."

"Great," I said, throwing my hand in the air. "What's that supposed to mean? 'Thinking outside the box'?"

"Seeing beyond what's there, developing your own meanings for the runes. After working with them, you'll find certain stones represent specific things to you."

I arched my eyebrow. "And, no doubt, those meanings will be very cryptic."

"Ophelia, you're looking for certainties, and there aren't any. Not in life and not with your gift."

"Okay. Okay. I may accept this, but that doesn't mean I have to like it." I took a quick look at the clock. "It's late and I'd better get going." Picking up the pouch and journal, I stood to go. "Oh, do you still want me to come to your big community meeting tomorrow night, don't you?"

She nodded. "Yes. The meeting could get sticky. The Department of Natural Resources, state legislators, members of the County Board of Supervisors, and, of course, Dudley Kyle will all be there."

"What about Harley Walters and his gang?"

Abby pursed her lips. "Yes, they'll be there. It'll be a challenge to keep Harley's group from turning the meeting into a circus."

Harley Walters fit the definition of *redneck* perfectly. Baseball cap, shirt with sleeves ripped out, jeans, and work boots. The scruffy two-day beard was optional.

He had the personality of a rock and hated my family for some reason. Especially my mother. Mention the name Margaret Mary Jensen to Harley and a big vein in his forehead would immediately stand at attention. I'd never been able to find out the reason for his hatred. Abby's response was always: "Ask your mother." And when I did ask my mother, her answer was: "It's not my story to tell." Finally I gave up asking and stayed as far away from Harley as possible. Not hard to do since we didn't exactly move in the same circles.

"Poor Edna," I said, "how did she ever wind up with a grandson like Harley?"

Abby sighed. "Harley's had a rough life. He was so young when his father died. His stepfather was a drunk and lost most of the land Harley's mother had inherited, so there are reasons for Harley's bitterness..." She sighed again. "But those reasons don't excuse some of his behavior."

"What behavior?" My ears perking up.

"Ask your mother."

Dang. Foiled again.

Crossing to where Abby sat, I leaned down and gave her a quick peck on the cheek. "Thanks for dinner. It was wonderful." Straightening, I moved toward the door.

"Wait, Ophelia."

The concerned tone of her voice made me look at her. "Yes?"

She hesitated. "Umm—please find the time to work with the runes while you're gone."

I watched her, perplexed. "Okay. I said I would, but why is this suddenly so important?"

Looking down, she picked up a spoon and tapped it on the table.

"Abby, what's going on? It's something about Brian's murder, isn't it? It's why you were insistent I talk to the police again." I walked back to the table and took the spoon from her hand. "You've had a vision."

She stood and put both hands on my shoulders. "There will be two men, both dark. One good. One evil. One who kills for a reason."

The blood slowly drained from my face. Brian's killer. Did Abby mean I would meet Brian's killer?

Three

My dinner sat like a stone in my stomach while I tossed and rolled in bed. Either it was the rich food or the runes poking me from beneath my pillow that kept me awake. Giving up on sleep, I reached for the journal on my nightstand. I squinted at the faint handwriting. Jeez, this had to be almost a hundred years old. The first words were the ones I had read at Abby's, but this time I forced myself to read the rest.

> *Thurisaz—giant, troll, demon, torturer of women, said to be used to evoke those from the under-world. The hammer of Thor. A rune indicating challenges, tests. Symbol of thorns—used both to defend and destroy. Brambles were used as enclosures to defend villages. Criminals were executed by being thrown on pikes [brambles] shoved into the ground...*

Once again, I slammed the book shut. Nice mental image—someone writhing in misery while the thorns punctured their body. Not good reading material before bedtime. Fluffing my pillow and turning off the lamp, I rolled over and tried to sleep. But with sleep came the dream.

I walked the silent streets, my steps splashing through dark puddles. Fog swirled around my ankles with a cold that clung to my legs. I knew evil hid in the shadows, beyond the faint glow of the streetlights. I sensed it, felt it wash over me in palpitating waves. There, ahead of me, lurking around the corner of the next building. My steps slowed. Did I want to see what lay around the corner? Did I have the courage to face it? I hesitated, remembering Abby's words, *True courage is facing what we fear.* I quickened my pace, determined to confront the evil.

Rounding the corner, I saw him. Dressed all in black, he carried a bundle, wrapped in a tarp, over his shoulder. His stride was long and I ran to catch up. But he stayed ahead of me. He slowed when he approached a Dumpster with pieces of garbage sticking out from beneath its lid. Stepping into the dim light, he quickly lifted the lid and dumped the bundle he carried inside the Dumpster. He turned and walked away.

I approached the Dumpster. Did I look inside or run to catch him? A sense of inevitability drew me to it. I had to see the truth. I lifted the lid and pulled the tarp back from the bundle he had thrown so carelessly inside.

Brian lay twisted on top of the garbage, with his head at an unnatural angle. Starting at his feet, my eyes traveled up his broken body. Defense wounds sliced across his opened hands and his shirt was ripped from the slash of a knife. But the worst was the wound that ran from his left ear to his right. Blood from the cut had ran down his neck and soaked his shirt. On his forehead, carved with deadly precision, was a five-pointed star. His dead eyes were wide open and still held the terror of his last moments. His lips were a dusky blue, and in my dream they moved with silent words.

Startled and sickened, I jumped back from the Dumpster and the lid shut with a *clang* that echoed in the alley. I whirled to see the dark figure retreating into the night. No. I would not allow him to escape, not this time. This time I would see the monster's face. I ran after him.

My heart pounded in my chest. Was it from running or from what I had seen? I didn't know. All I knew was that I had to catch the monster before he killed again. I chased him down the street and into an open field.

Turn around so I can see your face, I thought, but he kept up his pace. Air wheezed from my burning lungs as I ran faster. He came to a hedge and barreled through it. I followed, but before I could clear it, brambles reached out and snagged my clothes. Prickly branches wrapped around my legs and held me fast.

"Damn you. Turn around," I cried while the figure disappeared in the darkness.

My eyes popped open at the sound of my own voice. I scanned the room in panic while I struggled to sit up. Familiar shadows surrounded me: my dresser on the far wall and my reading chair by the window.

Okay, I'm in my own bed with all the covers kicked off and my body's drenched in sweat, not running through a park in Iowa City, chasing a murderer. I let out a shaky breath.

Placing my hand over my heart, I felt it pounding. Near my bed, I saw two eyes staring at me from out of the darkness. My dog, Lady. A mixed breed—half German shepherd, half wolf—her head easily reached the top of the mattress. She whimpered and pressed her cold nose against my bare arm.

"It's okay, girl," I said, patting her head.

I felt the bed suddenly dip at my feet and I watched a large black shape slink toward me, almond eyes glowing orange in the night. The shape crept up the mattress until it reached my lap, and with a pounce, settled on my legs. A loud purr rumbled in the silence of the room as my cat, Queenie, began to give herself a thorough cleaning.

I tried to wipe the image of Brian lying in the Dumpster from my mind, but the scene danced in the shadows of my bedroom. The blood, the terror in Brian's sightless eyes, his blue lips. My hand stroking Queenie's soft black fur trembled.

That dream, that vision of horror, was the one that haunted me five years ago. It started the night of Brian's murder, the night I wasn't able to save him with my magick, my powers. The guilt caused a breakdown and changed my life. It had been a long time since I'd dreamed of Brian's murder. Why tonight?

I reached over and flicked on the lamp and the soft light chased the remaining shadows away. Looking at the nightstand, I saw the journal. Did reading about brambles, demons, torture, trigger the dream? Was it only random firings of the subconscious brought on by the words I'd read? Or was it more? Was it a manifestation of my so-called gift?

Frustrated, I threw myself back against my pillow, disturbing Queenie. With an indignant look at me, she jumped off the bed and marched over to where Lady had settled. Plopping down, she resumed her bath.

I rubbed my temples while thoughts of Brian's murder bounced through my brain. What good is my gift if it doesn't answer my questions? Wait a second. The dream was different tonight. I'd never dreamed of chasing the killer before. And something else was different tonight. What was it? I forced myself to close my eyes and think, relive what I'd seen.

Oh my God. I jerked away from my pillow. Brian's mouth had moved and I remembered, remembered what his soundless words were.

"Help me."

Four

My lack of sleep the night before had made for a long day at the library and the last thing I wanted to do was attend a community meeting about hogs. But I had promised Abby.

The parking lot of the First Methodist Church was full by the time I arrived. Every car in town was there— the sedate sedans driven by the senior element, SUVs purchased to hold growing families, and four-wheel drive trucks looking like something from a monster truck competition, with tires so large and so far from the ground that it would take a stepladder to climb into the cab.

I watched from my car as people walked to the door, stopping along the way to talk to neighbors in hushed tones. Everyone's face wore a serious look: no laughter, no jokes. These people were fighting for their homes, especially people like Abby who would be living near the hog confinement buildings and sewage lagoon. Health issues stemming from the close proximity to the lagoon, the stench, and dropping property values were all concerns. Everyone had a reason to look serious— and worried.

After exiting my car, I walked quickly to the building. As I did, I felt people watching me. No doubt, they were surprised to see me at the meeting, I thought. Until a few months ago, I'd kept to myself after moving to Summerset. It had only been recently that I'd begun to let people, other than Abby, into my life. Ned, Darci, and a few others made up the small circle of friends that I trusted. The stares I felt on my back made my skin tingle. I walked faster.

Once inside the church's meeting hall, I stopped. Currents of emotion flowed in the confined space. Fear, anxiety, anger—all eddied around me like swirling fog, the tendrils infiltrating my mind. I shut my eyes and concentrated on imagining myself in a bubble, a shield against what I sensed. A wall to hold the feelings of others at bay. When my wall was firmly in place, I opened my eyes and scanned the room.

A long table had been placed at the front of the room and chairs were assembled in rows. Several of the rows were already full, but a lot of people stood milling around. I spotted our local state representative, George Saunders, going from group to group, shaking hands and doing a bit of backslapping. His face didn't mirror the worried expression of his constituents. Instead, he wore the practiced look of a seasoned politician. Concerned and attentive. But I noticed how, occasionally, his eyes would slide around the room, marking the next group to schmooze. After a final handshake and a firm pat on the shoulder, he'd move on.

Harley and his boys stood to my left, leaning against the wall. Some had their hands shoved in their pockets. Others stood with their arms crossed tightly over their chests. And all of them appeared ready for a fight.

Dudley Kyle and his group stood on the opposite side

of the room from Harley. Dudley was dressed in navy Dockers and a navy and white pinstriped shirt. His tasseled loafers screamed "expensive."

My gaze moved from Dudley to Harley over by the wall. He watched Dudley too. His eyebrows were knitted tightly together above eyes full of hostility, eyes that never left the spot where Dudley stood. The corners of his mouth dropped down in a scowl.

Dudley knew Harley watched him. Quick looks in Harley's direction were accompanied by a lot of nodding and low voices from the group knotted around Dudley. I recognized one of them as a member of the County Board of Supervisors. Talk about sleeping with the enemy.

But the tension was what I noticed the most. It stretched like a cord between the two men, taut and ready to break. Abby was right. The meeting could get sticky.

From my position by the door, I saw Abby at the front of the room with a cluster of people around her—Stumpy all spiffed up in a shirt and tie, Edna Walters with her walker in tow, and several more of the senior group. Abby's eyes met mine and she gave me a *thumbs up*. I smiled in return.

Without warning, another emotion crossed my radar, trying to penetrate my wall. It didn't come from Harley or Dudley Kyle. And it wasn't vague or insubstantial. It was hard and driving and it battered against my protection, looking for a chink. My hand instinctively went to the talisman I wore around my neck. I closed my eyes, while in my mind, I fought to keep my wall intact.

"Hey, Miss Ophelia."

The battering stopped. I turned to see Gus Pike standing next to me.

"Gus. How are you?" I asked smiling and held out my hand.

I was surprised to see him at the meeting. Gus Pike had to be almost eighty and lived in a shanty out in the boonies, south of town. He was even more reclusive than I'd been and his main companion was his goat, Charlie. I'd met Gus while on a walk with Lady, after she'd tried to make friends with his chickens, much to their distress. He'd been so kind and understanding about Lady's misbehavior that we became friends.

Gus shyly took my hand in his. His bad eye, the one locked in a permanent squint, twitched rapidly while he gave my hand a hearty shake. "Fine, Miss Ophelia. Ever since you gave me this here necklace," he said, reaching around his neck and pulling out an amulet of malachite suspended on a copper wire. "It's working wonders against the arthritis."

"Good," I said, giving his hand another quick shake and releasing it. "I'm glad. How's Charlie?"

"Oh, tolerable. He had a bellyache last night. I figured he must'a ate something spoiled. But you know how goats are." He gave me a toothless grin. "They'll eat anything."

"What are you doing here tonight, Gus?"

His grin faded while he shook his head. "Bad's coming, Miss Ophelia. Don't know if it's this here feller with the hogs or what. But I can feel it in my bones. Thought I'd better come here tonight and see if it was him or not."

Abby had always said she thought Gus had some psychic ability. Maybe she was right. Before I could answer Gus, a sharp rap from the front of the room drew our attention.

"If everyone would please take their seats now, we'll get started," Abby said from the front table.

I looked at Gus. "Shall we find a seat, Gus?"

"Naw. I think I'll go stand by the door. Then I can

leave right quick when this shindig's over." Gus took my hand again and gave it a small pat. "You've been a good friend, Miss Ophelia. You take care now. Bye."

With that he released my hand and shuffled off.

"You're a damn liar."

Heads swiveled to watch Harley, still leaning against the wall and still glaring at Dudley Kyle.

The meeting had been going on for hours. Kyle, Saunders, and the county supervisor had wiggled around every argument and every question that Abby's group brought up without addressing the issues. Tempers were beginning to rise.

Turning back after Harley's remark, I observed the men sitting with Kyle at the front table. Saunders, the state representative, wore a tight smile, while the county supervisor passed a hand over his forehead as if he were wiping away perspiration. The other two men seated at the table shuffled the notes that lay on the table in front of them. The only one who met Harley's look straight on was Kyle.

"Why do you think I'm lying, Harley?" Dudley asked with a smug smile.

" 'Cause you are."

Great answer, Harley, I thought, shaking my head.

I glanced over at Abby. She gave me a slight shrug of her shoulders. She knew as well as I did that Dudley Kyle would make verbal mincemeat of Harley any minute now.

Dudley knew it too. His smile became wider. "Harley, it's a matter of public record that my house is located near one of our facilities. I couldn't lie about it."

"Yeah, well what about the flies?" Harley asked.

"What flies?"

"The flies that swarm around a hog lot in the summer. They're so bad, I heard people living near one of your lots can't go outside."

"Nonsense. My wife and I spend a lot of time outdoors in the summer."

"But Mr. Kyle, isn't it true you spend most of the summer in Minnesota and the rest traveling in Europe?" asked a voice from the back of the room. "Away from the hog lots?"

Kyle's smile slipped a little when he looked at the speaker standing near Gus.

Whoever the man was, he was a stranger to me. About my age, with dark blond hair, and blue eyes pinned directly on Dudley Kyle. The man held a notebook in one hand and a pen in the other. A reporter, maybe? Whoever he was, he wouldn't be as easy a mark for Kyle as Harley.

"You didn't answer my question, Mr. Kyle," the stranger said.

Dudley's smile slipped a little more. "Well…" He paused and leaned back in his chair. Picking up a pencil, Dudley rolled it back and forth in his palms. "Ahh, yes. We travel in the summer."

"And isn't it true that the remainder of the year, you're at your home in Colorado?" the stranger persisted.

"Ummm—"

"Look," the supervisor interrupted, rescuing his buddy. "This meeting isn't about whether Dudley has flies or how much time he spends in Iowa. It's about the impact this facility will have on our community."

Abby shot to her feet. "You're right. We do need to know the impact." Turning her head, she looked straight at Kyle. "Can you tell us, Mr. Kyle, how you plan to get rid of the twenty million gallons of raw sewage your hogs will produce in a year."

"We'll inject the manure into the cropland, enriching the soil," Kyle said.

"What cropland?" Abby asked, arching an eyebrow.

The smug look returned to Kyle's face. "You've seen the maps, Mrs. McDonald. You know what fields we'll use."

Abby squared her shoulders and gave Kyle a piercing look. "Yes, I have, Mr. Kyle, but have you? If you have, you know that those fields are considered at high risk for erosion. Any chemical, natural or synthetic, will wash down into the stream every time it rains, polluting not only the stream but the river it drains into."

"Yeah," hollered one of Harley's boys. "Instead of shit rolling downhill, the shit flows downstream."

A chorus of "Yeah" and "That's right" erupted throughout the room.

"Now, now," said the supervisor, waving his hands at the crowd. "Everybody settle down. Mrs. McDonald here has a valid concern. One I'm sure the Department of Natural Resources will take into consideration before they approve PP International's permit to build."

"It's more than a valid concern," Abby said, turning her eyes from Kyle to the county supervisor. "We intend to prove PP International's facility will pollute the water beyond the DNR's guidelines if they use the fields specified. And without those fields, PP International doesn't have enough cropland set aside to handle the manure from their facility. The DNR will have to reject their permit."

The room went silent and a shiver of fear tickled up my spine. Abby had issued a challenge, and from the look on Kyle's face, he didn't like it. He was a powerful man, working for a powerful company. Abby was a senior citizen running a greenhouse. And there'd been rumors about what had happened in other towns to people who'd crossed PP International. I didn't want Abby to be one of those "people." Worry squeezed at me while I skimmed the faces of Abby's neighbors. Who would support Abby if trouble came? Or would she face it alone? Was that what Gus meant when he said, "Bad's coming."

The stranger in the back of the room caught my eye and winked.

"Excuse me," he called out, stepping forward. "Will the DNR also take into consideration the Clean Air Bill pending before the state legislature?"

Hmm, maybe Abby had an unknown ally? The pressure in my chest eased.

"Maybe you'd like to answer that question, Mr. Saunders?" the stranger continued.

Saunders shifted his weight from side to side, squirming in his seat. "Ahh, the DNR can't consider the bill, because it hasn't passed yet."

"The bill hasn't passed because it's held up in committee. Right, Mr. Saunders?" asked the stranger.

"Ahh, well . . ." His eyes darted toward Kyle, but Kyle ignored him. Saunders cleared his throat and straightened in his chair. Looking out over the crowd, he folded his hands on the table and tried to look earnest. "I can assure everyone we'll examine the bill closely. The health of our citizens is of utmost importance. But we must be careful that the bill isn't so restrictive that our most important resource, the family farm, is put in jeopardy," he said and gave the crowd a sanctimonious smile.

Nobody cheered at his statement and a look of

disappointment crossed Saunders's face. *Too bad,* I thought sarcastically, *that same line worked* so *well during his campaign.* I dismissed Saunders and turned back to the stranger.

He gave me a slight nod and stepped back into the crowd.

The meeting soon ended after Abby fired her salvo at Kyle. People again gathered in clusters, talking. Dudley Kyle and group beat a hasty retreat out the door without speaking to anyone. Score one for Abby's side.

Winding my way through the crowd, I made my way to where the stranger stood. By the time I reached him, Gus had left and the stranger stood alone.

"Hi," I said, extending my hand. "I'm Ophelia Jensen."

"Charles Thornton," he said, taking my hand and giving it a firm shake. "Nice to meet you."

Up close, his eyes were cobalt blue and mesmerizing. Not wanting to stare, I focused on a spot near the toe of my left shoe.

I shoved my hands in my pockets and looked again at Charles. "I'd like to thank you for speaking up, but how did you know about the Clean Air Bill? Are you a reporter?"

Charles gave me a big grin. "No, but the notebook and pen works well to give that impression, don't you think? It fooled Saunders."

I smiled back. "Yeah. He squirmed when you mentioned the bill. I think big bold headlines reading 'Saunders Stalls Clean Air Bill' flashed through his mind. But if you're not a reporter, why are you here?"

"I'm a freelance photographer and I'm in the area photographing the covered bridges for an East Coast magazine."

"Oh." I frowned, perplexed at his answer.

He grinned once more. "But that doesn't answer your question why I'm here does it? Or how I knew about the Clean Air Bill?"

I shook my head. "Not really."

"I've worked for a lot of different environmentalist groups over the years and I have a personal interest in those issues. When I heard about the meeting, I checked with an old friend who's in an environmental watch group. He was the one who told me about the bill. I thought the meeting would be interesting." His face grew serious. "Your grandmother has a tough battle ahead, fighting PP International."

My eyebrows shot up. "How did you know Abby's my grandmother?"

"It's a small town, Ophelia. It doesn't take long to learn about the people who live here. Especially someone as well liked as your grandmother. People enjoy talking."

Boy, they sure do. Tonight would be hashed and re-hashed over coffee tomorrow at Joe's Café. Would the talk be for Abby or against her? I looked over my shoulder to where she stood by Stumpy, listening to whatever he was saying. She appeared so somber that the worry I'd felt earlier started to snake around me again. A woman her age shouldn't be the one to fight a corporation like PP International.

A light touch on my arm brought my attention back to Charles. He watched me with a puzzled expression.

"Excuse me, did you say something?" I asked.

"I said you look troubled. Are you concerned about your grandmother?"

"Yeah," I said while I absentmindedly tucked a strand of hair behind my ear. "A little. We're very close and I don't like the stress this puts on her."

Charles nodded in sympathy. "I understand. I know what it's like to worry about the people you love." He hesitated while his eyes traveled to Abby. "And to be powerless to protect them."

A shadow crossed his face. The conversation we were having was becoming too personal for my comfort zone. And I didn't want to know what caused the sudden change in Charles. I had enough problems of my own. The trip to Iowa City, Abby, and PP International, sleeping with rocks under my pillow, and oh yeah, finding Brian's killer. A tiny headache began to pulse and I searched my mind for a polite way to excuse myself.

Charles unexpectedly extended his hand. "It was nice talking with you, Ophelia. It's late and I'm afraid I'm keeping you."

"Right," I replied, quickly shaking his hand. "It was nice meeting you, Charles."

Baffled by his abrupt good-bye, I watched Charles move through the crowd and out the door. A sudden chill announced its arrival and the energy that had pummeled my defenses earlier flowed around me. But this time the energy wasn't centered on me.

Charles. It followed him like a vapor trail.

Five

I watched the flat landscape fly by the car windows. In the fields the rich black dirt glistened in the early morning sun. Farmers, up since sunrise, pulled huge disks behind their tractors, breaking up the shiny black clods. But the scene barely registered in my brain. The same nagging headache from last night throbbed behind my left eye, distracting me. A headache probably helped along by sleeping on those damn rocks.

While Darci drove, her constant stream of conversation provided background noise for my thoughts. Her words passed right over my head. As long as I nodded occasionally and grunted once in a while, she didn't question my inattention. Thoughts of my dream, my conversation with Abby, beat in rhythm with the throb in my head. Why was the dream different this time? Was Brian asking for my help from beyond the grave? I believed what Abby told me about the men, but would I recognize Brian's killer when I met him? I pressed my closed eyes gently with my fingertips to stop the throbbing.

"You haven't heard a word I've said." Darci's eyes darted in my direction. "What's the matter? Got a headache?"

I continued to massage my tired eyes. "Yes."

"Hmm—I wondered why you looked crappy this morning."

"Thanks a lot, Darci."

"You're welcome," she said, smiling. "While we're on the subject, you've been grouchy too. More than usual. What's up? Is it the headache or is there something else I need to know about? More psychic stuff, another adventure coming up, maybe?"

I groaned, ever since last fall, Darci envisioned herself as a Dr. Watson to my Sherlock Holmes. Should I tell her about Abby's prophecy? No, since our "adventure" last fall almost led to murder—mine—the risk would be too great. If Darci found out I was searching for a killer, she'd insist on helping me. And I'm not sure I could protect her.

"Darci, you don't need any more adventures. You were lucky you weren't with Rick and me that night in the machine shed. You could've been killed."

"But I hated missing out on all the excitement."

"Trust me, getting shot isn't all that exciting."

"Speaking of Rick—"

"I didn't know we were."

Darci smiled. "You mentioned him. What's up with him?"

"Nothing's up. I haven't heard from him for a couple of months."

"That's too bad."

"It's okay. I knew from the beginning that he wasn't the one for me. He has his life in Minneapolis and he loves it. He told me once he couldn't imagine doing anything else." I shook my head. "I don't see him giving it up, ever. We were two people thrown together under unusual circumstances."

"Ships passing in the night," she said thoughtfully.

"Trite, but true." I replied, my tone noncommittal.

"What about Ned?"

"Dang, Darci, are we going to spend the whole trip discussing my love life?"

"From what I hear, there isn't much to discuss."

I laughed. "Yeah, you're right. Ned and I are only friends. I don't see it going any further than that. There isn't the chemistry."

"Not like with Rick, huh."

"What did I miss?" I asked, ignoring her question.

"What?" Her eyebrows drew together.

"You said I hadn't heard a word you said. So what did you say?"

"Oh." Darci's face brightened. "I asked you if you'd read that article in *People*? The one about the skeleton found under the pile of rocks near a small town in Massachusetts?"

"A skeleton?"

Darci gave a long sigh. "I guess you didn't."

"Okay, I didn't read the article. Why don't you tell me about it?"

She wiggled in her seat and gripped the wheel tighter. "Well, I think the name of the town was Brookton," she said squinting her eyes. "Anyway, some guy's dog fetched home a human skull. Can you imagine that?"

It was my turn to sigh. "No, I can't, and I'm not sure I want to."

"Come on, it's a really interesting story."

Staring at the flat black fields flying by the window, I decided, ever since last fall, Darci's interests had taken a macabre twist. But she didn't give me the chance to point it out to her.

"Naturally, a search was conducted. They finally found a woman's skeleton, without the skull, of course—"

"Of course," I interrupted, turning to look at Darci. "The dog had it."

"Right," she said, nodding her head empathetically. She stopped midnod and pursed her lips in a pout. "Oh, now you're teasing me. Do you want to hear the story or not?"

"Sorry. I want to hear the story."

Placated, she continued. "The skeleton was under a pile of rocks clear out in the middle of nowhere, in the woods. The local sheriff believes it's the remains of a woman who disappeared fifteen years ago."

"A young woman?"

"No, the woman was in her mid sixties, a recluse who made her living doing laundry. She was single, never married, and lived in an old cabin not too far from where they found the body."

"But why do they think the skeleton is hers?"

"The missing woman had a limp; she'd been born with one leg shorter than the other. The skeleton's left femur is shorter than the right and that person would've walked with a limp too. Like the missing woman."

"Was it murder?"

"Of course it was murder," Darci scoffed.

"Not necessarily. She could've died from natural causes and someone buried her out in the woods."

"No way. The article said the medical examiner thinks she was still alive when the murderer started piling the rocks on her."

My eyes widened. "You mean she was slowly crushed to death?"

"Yup."

"That's horrible!" I said while my stomach knotted at the thought of the poor woman's death. "What an awful way to die!"

"Yes, it is, but I haven't told you the most interesting part. The article hinted that it might be a case of *pressing*."

"What's that?"

"Come on, with your heritage, you don't know what *pressing* is?"

"No. What's pressing got to do with me?"

"It was used in Salem."

I still didn't get it.

"You know, the Salem Witch Trials?" Darci explained. "They used pressing to kill someone accused of witchcraft. The executioners would continue to pile rocks on the victim until they confessed." Darci stole a quick look at me. "It took about three days before the accused witch finally died."

A sick feeling settled in the pit of my stomach. I quickly rolled the window down a crack and took a deep breath of fresh air. "Can we talk about something else?"

Darci gave me a sympathetic look. "Okay, back to Rick—"

I held up my hand, stopping her. "I thought we'd finished with the subject of Rick."

"Okay. Whatever's eating on you isn't Rick and it isn't Ned. What *is* bothering you?"

"I guess I'm worried about Abby. She's upset over this hog confinement issue." I rubbed my eyes again.

Darci frowned. "We all are."

"It's a mess." I rested the back of my head against the seat. "And Abby's right in the middle of it."

Darci reached out and touched my shoulder. "Hey, don't worry. Abby can always hex 'em."

"No, she wouldn't do that. It's against everything she believes in. It sends negative energy into the universe and, according to her, would return to her three times over."

"Wow. Lot of bad vibes."

"No kidding. No, she'll try to stop PP International the normal way. Anyway, it's wrong to use magick to bend others to your will."

"I'm sure you're right, but it's gotta be tempting."

I turned my head and stared out the window. Tempting? What if I *did* find Brian's killer? What would I be tempted to do to him?

Thoughts of Abby filled my mind and along with them came a need to talk to her. But the seminars at the convention lasted forever. When I finally walked in the door, the phone was ringing. Abby.

"Hi, how are you? You've been on my mind all day."

"I'm fine, sweetie."

Bull, her voice sounded too tired. I shut my eyes and concentrated on Abby's face in my mind, but her laugh interrupted my thoughts.

"Sorry, it won't work, Ophelia."

"What?" I asked my voice defensive. "What won't work?"

She laughed again. "You and I both know you were trying to 'read' me. Like I said, it won't work."

Rearranging the pillows on the bed, I plopped down. "Darn, why not?"

"Advantage of being psychic. I sense someone's mind trying to touch mine."

"You never seem to have any problem reading mine."

"Well, I've had more practice at blocking than you've had. The more you work with it, the more successful you'll be. Now tell me about the seminars."

"I'd rather hear about what's going on with you. You sound worn-out."

Abby sighed. "I am, a little. It's been a long day. We had a strategy meeting and learned the Clean Air Bill is in danger of being watered down. And there's going to be an 'invitation only' dinner to raise campaign money for some of the key legislators. It's sponsored by—guess who?"

"Dudley Kyle and PP International."

"Right. One thousand dollars a plate. A lot of money for the politicians."

"But there are still some legislators that support the bill, right?"

"Yes, but will it be enough? We don't know. The good news is that PP International is having their share of problems too. I guess it was discovered they're using migrant workers, illegal aliens, in one of their operations in Minnesota. Now they're under investigation. We're hoping it brings some publicity our way. And if they're fined, it could cut into their expansion capital."

"Making it difficult to build the set-up in our county."

"Exactly."

"Have you learned who the investors are yet?"

"No, since it's a private company, there's no record. But we still have people checking into it." Abby sighed again.

Abby's voice sounded so discouraged and not at all like her. My face settled into a frown.

"What else is going on?" I asked.

"Oh, I'm worried about Harley."

Harley? Had he threatened Abby? I felt my hand tighten around the receiver. "What's he done now?"

"Arthur said—"

"Arthur?"

"Stumpy?"

"That's right. I forget he has a real name. Sorry, go ahead. What about Arthur?"

"When we had dinner after the meeting, he said Harley's been in the bar making rash statements about what needs to be done to stop the building project. Harley's operating from emotions, not logic. If he continues, he could hurt the group's credibility."

So Harley was shooting his mouth off at the bar, not harassing Abby. I loosened my death grip on the phone. "Can't you muzzle him?"

"Nice idea, but no. Harley is a bitter, unhappy man. Edna told me he had hoped coming back to farm his mother's place would solve his problems. He used to drive a semi, you know, and he hated it. But things haven't worked out like he thought they would. His wife left him five years ago, taking his sons with her. And now he thinks PP International will squeeze him out. I also sense he likes the attention he's getting. People are listening to him, especially when he spouts off about the hog confinement issue." She paused. "But enough of that—let's talk about you. Tell me about the convention. Are you having a good time?"

"It's okay—you know how it is. Some of the speakers are good, some aren't. Darci is enjoying herself. She met a product rep, thought he was cute, now she has a date with him tonight."

Abby chuckled. "Darci's good at making her own fun, isn't she? This friendship is good for you; you might learn something from her."

"Hey, I have fun."

"Yes, but not enough. You need to get out more."

"Sounds like you've been getting out. This is the second time in a week you've had dinner with Stumpy, excuse me, Arthur. Isn't it?"

Over the long distance I felt Abby weighing her words.

"Umm. Well, yes, it is. He's a good man. When he was young, he worked in the logging camps in Minnesota. He saw firsthand what man does to the environment if he's not careful. I have a lot of respect for him."

"That respect doesn't include sharing information of your talents, does it?"

"No, of course not. But if I did, I think he'd understand."

"Abby—"

"Oh, don't worry, I've kept my secrets for a long time, and I'm not planning on changing. But while we're talking about talent, how are you doing with the runes?"

Twisting the phone cord around my finger, I thought about it—how was I doing? I'd studied the journal, understood how to place the runes for a reading, but that was it. I hadn't tried to do an actual reading yet. Maybe I was afraid of what they would tell me.

"Ophelia, are you still there?" Abby's voice broke into my thoughts.

"Yeah, I'm thinking." I blew out a breath. "I really haven't done much. I feel their energy when I handle them, but I'm scared to do more."

"It's good to respect their power, but there's no need to fear them. They're only rocks."

"Yeah, rocks that give me nightmares."

"Nightmares?"

"Yup—the first night you gave them to me, I dreamed I chased Brian's killer, but I couldn't see his face. In the dream I got tangled in brambles and couldn't get loose. My struggling and yelling woke me up. Does it mean anything to you?"

"Well, it could mean you've begun to connect with the killer on some level."

Crap. That wasn't what I wanted to hear.

"I don't want to connect with that sick SOB," I said evenly. "I want to catch him."

"You *are* going to the police station?" Abby's voice rose with excitement.

I looked at my hand. The telephone cord was twisted so tight around my fingers that they were turning purple. Abby was right; I would talk to them about Brian's murder.

Six

A fake plant sat in the corner, a sad attempt at giving the room a "homey" touch. Its faded green leaves were coated with a thin layer of dust. The pale walls surrounding the plant were covered with bulletin boards announcing community activities, garage sales, and criminals to be apprehended.

The last one made me pause. If Henry Comacho would've had his way five years ago, my picture would've been up there with the rest of the thieves, rapists, and murderers. Memories of the pain, the fear, I'd felt the last time I was in this police station made me break out in a cold sweat. Memories that were tied to Detective Comacho and his endless questioning five years ago. He'd been like a bulldog gnawing on a bone and I was the bone. *Chew, chew, chew.* I would rather walk on glass in my bare feet than talk to him again. But, according to Abby, I had no choice. God, I hated it when she was right.

Taking a deep breath, I walked to the desk where a uniformed policeman sat.

"Excuse me, I'm looking for Detective Comacho. Is he available?"

The man looked up from the newspaper he was reading. "No. Henry isn't a detective here any more. Is there someone else who can help you?"

My stomach actually quivered with relief. I wasn't going to have to face Comacho again. Yippee.

"I know this sounds odd, but a friend of mine was murdered here five years ago. I wanted to know if the case is still open and if you had any new leads."

"Murder cases never close, but the detective who handles cold cases is Perez." He pointed down a hallway to my right. "His office is the first door on the left."

Walking down the hall, the clicking of my heels on the worn tile echoed in my ears. What would I say to this man? Had I met him five years ago? The name didn't jog my memory, but a lot about that time period was a haze. Taking another deep breath, I knocked on the door.

"Come in," said a deep voice.

I turned the knob and opened the door.

A dark-haired man sat behind the desk, looking at me. Over his left shoulder, cluttered on the bookcase, I saw pictures of a woman and children. A chair faced the desk. In it was another dark-haired man. The man shifted his body around so I saw his face. Familiar brown eyes stared at me.

My fingers curled tight around the doorknob while my heart boomed in my chest. My knees bent of their own volition.

Dang! Comacho!

I felt those brown eyes taking in every aspect: my clothes, my hair, how I stood. I straightened and released my death grip on the doorknob.

Both men stood when I took a shaky step into the room. Comacho spoke first.

"It's been a while, Ophelia." He studied me again and then turned to Detective Perez. "Joe, this is Ophelia Jensen. She was a friend of Brian Mitchell's."

"Oh yeah, I remember." He extended his hand from where he stood behind the desk. "How do you do, Ms. Jensen? Have a seat."

After I shook hands with Perez, Comacho stepped aside and allowed me to sit in the chair. I felt him hovering behind me. Neither man spoke and, from behind his desk, Perez watched me.

I plunged right in. "I want to know if there's anything new with the investigation of Brian's murder?"

Perez looked over my head at Comacho.

Looking back at me again, he asked, "It's been five years, Ms. Jensen. Why the sudden curiosity?"

"Umm, well—" The words I wanted to say dried up in my mouth.

Comacho moved from behind me and perched on the edge of the desk. "Do you have any new information?" he asked, zeroing in on me.

"N-no," I stuttered.

Damn, I sound guilty of something. Get some spine, Jensen, I thought. Squaring my shoulders and ignoring Comacho, I met Perez's stare.

"No, of course I don't have anything new. If I did, I would've told you by now."

Perez eyed me with curiosity. "Then why are you here?"

"I'm in town for a librarians' convention and I wanted to know if the murder is still being investigated," I said, twisting the strap of my purse around my fingers. Glancing at Comacho, I saw him watching my hands twist the strap. Dropping it, I clasped my hands in my lap. Comacho's mouth twitched at the corner.

"Look, I know it seems funny, after all this time, contacting you, but there's never been any closure for me after Brian's death. I want to see his killer caught. It won't bring Brian back, but it might provide some peace to his family and me to know you haven't given up."

Perez leaned back in his chair, putting his hands behind his head, and looked at Comacho. "The Iceman never gives up. He doesn't appreciate loose ends, do you, Enrique?"

Comacho gave Perez a cool glance. "No, I don't."

Confused, I looked at Comacho. "But the officer at the desk said you weren't assigned here any more?"

"I'm not; I'm with the Iowa Department of Crime Investigation."

"The DCI?"

"Yeah, I was in town, so I thought I'd drop by."

Right. After my experience with him five years ago, I knew every question he asked, every action he took, had a reason. But what was that reason? I didn't have time to worry about it now.

"You're still investigating?"

"Yes," answered Perez. "But unfortunately, we don't have any new leads. We know there've been other murders in the past five years that we believe were done by the Harvester. Yeah," Perez said noticing the shocked look on my face. "He has a name now, thanks to a clever reporter. The victims were all successful men who were homosexuals and all were murdered the same way. But the killings have been sporadic and over several states in the Midwest."

"And the DCI's involved now?"

"Yes, and the FBI." Comacho studied his hands. "You haven't been contacted by the killer, have you?"

"Who, me? How would he contact me?"

Perplexed, Comacho watched me. "The usual way: anonymous phone calls or letters."

I stared at the cracks in the floor. Sure, I could tell him the killer had contacted me in my dreams. And that I'm starting to have this weird mental connection with him. Oh, and by the way, may I use my runes to help you find him? What would the logical Detective Comacho do if I said that? He already thought I was nuts.

I shook the mental image away and said, "Why would he do that?"

"Well, thanks to Fletcher Beasley and his articles in the paper, your connection, your friendship, with Brian Mitchell was well known and sometimes serial killers think it's fun to taunt the friends and families of their victims. It extends their feelings of power and control," Perez explained.

"No, nothing like that has happened."

"But you'd tell us if it did?"

"Yes, I would." I stood to leave. "Thank you, Detective Perez. I appreciate you taking the time to talk to me, but I must go."

"I have to go too. I'll walk you to your car, Ophelia," Comacho said.

"That's okay. It's not necessary."

"No, I insist. Joe, great seeing you again. Tell Marcella hi and give her a kiss for me."

"Sure thing, Iceman. Take care, *hermano*," Perez said, doing a macho handshake thing with Comacho.

I hurried from the room, but Comacho caught up with me in the hallway. We walked down it in silence. I didn't have to look at him to be aware of his presence. It was like walking next to an iceberg. He knew I hadn't told the truth today and he knew I hadn't told the truth five years ago. I didn't need my psychic talent to know

Comacho didn't have much use for liars and his disapproval of me rolled off him in frigid gusts.

He held the door to the police station open for me and I stepped out into the bright sunshine. Right into Fletcher Beasley.

Wonderful, my second least favorite person in the world.

Beady little brown eyes in a sharp skinny face lit up in anticipation when he saw me. He was so excited that I saw the coffee cup he always carried tremble in his hand.

"Hey, if it isn't Ophelia Jensen. Long time no see. What's going on? Comacho finally arrest you?" Fletcher asked, his little ferret face gleaming.

Comacho stepped in between us. "None of your business, Beasley. What are you doing here, instead of chasing an ambulance, looking for some story to sensationalize?"

"Comacho, you wound me," Fletcher said, grasping his chest with his free hand.

"Nonsense. You have to have a heart before you can be wounded, Beasley."

Comacho took my arm and guided me around Beasley, down the steps. I felt his anger vibrating in his touch. He may be the Iceman outside, but he was burning inside.

Fletcher ran to keep up with Comacho's long strides.

"Hey, wait a second. I could ask you and Ms. Jensen here the same question: What are you doing at the police station?"

"Get lost, Beasley," Comacho said over his shoulder, never breaking his stride.

Out of the corner of my eye I saw Fletcher stop and slick back his thinning hair. Evidently, he decided to take Comacho seriously. After taking a gulp of coffee, he walked back to the station.

"Okay, you can let go," I said, trying to pull my arm out of Comacho's grip. "He's gone now."

Comacho released me, but I still felt the heat where he had clasped my arm. I rubbed the spot.

"Sorry, I didn't mean to grab you so hard. It's Beasley; he's always annoyed me. The guy's a jerk."

What do you know? Comacho and I finally agreed on something.

"Well, I know why I don't like him. He dogged my every step five years ago, but why don't you?"

Comacho ran his hand through his hair. "When I was on the force here, many times I watched him intrude on a family's grief during a tragedy, all in the pursuit of a story. And he'd take that grief and parade it on the front page. Helped sell newspapers." He shook his head. "He's a parasite."

Wow, Comacho actually had a heart.

Taking a pair of sunglasses from his pocket, Comacho slipped them on. "Ophelia, you've always been a loose end in the Mitchell case. I don't like loose ends—"

"Any better than parasites."

"Less."

Guess I was wrong. He didn't have a heart.

Looking at him, I saw my distorted reflection in his sunglasses. Even at this distance, I noticed how pale I looked. And frightened.

"I know you're either hiding something or lying about something."

"Am not."

My response sounded childish, even to my ears. I noticed the corner of Comacho's mouth twitch.

"Really, I don't know anything. I only want Brian's

killer brought to justice. I don't know why you think I'm hiding something."

Comacho's mouth twitched again. He's enjoying this. He likes watching me squirm. It was starting to tick me off.

Standing as tall as my five-foot-four frame would allow, I narrowed my eyes at Comacho. "Would you mind taking off those sunglasses? I hate talking to people when I can't see their eyes."

He shrugged. "Yes, ma'am."

"Thank you. Let's get this straight, Comacho," I said, propping my clenched hands on my hips. "I came here of my own free will because I want to see Brian's killer caught. To me, Brian's death isn't a loose end, like it is to you. He was a good person and my friend. He deserves justice."

Comacho's eyes never left my face. "You're stronger this time, aren't you?"

"You have *no* idea." I reached in my purse and pulled out a pen and a piece of paper. Using the top of my car as a hard surface, I scribbled my phone number and address on the paper. Whirling around, I shoved the paper at Comacho. "Here. It's my phone number and address. Give it to Perez or keep it—whatever. If anything new develops, let me know."

I got in my car, slammed the door, and drove away. I was so angry at Comacho that I didn't see the other car follow me.

Seven

"Grandpa. Grandpa. Stop the swing. I can't hear you."

I stood on Abby's wide front porch. The scent of newly plowed earth floated on the spring air that drifted around me while the stars glittered in the night sky like diamonds cast on black velvet. My grandfather sat in the swing and next to him sat Henry Comacho.

I knew it was a dream, but I couldn't wake myself up. Nor, in the dream, could I move from my position near the porch railing. It was as if my feet were frozen to the shiny gray boards.

Squeak, squeak. The sound was so loud that I couldn't hear their voices over it.

"Grandpa, stop. Don't tell him anything. We can't trust him." I struggled to move closer to them.

Squeak, squeak. Henry sat, not talking, with his head tilted, listening to my grandfather. While Grandpa talked, he stabbed the air with his finger, as if to make a point. Henry nodded.

My panic rose. I couldn't let Grandpa tell Henry our secrets.

"Stop!"

Suddenly the dream shifted, as they often do, and I

wasn't on Abby's porch. Instead I stood in an open field, the same field I had dreamed of a few nights ago. Only this time I realized it wasn't an open field. It was a park. In the darkness I made out the shape of the slide and merry-go-round. To my left was a Civil War monument. I knew this park.

Yes, Wallace Park, that's where I was. Brian and I had come here often in the summer. It was close to the university and a popular place for both the students and the staff. Surrounded by a tall hedge, its gravel paths wound through the trees. They had found Brian's mutilated body nearby.

The killer. He had left Brian's body in the Dumpster and walked through this park. Was he still here? I strained my eyes searching the empty spaces, but saw nothing, only shadow.

In the last dream what path had the killer taken? I spun around. *Think, Jensen, think. Remember the dream. Yes, he went to the north, through the hedge.*

I ran down the gravel path. It exited the park on the north side, on First Street. Would I catch him this time? Would I see his face? I ran faster.

Rounding the corner, my feet slid in the loose gravel when I skidded to a halt. There, on the street, a blue van. Moving toward it was a dark figure, Brian's killer.

"Stop!" I yelled.

He heard me and looked over his shoulder, but it was too dark for me to see his face. Yanking the door open, he got in and the van peeled away from the curb. Its red taillights disappeared around the corner of First Street.

Dang, I missed him again. Frustrated, I stood staring down the empty street.

The sound of pounding jolted me awake. Where was I? Oh, yeah, the hotel and somebody was pounding on the door to my room. Shaking my head to clear away the dream, I stumbled to the door. I opened it to see Darci with her fist raised. Her blonde hair was tousled from sleep and, dressed in her pink satin robe, she looked like a model from a lingerie catalog. Except her robe was on wrong-side-out. She must've thrown it on in a hurry.

"What's going on? I could hear you shouting through the wall. Are you okay?" she asked, her words tumbling out all at once.

Dang, did I wake up the whole hotel? A quick look down the hall assured me no one else stood peering out their door. I grabbed Darci's arm and pulled her in the room, shutting the door behind her.

"Yeah. I was dreaming." I walked past Darci to the bathroom and filled a glass with water. The cool water felt good as it slid down my burning throat. Looking at myself in the mirror, the face staring back at me looked wild. My pupils were dilated and my hair was tangled and knotted. I ran my fingers through my hair to straighten it. Taking a deep breath, I returned to the bedroom where Darci sat with her legs tucked underneath her on the bed.

"Okay, are you going to tell me what's going on or not?" A determined look settled on Darci's face. "I know this isn't just about Abby."

Sitting in the chair across from the bed, I tried to think of an answer. It wouldn't do any good to lie to Darci. Most people passed her off as a dumb blonde, but I knew better. She'd keep digging till she learned the truth.

"If I tell you, you have to promise me you'll stay out of it. Let me handle it this time."

Darci made a face. "All right. I promise."

"I don't know where to start," I said, shaking my head.

"The beginning is good," Darci said, smiling.

I tried to return Darci's smile, but my lips wouldn't

bend. "Well, it seems, according to Abby, I'm supposed to find justice for Brian."

"How?"

I tugged on my lip before I answered. "Find the serial killer who murdered him."

Darci's eyes widened. "Wow. You're going to catch a serial killer?"

"I don't know if I'm supposed to *catch* him, exactly. Maybe I'm only supposed to figure out who he is, then pass the information to the police." I rubbed my palms on my legs. "At least, I hope that's what I'm supposed to do. I've already been to the police station—"

"Without me?"

"Yes, without you. I told you, I don't want you involved. I don't know what's going to happen or if I could protect you."

Darci made another face.

I smacked the arm on the chair. "I mean it, Darci. You promised you'd stay out of this. If I do run into Brian's killer, it'll be dangerous. The man's a butcher. You don't exactly fit his victim profile. You're the most heterosexual person I know, but the profile could change. I've already lost one friend. I don't want to lose another."

She plucked at the bedspread. "Okay, how are you going to do this?"

"Don't know." I ran my hands through my tangled hair in frustration. "I've started dreaming about the murder again. In the dream I see the killer put Brian's body in the Dumpster where he was found. And I chase him. Tonight in the dream I recognized where we were, Wallace Park, but before I caught him, he got in a blue van and sped off."

"In the dream did you see his face or the license plate?"

"No. It was too dark. But for some reason, I know the van was stolen."

"What are you going to do?" Darci asked, spreading her hands wide. "Keep dreaming until you see his face?"

I cleared my throat. "Umm, Abby kind of said I'll meet him. According to her, I'm going to meet two men: one good, one evil."

"You *are* going to find the killer," Darci said, her excitement rising.

I tried to keep my tone neutral. "I suppose."

"And because of your dreams, you'll recognize him when you meet him?"

"I don't know, maybe." I shuddered. "That's what I hate about this psychic gift: What I see is always vague. Abby said to trust in my spirit guides and I'll be shown the way. She also gave me my great-grandmother's runes. They're to help me too."

"Cool." Darci's eyes gleamed. "May I see them?"

"Sure." I walked over to the bed and removed the bag from under my pillow. Sitting cross-legged on the bed next to Darci, I spread the runes on the bed.

She reached out her hand to pick one up.

"No," I said, touching her wrist and stopping her. "You can't touch them. Only the person they belong to may handle them."

"Of course, like with the crystals Abby gave me. If someone else handles them, it messes up the energy, right?"

"Right. Your crystals are in tune with your specific energy. If someone else handles them, it can imprint their energy instead of yours."

"Got it. Then you have to cleanse them."

"Yeah, and it's a pain," I said, frowning. "All that smudging and rededicating. It takes forever."

She hunched forward, with her hands clasped in her lap, and studied the runes. "How do you use them?"

"A lot of different ways—divination, magick, spells. My great-grandmother wrote some of their history in her journal. The Vikings would use a *niding pole,* a pole to cast a spell, against a neighbor who had done them harm," I explained, nudging the runes with my finger. "The *vitki*—runecaster—would stick a pole in the yard facing the offending neighbor, stick a carved horse head on the top, and ritually carve his curse in runes on the pole. Or they'd write specific runes on a piece of wood to create a spell. Believe it or not, the placement of the timbers on the old half-timbered houses in Northern Europe were actually a combination of rune symbols. Usually for the protection and prosperity of the household."

"What about divination? Have you tried it?"

"No, not yet. There are a lot of different castings one may use. Seven runes, five runes, or cast them all on a cloth, imagine a circle around them, and interpret the runes according to their position to one another. Whether they're upside down, right side up."

"The last one sounds difficult."

"Uh-huh, I think so, too. From what I've read, the easiest is the three-rune casting. It represents the *Norns, Urdhr, Verdhandi,* and *Skuld*—the past or problem at hand, the present or path one should take, and the future or what will happen if you follow the advice of the runes."

"Why don't you try it?"

"Now?"

"Yeah, why not? Other than learning the van was stolen, your dreams aren't showing you much. Maybe the runes will. It's not like you've got anything to lose, is it?"

"True. Okay," I said, picking the runes up and putting

them back in their pouch. When I touched them, their energy vibrated in my hand. After all these years of lying forgotten in their sack, were they excited to be of use once again?

I cleared my mind as Abby had taught me. Silently, I asked for my eyes to see only the truth, my ears to hear only the truth, my mouth to speak only the truth, and my heart to know only the truth. With a request for protection and guidance, I formed my question in my mind. *Will I find justice for Brian?*

Reaching in the bag, I slowly ran my hand through the bag, letting the runes slip through my fingers. One made my hand tingle more than the others did. I drew it out and placed it on the bed in the exact position it was when I selected it. Repeating the process, I drew two more and placed them in a row next to the first rune.

I studied them for a moment. The symbol for the first one, the present, was upside down. Murk-stave, not good. The other two were right-side-up.

"Well? What did you get?" Darci asked impatiently. "What do they mean?"

"Hey, give me a minute. I'm new at this and I need to think." Reaching over to the nightstand, I pulled out Great-Grandma's journal. The old pages crackled while I turned them, looking up the symbols.

Slamming the journal shut, I stared, mesmerized, at the first rune, the upside-down one, *Urdhr,* the problem at hand. Maybe if I stared long enough, it would turn right-side-up.

Elhaz—grave dangers lie hidden; possibility of being consumed by unknown forces…

Nope. Not good, not good at all.

Eight

"What is it? You're three shades whiter than milk. It's bad, isn't it?" Darci said, reaching over and touching my arm.

Her touch brought me out of the thoughts. I took a deep breath and blew it out slowly.

"The present is *Elhaz*—"

"How did you pronounce that?"

" 'Ale-hawz.' The second is *Eihwaz*—'eye-wawz,' the third is *Tiwaz*—'tea-wawz,' " I said, pronouncing each rune twice slowly.

"Are they all bad?"

I shook my head. "There aren't bad or good runes. They just *are*. And they're damn subtle too."

Darci patted her hands on the bed. "Will you please hurry up and tell me what they mean?"

"Sorry. Okay, the first one, the problem, indicates grave dangers lie hidden. If I'm stubborn and refuse to prepare for the challenge, I could be consumed by unknown forces."

"Humph." Darci snorted. "That doesn't sound too subtle to me, especially the stubborn part. They've got your number on that one. What about the rest?"

"The middle one, the path I should take, is *Eihwaz*. It means I have protection, toughness, and the power to defend myself. The last one is *Tiwaz*. It stands for justice, good over evil," I said, picking up the last rune and rolling it in my palm.

"But that's good, isn't it? It means you'll win in the end and Brian's killer will be caught."

"Yeah, yeah, that's probably what it means," I said, picking up the rest of the runes and putting them back in the bag. "Listen, it's late and I need some sleep. I can't be dozing off in the seminars tomorrow. You still want to go out tomorrow night?"

"You bet. I want to go to this really cool bar. Tim took me there on our date. It has a great dance floor."

Darci got up and walked to the door. Stopping, she turned and looked at me still sitting on the bed.

"After all of this, it would do you good to get out and have a little fun. Forget about killers, runes, and dreams for a while," she said.

"You're right. I'll look forward to it," I answered, smiling.

After she left, I walked to the door, locked it, and put the chain in place. Leaning against the door, I looked at the bag with the runes lying on the bed.

Darci thought it was the first rune that had scared me. Its prediction of grave danger wasn't a surprise. I was dealing with a serial killer, after all. And Darci was right about the rest of the reading. The runes showed my stubbornness and my reluctance to accept the challenge I had to face. Also that I had the power to protect myself—if only I would use it.

But Darci didn't know the whole truth about the last rune, the one that scared me.

It did mean justice and success, but it was also the

symbol for the Norse god Tyr, the god of war. According to the sagas, a wolf was about to devour mankind, but Tyr tricked the wolf by placing his right hand in the wolf's mouth. The trick distracted the wolf long enough so that he could be bound and stopped from eating all the humans. When the wolf discovered Tyr's trickery, he chewed the hand off. Tyr sacrificed his hand to protect man.

Self-sacrifice. What would I be called on to sacrifice in order to stop a killer? My life? Someone dear to me? Unfortunately, the runes didn't answer that question.

Half-asleep, I rolled over to shut the alarm off. I did not want to get up. To hell with the seminars. I'd stay in bed for the rest of the day. But I couldn't find the *snooze* button. Where was it? Aww, here it is. I pushed it again and again, but the clock wouldn't stop ringing. Finally, it penetrated my sleep-fuzzed brain that it wasn't the alarm. It was the phone. Dang.

"Hello," I said, my voice sleepy.

"Hi, dear. Sorry to wake you, but I wanted to catch you before you left for the day. What happened at the police station?"

Abby. I should have known. I glared at the clock: 6 A.M. I sat up in bed and clicked the alarm off.

"Ophelia, are you there?"

"Yeah," I said and scooted up in bed. "I was shutting off the alarm."

"What happened?"

"How do you know I went to the police station?"

"Please—"

I cut her off. "Okay, dumb question. I went, talked to a Detective Perez. The case is still open. There have been other killings they think are related, but he wouldn't say if they were any closer to catching the killer. The DCI and the FBI are involved now."

"I see. Hmm—interesting."

"Oh, and I ran into not only Henry Comacho, but also Fletcher Beasley."

"How unpleasant for you. Did you speak with either one?"

"Oh yeah, Comacho insisted on walking me to my car. He's still cold and calculating, still convinced I'm hiding something, and still determined to find out what it is."

"What about Beasley?"

"I didn't speak with him, Comacho did. Seems he doesn't like Beasley any more than he likes me. Are you getting any vibes on him when I mention his name?"

"No."

"Shoot." I let out a long sigh. "Well, I gave him my number and told him to call me if there are any new developments. Oh, and Darci now knows. I had a dream last night. She heard me shouting and came to my room."

"What did you dream?" she asked.

I plucked at the sheet, not answering. Did I tell her about Grandpa?

Abby continued. "Was it the same as before?"

I made my decision. "Sort of. But it started with Grandpa and Comacho sitting on the swing on your front porch. They were talking, but I couldn't hear what they were saying. Grandpa was doing all the talking and Comacho was listening. I remember I was afraid Grandpa was telling him our secrets. What do you suppose it meant?"

"I don't think that part of the dream was necessarily prophetic. My house represents security to you and the detective threatens it with all his questions. What was the rest of it?"

"I was in the empty field, same as before, only this time I recognized where I was. Wallace Park. I chased the killer again, but he got away in a blue van. I didn't see his face, but for some reason, I know the van was stolen."

"Interesting. Are you going to tell the police?"

"Why would I?"

"Maybe a van was stolen around the time Brian was murdered."

"Yeah, but it was five years ago. There surely wouldn't be any evidence left by now, even if they found the van."

"It seems to me, each time you dream, you're getting a little closer to the killer. Each time you learn something new."

"Seems that way to me too. Oh, and I also did a rune reading."

"Good for you. What did the runes say?"

"I'm facing grave danger. If I don't use my resources correctly, the outcome won't be good. But I have the gifts I need. If I use them, success will be mine."

"Very good."

"Did you ever try the runes?"

"Yes, my grandmother tried to teach me, but they don't speak to me like they do you. I have better results scying with a candle."

"I don't. No matter how long I stare at the flame, I don't get any insight into my questions."

"Maybe we're trying the wrong element. Your zodiac sign is a water sign, not a fire sign. Maybe a bowl of water, with some crystals to help your concentration, would work." Abby sighed. "I wish we had more time."

I felt fear squeeze my heart. "What do you mean, 'more time'?"

"I can't shake the feeling things are happening faster than we think. And I think this is going to be a path you'll walk without me."

The fear squeezed tighter. "But you'll be there if I need you, won't you?"

"Of course, always."

"No matter what?" My voice squeaked.

"No matter what," Abby said, her tone reassuring.

The fear loosened its grip a little. I couldn't imagine Abby not being with me. The emptiness I would feel without her would be unbearable.

"I'm more worried about you right now. How are you? And how's the battle going?"

"Poorly. If you haven't seen the paper, the legislature overturned the DNR's recommendation on the level of hydrogen sulfide emissions in the air. The argument was made that it would penalize all livestock operations, including those on small family farms. Our group disagrees. We feel the only ones who would have to modify their operations are the large corporations. But the legislature doesn't seem to be listening to us."

"What are you going to do?"

"For now, concentrate on stopping PP International from building the new hog confinement. We have good people working on it. If the radicals would work with us, within the framework of existing laws, we might be successful. Instead, someone's being stupid."

"What happened?"

"Someone slashed the tires on a truck belonging to one of PP International's managers, the one who oversees their farrowing operation. It happened night before last. Everyone suspects Harley and I know Sheriff Wilson talked to him, but they can't prove anything."

"I hope Bill put the fear of God into Harley."

"I'm sure he tried, but I doubt Harley will listen. Edna's worried about him."

"Abby, are you sure you want to continue with this fight? Things could get messy and I don't want you hurt."

"Don't be silly. I'm not going to be hurt. It'll be fine. We need to convince these people to work within the law. If it gets worse, I'll talk to Harley myself."

"I don't know if that would be such a hot idea, Abby. Harley's got a bad temper and if Bill can't intimidate him—"

"I can be more intimidating than Bill."

Well, she was right about that. I'd seen her stop someone with a look. But I didn't want her talking to Harley alone.

"Will you promise me that if you do talk to Harley, you'll take Stumpy, sorry, Arthur, with you?"

"If it'll make you feel better, I'll promise. But I told you: Quit worrying. You've got enough to think about now. Concentrate on what's going on around you, on developing your gifts, please. Use them to find the solution. Remember, the runes said you're in grave danger."

"All right, all right, I will. But *you* be careful."

Before Abby answered me, I heard a loud noise in the background and a male voice talking, but I couldn't make out the words.

"Abby, I hear someone. Do you have the television on?"

"No, it's Arthur. He's here for breakfast. Got to go," she said in a rush. "I'll talk to you tomorrow when you get home."

Click. Abby had hung up. I sat staring at the receiver in my hand. Arthur? Breakfast? My God, it was what? I looked at the clock, six-thirty in the morning. What was he doing at Abby's at six-thirty? A thought popped into my mind. No, no, couldn't be. The woman was seventy-four years old. And he had to be at least the same age, if not older. I wiped the mental image away. I'd think about it later. Right now I had something to do.

In the bathroom I grabbed a washcloth. After looking up the number in the phone book, I dialed it. On the second ring, a woman answered.

"Police Station. May I help you?"

Placing the washcloth over the receiver, I said, "Tell Detective Perez to check the stolen vehicle records from five years ago, from the month of November. He's looking for a stolen blue van. It might have been used in the Brian Mitchell murder."

As I hung up the receiver, I heard her say, "Wait, who is this? What's your name?"

The washcloth trick always worked in the movies, didn't it?

Boy, I hope so.

Nine

The colored lights above the dance floor flashed to the rhythm of the music while hot sweaty bodies moved to the same beat. Cigarette smoke hung in the air in gray wispy clouds. Darci's bright red lips were smiling and her eyes surveyed the room, taking it all in.

"Isn't this great?"

"Well—" I eyed the room skeptically.

Darci's head swiveled in the opposite direction. "Oh, look over there. At the couple by the steps. That guy's a good dancer, isn't he?"

"Well—"

"What about that guy over there? Do you think he's cute?"

I leaned back in my chair and folded my arms across my chest. And waited.

Darci's head swiveled back. "You know, Ophelia, you might have more fun if you tried talking a little more."

Shaking my head, I smiled at her. "Darci, how can I? You won't let me finish a sentence."

"Oops. Sorry. I guess I get carried away sometimes, but honestly, isn't this just the best? I wish Summerset had a place like this."

"Summerset and a singles bar, huh? Let's see how many single men are there in Summerset? Five? I don't know if that would be enough to keep the place open."

Darci laughed. "Yeah, you're right. And their work boots would scratch up the floor." She laughed again. "I guess we'll have to go to Des Moines next time."

I groaned. Crud, now she'd want me to party with her all the time. I saw visions of my nice, quiet life slipping away in a haze of booze and men. I groaned again.

"Oh, stop it," she said, narrowing her eyes. "You're going to have fun tonight if it kills you. Something has to get your mind off all the stuff that's going on."

She might be right. I guess my life wasn't that quiet to begin with—serial killers, weird dreams, and a grandmother who practiced magick by the light of the moon. Nope, not quiet at all.

Abby was right too. My friendship with Darci was a good thing, a very good thing. And I knew no matter how many times Darci promised me to stay out of it, she wouldn't. How in the devil was I going to find Brian's killer and protect her at the same time? The thought scared me.

Darci reached across the table and lightly touched my hand. "I told you to stop it."

"Stop what?" I asked, shrugging a shoulder. "I'm just sitting here."

"Yeah, with a frown plastered on your face." Darci settled back in her chair. "Relax, forget about the runes and the dreams. It'll be okay, really. I've got faith in you. You'll handle the trouble when the time comes."

She had more confidence than I did, I thought, while my eyes scanned the bar. In the dim light my eyes locked on a man standing near the bar. He looked familiar, wearing a baseball cap and a shirt with the sleeves cut off at the shoulder. Damn, he looked like Harley Walters. Why would Harley be in Iowa City?

"Darci, is that Harley Walters standing at the bar?"

Darci spun around in her chair to look. "Where?"

"Over there," I said, motioning with my head. "Baseball cap, shirt with sleeves cut out."

She shook her head. "I don't see him."

I peered around Darci. The man I had seen was gone. Oh well, couldn't have been Harley. He was too busy causing Abby trouble to come to Iowa City.

"Hey, look at the guy over there. Now, he's cute," Darci said, her eyes widening.

I looked around the dance floor. "Which guy?"

"The one with the black hair, red shirt, tight jeans. Ohhh, he's got a great butt too."

"Dancing with the redhead?"

"No, not him. The one with the brunette. He has his back to us now."

Scanning the dance floor, I saw the man Darci was talking about. He had his back to me and I couldn't see his face. Dark hair, wide shoulders tapering to a narrow waist. And, yes indeed, his butt wasn't bad. Perfect, really. He danced well too. His perfect butt swayed in perfect rhythm with the music. It was a pleasure to watch him.

His partner thought so too. Her eyes never left his face and she'd toss her hair and smile at him. She danced in close to him and grabbed his waist. Soon her hips were moving with his to the same rhythm.

"Jeez, why don't they just get a room," I said to Darci. Glancing over at her, I saw her eyes were focused on the couple too.

"Wow, he is *so* hot. And she's trying hard to pick him up."

"The way they're dancing," I said, not taking my eyes off the swaying couple. "I'd say she's succeeded."

"Umm, I don't know. I don't think so. If you notice, it's her hanging on to him, not the other way around. Watch and see what happens when the song ends."

When it did, the man took one step back, away from the woman. Maybe Darci was right and they weren't together. He took the woman's arm to escort her off the dance floor, and when he did, he turned.

No, not again, not twice in the same week! The man was Henry Comacho. Ewww, I'd been having lascivious thoughts about Henry Comacho's butt. I'd be scarred for life.

"What's wrong with you? You look like you swallowed something sour."

I reached across the table and grabbed Darci's wrist. "We've got to get out of here. It's Comacho."

"Who?"

"Comacho, Henry Comacho. You know, the detective, the one I refer to as the spawn of Satan?"

"Oh, *that* Henry Comacho."

"Yes, and we have to leave before he spots me," I said, ducking my head and slinking down in my chair.

Darci looked over her shoulder. "Too late—here he comes." She looked back at me. "Sit up straight. Act as if nothing's wrong. It's not like he's going to arrest you."

"Maybe it would be better if he did. I wouldn't have to talk to him. Jail might not be bad." I felt my eyes glaze over. "Three meals a day, my clothes picked out for me every day..."

Darci leaned forward and shook my arm. "Shh. You're babbling."

I clamped my jaws together to stop my runaway tongue.

"Hi, Ophelia, we meet again. What a coincidence. Haven't seen you in five years, and now, twice in the same week. Odd, isn't it?"

"Yeah, real odd," I said through my clenched teeth.

He turned his head and looked at Darci, waiting for me to introduce them. Darci took the initiative.

"Hi, I'm Darci West, a friend of Ophelia's," she said, extending her hand.

"Nice to meet you, Darci. I'm Henry Comacho. Mind if I join you ladies?"

Before we answered, he pulled the chair out and sat. I picked up my straw and bent it back and forth in my hand while my knee bounced up and down of its own volition. *Dang, that man makes me nervous.* Silence settled on the three of us.

Darci broke the silence first. "Uhhh, Ophelia told me you're a police detective here?"

"Was, now I'm with the DCI."

"In Des Moines?"

"Yes."

"That's close to Summerset."

I nudged Darci's ankle with my foot. Comacho didn't need to be reminded of how close Summerset was to where he worked. He might decide to pay the town a visit.

"Yes, I suppose it is."

"And you investigate serial murders, don't you?"

I nudged her harder this time. Now was not the time to discuss serial killers.

"I assist local police anywhere in the state with homicides, not only serial ones."

"Oh, were you in—ouch!"

Whoops, nudged her too hard.

"Excuse me?"

"Nothing. My purse fell on my foot," Darci said while she nudged *me* under the table and glared.

A man came up behind Darci and laid his hand on her shoulder.

"Excuse me, would you want to dance?"

"Sure, love to." With one last glare at me, she stood and walked to the dance floor.

I watched Darci dance. She was smiling. And when her partner said something to her, she threw back her head and laughed. She was having such a good time and I couldn't help but smile myself, watching her.

"Your friend's nice."

"What?" I asked, turning my attention away from the dance floor.

Comacho leaned toward me. "I said your friend's nice."

"Yes, she is. And if you try to pull her in on your investigation of Brian's death, I'll have to hurt you."

His eyes widened in surprise and he laughed.

"What's so funny?"

"You. I didn't know you had a sense of humor."

"Yeah. Well, I didn't know you knew how to laugh. And why is the idea of me protecting Darci funny?"

"First of all, it's illegal to threaten a police officer—"

"You're not on duty now," I interrupted.

"Doesn't make a difference. And second, I'm twice your size. You think you could take me, Jensen?" He leaned closer.

"You might be surprised," I said with a confident look.

He nodded his head, smiling. "Yeah, maybe I would." The smile disappeared while his eyes searched my face. His eyes broke contact when a waitress set a drink in front of him.

"Here's your Cuba Libre, Henry," the waitress said.

"Thanks," he replied and looked back at me. "Do you want anything, Ophelia?"

"No, I'm fine."

"Keep the change, Jill," he said, handing her a five-dollar bill.

"Thanks." And she walked away.

Henry took a drink and looked at me again. "You're not the same person you were five years ago, are you?"

I shrugged.

"Didn't think so. Moving to Summerset after you left the hospital evidently did you good."

I gasped. After Brian's death, I'd spent two weeks in the psyche ward, being treated for Post Traumatic Stress Syndrome. "How did you know about the hospital?"

"I keep tabs, especially when it's related to a case like Mitchell's."

"I'd rather not talk about it," I said, leaning away from him.

"Hey, it's okay. I understand. When I was in the service, a lot of guys had problems when they came back from Kuwait, the ones who had watched their buddies get killed." He shook his head. "'Survivors' guilt,' I think they call it. Nothing to be ashamed of."

Wow, understanding from Henry Comacho. Amazing.

Not able to meet his eyes, I looked around the room. From where he sat at the bar, Fletcher Beasley raised his glass to me.

I shut my eyes. This was surreal: Henry Comacho *and* Fletcher Beasley.

"What's wrong?"

I opened my eyes to see Comacho staring at me.

"Are you and Beasley joined at the hip or something?" I asked sarcastically.

"Huh?" His forehead wrinkled in a frown.

I nodded my head toward the bar. "Beasley. He's sitting at the bar and just tipped his drink at me."

Henry shifted in his chair, looking for Beasley. After spotting him, Henry turned back to face me. "That man's a nuisance. Not even his colleagues like him. He's screwed too many of them out of bylines. In fact, his nickname in the newsroom is 'Weasely Beasley.'"

"Well, I've never liked him very much."

Understatement of the century.

"I know why. I know he made your life miserable during our investigation of Mitchell's murder." Henry picked up his glass and drained it. "I've always been sorry about that."

First understanding and now an apology?

Comacho saw the shock on my face. "What? You look surprised. I'm a nice guy, really."

"You're so nice that your friend, Perez, calls you the Iceman?"

He smiled. "It's a joke. Joe and I are old friends. We were in the Army together. When we got out, he helped me get on the force here. Went through the Academy together. He's my *hermano*."

"Brother?"

"Yeah."

"He called you Enrique?"

"That's my real name. Henry's the Anglo version."

"Oh."

Silence hung over us again, but this time it wasn't a bad silence. Not a heavy one like before.

Henry swirled his drink in his glass, making the ice cube clink.

"Ophelia, there is something I want to ask you."

"Yes?"

"Last fall you were involved in another murder. You and some reporter from Minneapolis. Want to tell me about it?"

That rat! He had been nice in order to lull me into spilling my guts. The apology, the sympathy, it was all an act. I felt the blood rush to my face.

"You really are a jerk, Comacho. No, I'm not telling you anything," I said, my temper blazing.

"Hey, simmer down. I read the report and was curious."

"Then you know I had the misfortune of being in the wrong place at the wrong time."

Comacho shook his head. "I don't know, second murder in five years. Most people go through their whole lives without being involved in a murder investigation. You've been involved in two."

"It was an unfortunate coincidence."

"Pretty unfortunate for the victims too."

"Look, I didn't even know the man whose body I found in the woods last fall. I'd never seen him before. And Adam Hoffman confessed to his murder."

"But you helped catch Hoffman."

"No, I didn't. I blundered into an ongoing investigation. They would've caught Adam regardless."

"Maybe, maybe not. I thought the report was missing a lot of information, especially about what happened that night in the shed. When you and Delaney got away. For instance, how *did* you manage to escape? The report said you were tied up."

"I don't want to talk about this."

I stood to go.

Comacho looked up at me. "There are a lot of things you don't want to talk about, aren't there, Jensen? What if we talk about a tip Joe got today, about a stolen blue van? But maybe you don't want to talk about that either?"

I leaned over and got right in Comacho's face. "You still think I had something to do with Brian's murder? Prove it."

His gaze never left my face and his eyes were as hard as crystals. "Be careful, Jensen. That remark sounded an awful lot like a challenge."

Straightening, I looked down at him. "Can't prove something that isn't true, Comacho."

I turned and began to walk away when Comacho called to me.

"Hey, Jensen, don't trip over any more dead bodies."

Looking over my shoulder, I gave him the one-finger salute. I was sick and tired of that man hounding me. I was getting the hell out of here, out of this bar, out of Iowa City. It was a mistake to come here in the first place.

I marched up to Darci on the dance floor. "Come on, we're leaving." I grabbed her arm and pulled.

"Ophelia, wait. Wait." She jerked her arm away. "Would you wait a second? Calm down."

Turning to her dance partner, she said, "Excuse me, Tom. Ophelia normally isn't like this. Ophelia, this is Tom."

Great, I've got Comacho and Beasley on my tail and she wants to introduce me to some guy? I tried to pull myself together and plaster a tight smile on my face.

"Hi, Tom. Sorry to interrupt, but we have to go now. Nice meeting you."

I grabbed Darci's arm again and pulled her off the dance floor. We walked fast, past the tables and through the door.

"Would you slow down? What is wrong with you?"

"Comacho started asking questions about last fall, but first he pretended to be nice to soften me up. Then he *happened* to mention the blue van. I never should've called that tip in. But they can't prove it was me right? Right?"

Darci gave a careless shrug. "Not unless they trace all their calls."

So much for having fun tonight.

Ten

The winding lane that led to Abby's house stretched endlessly before me. On either side, the barren plots of ground stood waiting for Abby to till and sow her seeds. On the left, she'd plant her sweet corn. On the right, she'd plant other vegetables: tomatoes, peas, green beans, all to be sold later on in the summer.

The greenhouse itself sat around the first bend. Inside would be her herbs and bedding plants. Soon everyone in the county would be coming to buy them. They all knew her plants were the best, the healthiest. When I drove by, I saw no activity in the greenhouse, which meant Abby was still at the house.

Rounding the second bend, I saw Abby's house. The house, white with green shingles, looked solid and strong in the warm April sunshine. The wide porch, the one in my dream, wrapped itself around the front of the house. I saw the swing swaying in the breeze. This house, this home was my refuge, my sanctuary, and the idea of Henry Comacho invading it, as he had in my dream, nagged at my thoughts. Shoving them aside, I got out of the car and walked up the porch steps.

Opening the door, I called to Abby, but she didn't

answer. Instead I heard the scrambling of toenails on the wooden floor of the kitchen. Lady bounded down the hall and flung herself against me. Queenie strolled out the door leading to the living room. She arched her back in a stretch and gave a wide yawn before meandering down the hall toward me.

Crouching down, I scratched Lady's ears. "Hey, girl, how ya doing?"

Lady's wet pink tongue snaked out and licked my cheek while Queenie rubbed up against my back.

"Yeah, I'm glad to see you too," I said, laughing. I stood, picked up Queenie, and walked through the house to the back porch. Lady followed closely at my heels.

Looking out the screen door, I saw Abby's summerhouse. It sat behind the main house, near the woods that crept close to the backyard. It was Abby's personal space. She often went there when she needed to think over her problems.

"You stay here," I said, pointing at Lady. After setting Queenie on the floor, I opened the screen door and walked to the summerhouse.

The windows were covered with old curtains shirred at the top. One wasn't pulled completely shut. I peeked through the crack and saw her, dressed in one of her cowled robes, sitting on the floor. The crystals placed in front of her sparkled in the soft light of candles burning around the room. And even though the light was dim, I knew she sat within a circle of salt. Abby was casting a spell.

Closing my eyes, I tried to read the energy that seeped out of the building.

Sadness. Hurt. The desire to heal and protect.

Yes. I understood. The spell was to protect the earth from Dudley Kyle and his group.

Not wanting to disturb her, I walked back to the house

and waited for her in the kitchen, where Lady was curled up on a rug, chewing a dog bone, and Queenie was stretched out, sunning herself on the kitchen floor.

It didn't take long for Abby to join me. I turned from my place at the kitchen table when I heard the screen door on the back porch slam.

Abby's face lit up with a wide smile when she saw me.

"Ophelia, you're home," she said, walking over and giving me a quick hug.

"Yeah, I dropped Darci off and I came straight here." I studied her face and noticed more fine lines etched around her green eyes. "I've been worried about you."

"There's no need to worry, I'm fine," she said, giving me another hug.

"You don't look fine. You look tired."

Abby waved her hand in the air as if to shoo my concerns away and sat across from me. "I'm a little drained right now, that's all."

"I can imagine. When you weren't in the greenhouse or in here, I walked out to the summerhouse."

"You know I was casting a spell."

"Yeah. Do you really think it'll do any good?"

"Of course. If I didn't believe, the spell wouldn't work. It might manifest itself in ways I don't expect and I might not see it happening, but it will work."

"Why does this stuff always have to be so subtle?" I asked, frowning.

She laughed. "You always want everything done yesterday, don't you? You must learn patience if you want to be effective."

"I don't see why. Why can't a spell be, *Boom*"—I said, snapping my fingers—"everything fixed."

"The universe doesn't work that way."

"Well, it should. What good is my power if it won't do what I want it to?"

"Ophelia, that's pride talking. One of the things you need to work on. You have to surrender your pride if you want to make full use of your gifts. The power isn't yours, you know. You are simply a tool, a vessel that can channel the energy in a specific way. To think it belongs to you is dangerous."

"How's it dangerous?"

"It leads you to believe you can bend the world and fate to your will and you can't. And to try and do so is wrong."

"But if it helps people?"

"Who are you to decide what helps and what doesn't?"

"Right is right. If I see something's wrong, I should fix it."

Abby reached across the table and took my hand in hers. "Sometimes things are wrong for a reason—a reason we can't see—but in the end, good will come from it."

"And if I mess with it, I screw up what's supposed to happen?"

"Yes."

Frustrated, I stood, walked over to the counter, and poured a cup of coffee. Holding the warm cup in my hand, I turned around and stared at Abby. "How in the hell am I supposed to know the difference?"

"By surrendering your pride, your sense of self. By letting yourself be guided. By exercising patience."

"That's hard."

Abby smiled. "I never promised you easy. Things worth having aren't. But you will grow spiritually."

"Abby, I don't think I can do it."

"Sure you can. It is a hard lesson to learn, but you'll learn it. Trust that you'll be helped along the way."

"The spirit guide thing?"

"Yes. But they can't reach you if your pride is blocking them."

While I thought about what Abby had said, I glanced around her kitchen. Stacked in the corner were placards.

"Hey, what are the signs for?"

"Oh, those," she said, glancing at them. "They're for the demonstration tomorrow."

Great, another demonstration. I'll be bailing her out of jail yet.

"What demonstration? You're not doing another sit-in at the four-way, are you?"

"No. I don't think Edna could handle another sit-in. She barely made it to her feet last time," Abby said, smiling. "We're picketing PP International's farrowing operation. The news media both here and in Des Moines have been notified and we hope to get coverage. Hopefully, it will help educate people to what's really happening in these units."

"Such as?"

"The fact that the sows spend their entire lives in crates, only big enough for them to either lie down or stand up; that the baby pigs are weaned after only ten days and the breeding process starts all over again. You know the animals can't handle this forced reproductive cycle. After only two or three litters, they're worthless. And it's off to the sausage factory."

"The operation sounds like an assembly line for the production of pork."

"It is. Confinement setups aren't operated like farms. Their goal is to produce large quantities of meat in a short amount of time. But these corporations are hiding behind laws made to protect the family farm. It's one thing we want changed." She looked down at her hands, folded on the table. "I'd like you to go."

I placed my hand on her shoulder. "Of course, I'll go."

She reached up and patted my hand. "Thanks. I know this is a difficult time for you."

I sat next to her. "You know, I thought about everything that's happened all the way home from Iowa City. I did call the police station about the van I saw in the dream. Maybe that's all I needed to do? Maybe they'll find the van, find the clue they need to lead them to the killer? It could happen, right? And I haven't had any more dreams since the one with the van."

Abby shook her head and smiled. "You sound desperate, dear."

"I *am* desperate. I don't want to face Brian's killer. I'm not ready."

"Guess you'd better get ready," she said with a quick nod.

"Thanks. You're a lot of help. Oh, and you were wrong about meeting two men. The only men I really talked to were Comacho and Beasley and I already knew them. I did meet some guy Darci was dancing with at the club, but it was a 'Hi—got to go' kind of a thing."

Abby shot me a stubborn look. "I know what I saw— two men, both dark, one good one, one evil."

"But was it Brian's killer?"

"One killed for pleasure. And you've felt a connection with his killer in your dreams."

"Okay, I met three men in Iowa City. Comacho is dark, Beasley's bald, and Darci's friend was blond. Except for Comacho, and he's a cop, none of them fit your description. Did you see their faces?"

"No, only sensed their presence."

"You couldn't describe them?"

"No."

"And this is supposed to help me *how*?" I said, arching my eyebrow.

"I don't know," Abby said, standing up. "I'm as frustrated as you are, Ophelia. I've tried and tried to see past the veil, but all I see is darkness and you alone."

My heart caught in my throat. *Alone?* I grabbed her hand. "What do you mean, alone? You told me you'd always be here for me?"

Abby squeezed my hand. "I will, but I've already told you, I've got a feeling I'm not going to be helpful this time. And I don't care for it. It's as if my gift is failing me."

I understood. I felt the same way when I saw Brian's murder but arrived too late to save him. Looking at Abby, the fine lines seemed deeper now. She was worrying too much about everything.

The urge to protect her from my problems overwhelmed me. I stood and hugged her. "Don't worry. You're the one always telling me to trust I'll be guided at the right time. I guess you need to have a little faith too." I stepped back and looked at her. A faint smile tugged at the corner of her mouth.

"This is a switch, you telling me to have faith, isn't it?" she asked.

"Yes, it is. And it'll be okay. After all, I've had the best teacher in the world, right?"

"I don't know about best, but I've tried." She nodded once. "You're right. The solution will come when it's supposed to. There is a pattern. All we have to do is follow it."

Follow the pattern. And at the same time, protect Darci, protect Abby, and find a killer. Piece of cake, right?

Eleven

Late, late, I'm late, I thought while I rushed up the steps to the library. I stopped on the seventh step. *Oh God, I'm beginning to sound like the White Rabbit in* Alice's Adventures in Wonderland. *I've got to get a handle on all the stress, or soon I'll be* seeing *white rabbits.* Shaking visions of rabbits from my mind, I proceeded up the steps.

When I shoved the door opened, and I hurried in and saw Darci hanging over the counter, talking to a man. It appeared she was having a great time flirting with him.

Something about him seemed familiar, although I couldn't see his face. Blond hair, slight build. Charles.

I stopped while I felt my face flush with pleasure. Charles's quick defense of Abby's cause at the meeting had impressed me. Even some of the neighbors Abby had known for thirty years hadn't had the courage to speak up. They'd sat back and let Abby do the talking. Charles, a stranger, had done more for her. His attitude was, well…endearing.

I did a mental shake. *Jeez, Jensen, get a grip. You do not know this guy. Get behind your wall and stay there until you learn more about him.*

While I stood there arguing with myself, Charles turned toward me and gave me a big smile. Darci gave me a wink. Lord, what had she been telling him?

"Ophelia, I'd hoped to catch you," he said as I walked over to him. "I stopped by the library last weekend, but the lady with the glasses told me you weren't in."

Returning his smile, I moved behind the counter and stowed my backpack. "That would've been Claire. I hope she didn't peer at you over the top of her glasses."

Charles laughed. "Well, yes, she did. A little. It was disconcerting."

I chuckled. I'd heard that statement before. Claire, president of the Library Board, had a habit of looking at people over the top of her glasses. Usually when she was annoyed. And I'd seen grown men shiver like school-boys when she gave them *the look*. Charles must be made of strong stuff if he only found Claire's look dis-concerting. My opinion of him went up another notch.

I gave Darci a sideways glance. Her mascara-rimmed eyes watched me with interest and I shuddered to think what might be going through her mind. The small nod she gave me confirmed my suspicions. Before the day was out, she'd have a hot romance between Charles and me manufactured in her mind. I shot Darci a warning look.

She answered the look with a slight shrug. Picking up a book, she flipped the cover open and checked the due date.

"Are you going to be in Summerset long?" I asked to try to cover the sudden lull in the conversation.

"I don't know." Charles traced his finger along the counter. "Darci said there's going to be a demonstration today."

"Umm—yes," I said, glancing at Darci again.

Darci gave me a quick smile.

"The demonstration will provide a good photo op. A small group fighting a large corporation. A David and Goliath kind of a thing. I also dabble with writing. It would make a good story." Charles frowned. "I've seen the effects firsthand of what careless stewardship of the land will do. Unfortunately, my family was careless. I've spent a lot of my time trying to correct the damage our factory caused."

"How admirable, Charles," I said.

"Not really," he said, his face turning a light pink. "I felt a responsibility. If everyone protected Mother Earth, we wouldn't have the pollution we do now." He blushed again. "I'm sorry. I tend to get carried away when I talk about the environment."

"Don't think a thing of it, Charles," Darci said. Turning to me, she said, "Has Abby met Charles yet?"

"No," Charles spoke up. "I haven't had the pleasure of meeting her, but I'd like to."

Darci shifted to face Charles. "You should. She's going to love you. You have a lot in common with Abby. Hey, I've got an idea." Her bright gaze settled on me. "Ophelia, why don't you introduce Abby to Charles?"

"I'd consider it an honor." Charles's blue eyes stared at me openly. "May I escort you and your grandmother to dinner? I'd enjoy talking to her about the situation she's facing. After the demonstration, of course. And if she isn't too tired."

"I don't know," I said, hesitating. "I suppose. I'll ask Abby after the demonstration."

"You're not comfortable with the idea?"

"Ahh, well..." I struggled to think of an explanation. A quick glance at Darci didn't help. She didn't seem to be paying attention, but I knew her attitude was an act. She'd soaked in every word.

Biting my lip, I moved my attention back to Charles.

"It's okay, Ophelia," he said gently. "I won't be of-fended if you don't want to have dinner with me."

"It's not that," I said, flustered.

Why didn't I want to have dinner with him and intro-duce him to Abby? I admired the way he spoke at the meeting. He was attractive, polite, and it seemed we had a lot in common. But something was holding me back. What?

Charles watched me closely. "You don't know me well enough to introduce me to your grandmother."

It wasn't a question. It was a statement—and he'd de-scribed exactly what I was feeling.

My eyes flew wide in surprise. "That's astute, Charles. How did you know?"

"I noticed at the meeting how protective you are of her. Comes with my job, I guess. Noticing things," he said shyly. "A freelance photographer is trained to look for subtle nuances and sometimes it's hard for me to shut the radar off."

Boy, could I identify with his statement. I'd spent my life trying to shut my radar off, not allowing my sensi-tivity to others to intrude into my life. I had never con-sidered others might have the same problem, but in a different way.

"It's not that I don't think you're a nice person—"

He held up his hand, stopping me. "I understand. But I would like to talk with you more. May I call you?"

"My number's not listed," I said abruptly.

"Oh," he said, his voice full of regret.

A sharp jab in my ribs from Darci showed how closely she had been paying attention.

It was my turn to blush. I felt the heat spread up my neck and into my cheeks. I slid my eyes over to Darci.

She lifted her eyebrows as if to say: *Give him your number, dummy. Thanks, Darci,* I thought and looked back at Charles.

"Ahh, well, ahh, I suppose I could give you the number," I stuttered. Slipping out a piece of paper from under the counter, I scribbled my cell phone number and handed the paper to him.

"Thank you, Ophelia," he said, taking my hand again. He looked over at Darci, but still held on to my hand. "It was nice meeting you again."

"You too, Charles."

"I'll look forward to talking to you soon," he said, his eyes meeting mine. He gave my hand another quick squeeze, pivoted on his heel, and left the library.

Darci was the first one to break the silence. "Boy, I thought for a minute there, he was going to kiss your hand."

"Darci did you—"

She held up her hand, stopping me. "Want to go out with him? Nope. He's not my type. He's cute, but too aesthetic for me. You, on the other hand—"

"Hold it. I'm only going to talk to him," I said, picking up the library cards to be filed. "That is—*if* he calls."

She chuckled. "Oh, he'll call. And I bet you wind up having dinner with him too."

"So," I answered with a shrug, "it would only be dinner."

"But who knows?" Darci tapped her chin. "Ned doesn't trip your trigger, but Charles might. That's why I told him about the demonstration and suggested you introduce him to Abby."

I dropped the cards. "The idea of introducing him to Abby wasn't spur of the moment? It was a setup?"

"Sure. I knew you wouldn't introduce a stranger to Abby without checking him out first. I'd hoped, after you said, 'No,' Charles would follow through and ask for your phone number." Darci fluffed her hair and gave me a satisfied look. "But you almost spoiled my plan when you didn't give it to him right away."

I rolled my eyes. "Honestly, you *are* the biggest manipulator."

"You bet I am. If you're not going to take care of your love life, somebody has to," she said with a smirk.

And to think, I once had typecast Darci as a dumb blonde. Boy, was I wrong.

Looking down at my watch, I said, "Dang, look at the time. I have to work on those files in my office. I told Claire I'd have them done before I left for the demonstration."

"She didn't care you're taking today off?"

"No," I said, sticking the books Darci had checked in under the counter. "I called her last night to ask if the Library Board would have a problem with my participation. She said since most of the board agrees with Abby, it shouldn't be an issue."

"Speaking of Abby, what did she say last night when you saw her? Did she say anything else about Brian's murder?"

"Not really. She's as frustrated as I am." I snorted. "Nevertheless, she is convinced I've met Brian's killer."

Darci arched an eyebrow. "Maybe you have?"

"I've been over this with Abby. The only dark man I met in Iowa City was Comacho and he's a cop."

"You said Perez was dark."

"Yeah, but he's a cop too."

"You know I've been reading about serial killers. A lot of them have a real fascination with authority and power. A cop has both power and authority. And what I read said the killers are like chameleons. They change their outward behavior to match the situation. Think about it—a serial killer using a cop's badge as cover. What a great way to hide. Be hard to catch him, wouldn't it?" she said thoughtfully.

I shook my head. "That's nuts. I think Comacho is a jerk and a sorry excuse for a human being, but it doesn't make him a killer. And Perez, from the pictures in his office, he has a wife and family."

"So do other serial killers," she insisted. "According to what I've read, organized killers, and I think this guy's organized, often do. People who know the killers are surprised that the person they knew had a secret, violent life."

"That may be, but I don't think the killer is either Comacho or Perez."

"Okay. What about the guy you saw at the bar?"

"You mean the one who looked like Harley Walters?"

"Yeah. Harley's dark. Did you ask Abby if Harley was out of town this weekend?"

"No. I'd forgotten about the guy in the bar."

"What if it was Harley? What if Harley's the Harvester?"

"Come on. Harley Walters, a killer? That's as crazy as suspecting Comacho," I scoffed.

"Who knows? Last fall would you have suspected Adam Hoffman of being a killer?"

"No."

"Exactly. You never know from the outside what's happening in someone's life." Darci squinted and stared off into space. "And Harley does kind of fit the profile. Right age, right sex, and right ethnic background. From what I know of his past, he had a rough time growing up.

His father died when he was young and his mother married a man that mistreated Harley. He had several run-ins with the police when he was a kid. He's volatile, sees himself as a victim of society."

"You could say the same thing about a lot of people, Darci."

"True." She cocked her head to one side. "Wouldn't it be interesting to find out if Harley was in the area when the other murders occurred? He did drive a semitruck and traveled a lot."

"Hey, stop right there," I said, frowning. "You promised me you'd stay out of this. I don't want you snooping around Harley's. Even if the guy isn't a killer, he's mean and volatile. You stick your nose in his business and he might cut it off."

"Okay, okay. But somebody's got to find some answers."

I touched Darci's arm. "Yeah, but it doesn't have to be you. I mean it; I don't want to see you hurt. Abby said the answers will come to me. We have to trust in that."

"I said okay," she replied, her eyes not meeting mine.

I tugged on her sleeve. "You promise you won't go out to Harley's?"

"I promise," Darci answered.

"I've got to get those files done," I said, glancing at my watch again. "I'm to be at Abby's in a couple of hours."

As I walked to the stairs to go to my office in the basement, I looked over my shoulder at Darci. She was still standing at the counter, staring off into space again. I could almost see her mind working.

I wondered how long she'd wait before she showed up at Harley's.

Twelve

Clouds of dust from the gravel road hung in the air—kicked up by the caravan of cars, SUVs, and trucks. Abby slowed her van and came to a stop near the drive to the PP International farrowing buildings. The other vehicles pulled in behind her. She got out and walked down the row of cars, giving last-minute instructions.

I looked across the road and saw Ned Thomas leaning against his red Ford Escort on the other side. Ned looked good—his blue jeans hugged his lean frame and the T-shirt he wore tucked into the jeans showed a trim waist. Nope, no spare tire there. In a way he reminded me of Charles. They had the same kind of build, but Ned's eyes were green, instead of Charles's unusual shade of blue.

I stepped out of the van and leaned in across the seat to hit the cargo door release. When I turned around, I found Harley Walters looming in front of me.

"Jeez, Harley, you startled me."

The baseball cap he wore low on his forehead made it difficult to see his eyes, but I watched while a slow smile spread across his face. He enjoyed catching me off guard. I thought about Darci's suspicions. Could Harley be a killer? Surely not, but his attitude was threatening.

"Hi, Ophelia," he said, not moving an inch.

Taking a step, I made a move to go around him, but he stopped me.

"Does your grandmother think this *peaceful* demonstration's going to scare PP International?" he said and twisted his lips in a sneer.

"Gee, Harley, why don't you ask Abby yourself?" I asked, shouldering my way passed him.

He made a derisive sound and strode away, not toward Abby, but away from her. He might try to intimidate me, but I noticed he steered clear of Abby.

"Harley giving you a hard time?"

Turning my head, I saw Ned standing by the front of the van. "He's trying."

"But knowing you, you're not going to let him," Ned said, chuckling.

"I certainly don't intend to," I said, pulling the cargo door open.

Ned strolled to the back of the van and stood next to me. "How was Iowa City? Did you have a good time?"

"Yeah, it was okay. Darci probably had more fun than I did."

Ned smiled. "You expected that, didn't you?" His smile faded. "Why didn't you call me when you got home?"

"Gee, I'm sorry." I drew a pattern in the gravel with the toe of my shoe while I thought about how guilty I felt at that moment. "Too much stuff to do, unpack, check in with Claire at the library, go see Abby. I guess I should've."

Ned gave me a rueful smile. "Listen, I know we're just

friends." He let out a chuckle. "Now there's a phrase every man likes using."

I looked down at the pattern I'd drawn in the gravel. "I'm sorry, Ned—"

He put a hand on my shoulder. "Would you quit apologizing? Friendship's good. I don't have a problem with it."

Relieved, I looked up at him and smiled. "I think friendship's good too, Ned."

"I'm honored you trust me enough to let me be your friend." His eyes sparkled. "Not many people can say that."

I grabbed a placard from the cargo area in the van. "Not many people *want* to say that. Believe it or not, some people think I'm difficult," I said, while I propped the placard on the bumper.

"No. Not you. Really?" he said, faking surprise.

I fisted my hand on my hip and gave him a withering look. "Ha, ha. Very funny. Here help me with these . . ." I paused and smiled sweetly. "Please."

Ned laughed and removed the rest of the placards from the back of the van. "Whether you know it or not, Ophelia, your rep's slipping. You're not as hard-nosed as you once were. Ever since last fall, you've changed."

"Oh yeah? Who says?" I asked defensively.

He laughed again. "You don't care for change, do you?" Ned gave me a light punch in the arm. "Don't worry about it, Slugger, you're still scary. Not many people are going to mess with you."

"Good," I replied emphatically.

Laughing and shaking his head, Ned walked away.

While he did, I watched him and thought about what I'd told Darci. It was too bad. Ned was a good man and we did have a lot in common. But all I felt when I saw him was warm friendship. I sighed. Oh well, with Ned here, at least Abby's group would make the front page of *The Courier*.

"Ahem—"

I looked over and saw Abby watching me watch Ned walk away.

"Yes?"

"I hope Ned isn't getting the wrong idea. You know he's not for you, don't you?"

"Yeah, I know. And Ned knows it too."

"Good," she said, picking up some of the stacked placards. "People in town have started pairing the two of you up, you know."

"Really?"

"Of course. You know how it is in a small town. You date someone twice and the town has you getting married."

Marriage? No way. Someday, maybe, if I met the right man. Ha, the right man? I rolled my eyes. Who in the devil would be the right man? Who could put up with—and understand—my life, my gift? Most men, including Ned, would think I was some kind of freak if they only knew what I really was.

Abby read my mind. "Let it go, Ophelia. You don't need to add that to your list. You've got enough on your mind for now."

"No kidding." I looked around at all the people getting out of their vehicles, searching for Charles, but I didn't see him.

"Is the young man you told me about here? The photographer?"

"I don't see him. Maybe he'll show up later," I said,

hoisting the rest of the placards in my arms. "Come on, you'd better get started."

"Don't forget to stay on the road. We don't want to be arrested for trespassing," she said.

Abby and I walked down the road toward the buildings. The gravel crunched under the soles of the tennis shoes we both wore and the warm April sun beat down on our necks. Around us drifted the smell of rotten eggs. The hydrogen sulfide from the sewage lagoons. Yuck. How could anyone work here?

I was concentrating so hard on blocking the stench that I didn't notice it at first, but I began to pick up something else in the air. Was it another smell? No. Not a smell. More of a feeling, pulsing underneath the smell of rotten eggs. I hesitated and, turning, looked at Abby.

"I know. I feel it too," she said. She stopped for a moment and I felt her mind reach out and probe the air.

"What is it?"

Abby squinted as her eyes scanned the landscape. "I don't know. I sense it—" she shook her head. "No, can't pick it up. Maybe it's everyone's emotions, all jumbled together, we're feeling." She resumed walking down the road.

Yeah, emotions, that's it. After all, everyone here had strong feelings about PP International and it only made sense Abby and I would pick up on them.

I spied Harley now standing in the middle of the road, right in front of the entrance to the property. Facing him was another man, Dudley Kyle. Talk about strong feelings. Even at this distance, I felt the anger flowing back and forth between the two men. Harley's dark complexion was mottled and he stood with both hands on his hips, legs spread wide. And he was right in Dudley Kyle's face.

Dudley was doing better at controlling his anger. His face wore a tight smile, but it was to mask the anger I felt rolling off him.

Abby tapped my arm. "Can you see it, Ophelia? Their anger? Concentrate."

I stared intently at both men, and instead of only feeling the anger, I saw it. Great waves of red, swirling around both men. The waves would hit one another and plume into the air.

"Wow. Yeah. I've never been able to see feelings before."

"It's their auras. I wondered if you'd eventually be able to see them." She shook her head. "We'll talk more about it later, but for now, I'd better get over there before Harley takes a poke at Kyle."

I watched Abby hurry up to Kyle and Harley. She laid a hand on Harley's arm, but he shook it off. She took a step closer to Harley and he moved toward her. I saw Harley's red aura reach out to encompass Abby. Shoving the signs at one of the demonstrators standing next to me, I took off at a run toward them. I didn't care if he did outweigh me by about a hundred pounds. If he touched Abby, I'd flatten him.

I'd almost reached her when Stumpy, oops, Arthur, stepped out of the crowd that had gathered around Abby, Kyle, and Harley. I skidded to a stop and watched him grab Harley firmly by the arm and pull him away from Abby and Kyle. Not bad. Pretty good for an old guy, I thought.

He escorted Harley to the other side of the road, never letting go of Harley's arm. He stopped, leaned in close, and started shaking his finger in Harley's face. It reminded me of when I got in trouble in second grade and Mrs. Jones would yell at me. I didn't envy Harley.

Looking back to where Abby stood, I saw Dudley Kyle had retreated inside PP International's property. He stood talking with another man. The manager of the facility, I suppose. They moved and walked away—in the direction of the manager's trailer. I watched them disappear inside.

The group that had gathered around Abby were all holding signs now and began walking back and forth in front of the drive, chanting. Crisis over.

Okay, what do I do now? Pick up a sign and join the demonstrators? No. I was better at observing. Go talk to Ned? No. He was busy photographing the group. Sticking my hands in my back pocket, I looked down the road and tried to decide what to do.

Suddenly it was almost as though someone had pushed me from behind, but I was standing alone. Turning around, I stared at the ditch on the other side. There, I felt it again. The same feeling I had when Abby and I were walking down the road. The pulsing. And it wasn't coming from the direction of the group.

I wandered toward the ditch, and as I did, the pulsing grew stronger. It seemed to rise from the bottom of the ditch like a murky mist, spilling out and over the steep slope. I felt the pulsing as it eddied and curled right above the surface of the road. Its tendrils seemed to reach out and wrap around my ankles, tugging me toward the side of the road, toward the pulsing's source. A source that lay somewhere in the bottom of that ditch.

But what? What was the source? The closer I got to the ditch, the more intense and rhythmic the pulsing became. With every step, the pulsing glided farther up my body. It moved smoothly from my ankles to my calves, up my calves to my waist. The pulsing crept higher until it drifted in a lazy circle about my chest.

Then swiftly, without warning, it coiled around me and squeezed, like a snake. And with every breath, every time I exhaled, it squeezed a little harder. I tried to take a deeper breath, but I couldn't seem to pull enough air into my lungs. I started to feel light headed, and little dark dots floated in my peripheral vision.

Great, I'm going to pass out on the road. And in the distance, I heard a car approaching. Gee, I hope they don't run over me.

But as the car got closer, the squeezing eased and stopped. I sucked in a great gulp of air and the dots went away. I recognized the car. It belonged to Sheriff Bill Wilson. Kyle must've called him from the manager's trailer.

The sheriff's car rolled to a stop and Bill and his deputy, Alan Bauer, got out. I watched as Abby walked over to them and said something. Bill nodded and leaned back against the door, crossing his arms across his chest. Alan stood next to him with his hands in his pockets. Abby walked back to the group.

Well, Bill's presence ought to make Harley think twice about starting trouble again.

I turned around and stared at the ditch. It was deep and full of dead weeds. Did I want to find out what was down there? Find out what was causing the strange pulsing? Nah, probably not. I bet all I'd find would be a bunch of rotten garbage someone dumped. Rotten garbage sending out negative vibes, that's it. I bet there'd be poison ivy down there too.

I started to walk away, but the pulsing began again. And with the same rhythm—*ta dum, ta dum*—the rhythm of a heart beating. It reminded me of what I'd felt at Abby's meeting, the energy that had battered against my defenses. But this time it didn't pummel me.

Instead, the pulsing tugged and pulled at me as it had a few moments ago, compelling me toward the bottom of the ditch, toward the energy's source. I had no choice but to follow.

The shoulder was soft with the loose gravel and I side-stepped off the road to avoid sliding down the slope. At the bottom, I picked up a stick and swung it from side to side to clear the weeds out of my way.

Phew, it smells worse than rotten eggs down here, I thought. The smell confirmed my original suspicion. All I'd find down here would be a big nasty pile of garbage!

Still swinging my stick, I took two more steps while I scanned the ground in front of me. Nope, nothing here. I can go now. Then my stick hit something solid. I moved the weeds to the side. Ewww, a dead hog. My stick had hit one of the legs sticking out from the bloated body.

Yuck.

I scrambled to get away from it, and in my haste, tripped over my own feet. Facedown in the weeds, I started to pull my knees up and get to my feet when I saw it. It was a piece of dirty blue cloth sticking out of the dirt in front of my nose.

Bamm, I was slammed back down, and my knees collapsed. While I lay there, spread-eagle, in the dirt, something held me down. My face ground into the soil and weeds poked at my cheeks, at my stomach through my thin shirt. The pulsing squeezed again—harder, tighter, faster. *Ta dum, ta dum, ta dum.* I couldn't breathe and the dots came back. Is this what would've happened at the meeting if I hadn't been able to stop the energy getting past my wall? I tried to breathe, to concentrate on building the wall again, but I wasn't strong enough. The dots danced closer and closer together till they blurred into one big black blob.

Behind my closed eyelids, a pinpoint of white light shone in the center of the blob. It spread wider and wider until a vision unfolded before my eyes.

An old man, dressed in overalls and a blue work shirt, knelt in his yard, and in the background, I heard the angry clucking of chickens. But I couldn't see the old man's face clearly; all I saw were the beads of nervous sweat covering his bald head. And I felt his fear.

Behind him stood a man with a knife. His face was hidden by the dark red aura swirling around him in a vortex. He was yelling, but I couldn't hear the words over the sound of the chickens. As he yelled, he poked the old man with the point of the knife. Each time he did, the old man's fear increased. Suddenly the old man grasped his chest with both hands and fell forward, face-down in the dirt. Dead.

Once deprived of his prey, the man's anger exploded and his aura reached out and covered the old man on the ground. Through the haze, I saw his foot swiftly kick the old man's body. Kneeling, the man rolled the body over and, with angry slices, carved something deep into the old man's forehead.

When the body was faceup, I struggled to see the old man's face through the mist, but it blurred his face.

With a grunt, the man rolled the body facedown again and left. Only moments later, he returned carrying a bottle. Shaking the bottle back and forth, he emptied the contents on the body. The sudden flare of a match glowed in the mist and I watched the flaming match arc through the mist and land on the old man.

The chickens quieted and the mist receded. The body, lying still on the ground, burst into flames.

I gasped, drawing air into my tight lungs. When I did, the picture in my head faded and, along with it, the pulsing. Sickened, I took another deep breath and rolled over onto my back.

Staring up at the clear sky, I knew I'd found the source of the strange pulsing. I recognized the piece of blue cloth sticking out of the dirt only inches from my head. The cloth was the same material as the old man's shirt in my vision.

Crap! I'd found another dead body.

Thirteen

I crawled up the slope of the ditch until I reached the top. Once there, I stood, but my knees felt shaky. Taking one wobbly step onto the road, my eyes searched the crowd for Bill. He was still standing by his car. I tottered over to where he stood.

"Jeez, Ophelia. Did you fall down or what? It looks as though you've been rolling in weeds," he said, looking me over.

"Yeah—something like that. Uhh—I think there's something you better take a look at," I said, waving my hand toward the ditch.

"What?"

"Something. Come on, I'll show you," I said, tugging on Bill's sleeve.

He glanced at Alan and shrugged. "Okay."

He followed me over to the side of the road. "What's this about?"

I pointed to the bottom of the ditch. "There. Do you see it?"

He scanned the weeds and frowned. "God, it stinks over here. Smells as if something's dead."

"There is. There's a dead hog lying at the bottom."

Turning to look at me, he raised one eyebrow. "That's what you wanted to show me? A dead hog?"

"Ummm. No. Something else."

I frowned and stared at the ditch. *Dang, how do I explain this one? How do I tell him I'm sure there's a dead body buried near the hog? Without telling him how I know?*

"What?" he asked, watching me.

"Well, near the hog, there's a piece of material sticking out of the dirt. And it looks as if something's buried there."

"What kind of something?"

"I don't know," I said, shaking my head. "But I thought I'd better ask you to check it out."

Bill studied my face. "All right. Where is it?"

"There," I said, pointing again. "Do you see where the ground's been disturbed?"

"Yeah. You stay here."

Bill followed the same path I had as he made his way down the slope. At the bottom he crouched down and, picking up a stick, scratched at the dirt near the piece of material. He stopped, dropped the stick, and shook his head. Over his shoulder, he called to me.

"Ophelia, go get Alan," Bill said in a flat voice.

I got Alan and brought him over to where Bill still crouched at the bottom of the ditch. We watched while Bill stood and made his way back up the slope, careful to stay in the same path as before.

"Alan, go back to the car and call the medical examiner's office in Des Moines and the DCI. We've got a body buried down there."

Alan's mouth dropped open and his eyes popped wide. Snapping his mouth shut, he said, "Yeah, yeah, sure thing, Bill." He pivoted and scurried away.

"And Alan," Bill called out, "use the bullhorn to tell everyone to go back to their cars. Go from car to car and take everyone's name. I want a list of everyone here."

"Yes, sir," Alan said and took off at a run.

I started to inch away, but Bill noticed and stopped me.

"Wait, Ophelia. You and I need to talk."

Crap. Here it comes.

"Why were you in the bottom of the ditch?"

"I thought I saw something."

"What?"

"The dead hog?"

"How did you see the hog from the road? I couldn't."

"I smelled it?"

Jeez, I'm making a mess of this.

"Then what?"

"I went down to investigate. Finding it startled me and I started to run, but I tripped and fell. That's when I saw the piece of material. I came and got you. See. Simple." I lifted a shoulder.

"Right. Simple. Except for one thing." He drew a handkerchief from his pocket, took off his hat, and mopped his bald head with the handkerchief. "You seem to be developing a real talent for finding dead people, Ophelia. This is the second body you've found in less than six months."

He stuck the handkerchief back in his pocket and settled his hat back on his head. While pulling the bill low on his forehead, his eyes drilled into mine. "Do us both a favor. Don't find any more," he said sternly and walked away.

Abby and I sat in the van, not speaking, while we waited until Alan gave us permission to go. While I sat there, I watched the road. Everyone, except Ned, Alan, and Bill, were in their cars. The three men stood near the edge of the ditch, talking. And they kept glancing at *me*.

Ned gave his head a quick shake and began to walk away. Bill reached out and grabbed Ned's arm, but Ned twisted away from him and kept walking. He marched down the road and up to the van.

When I rolled down the window, Ned leaned against the van and stuck his head in the window.

"Are you okay?"

"Been better," I said and wrinkled my nose against the sudden smell from the hog lot that filled the van. "How much longer before we can go home?"

Ned looked over his shoulder. "It should be soon. Bill's going over the list of names Alan made. When he's sure Alan didn't miss anyone, he'll let everyone go."

"Good," I said, closing my eyes.

"Is there anything I can do?" Ned asked, his voice concerned.

I opened my eyes and looked at him. "No, but thanks for asking." A shaky sigh escaped. "My mind doesn't seem to be functioning too well. Right now, I want to go home."

"Do you want me to come over and keep you company?"

"Nice of you to offer, but I think I'd be better off alone."

Ned reached in the van and brushed a strand of hair back from my face. "I'll call you tomorrow. Take care, okay?"

"I will," I said and rolled up the window.

Ned walked back to where Bill and Alan stood, but before he reached them, a large SUV pulled to a stop near Bill and Alan. The medical examiner had arrived.

And right behind it, another nondescript car pulled in. The car door swung open and out stepped Henry Comacho.

I felt like pounding my head on the dashboard. I didn't need the runes to tell me what Comacho's appearance meant. I wondered how long it would take him to hunt me down. When the time came, I'd better be prepared.

Before I could point Comacho out to Abby, Alan stepped into the middle of the road and made a *Move along* motion to the first car. The car slowly pulled away and the rest of the vehicles followed.

"You're sure you're okay?" Abby asked, her eyes fixed on the road ahead.

"Yeah," I answered in a low voice.

"You're lying."

"You're right, I am." I took a big breath and held it for a second before I spoke again. "I'm not okay. I'm scared spitless. The second car belonged to Henry Comacho. I'm sure you'll get to meet him," I said, watching out the window.

"Meeting him will be something to look forward to, won't it?"

"Right. About as much as a root canal." I shifted in the seat and stared at her. "Did you know I'd find the body?"

"No," she said, stealing a look at me.

With her eyes back on the road, her hands tightened on the steering wheel. "No, I didn't, didn't even have a sense of unease about today. That worries me. Usually, I have *some* feeling of danger, but not today. I don't understand it."

"You said last night you saw me alone. Maybe this is some cosmic test for me?" I snorted. "If it is, I wish it were a test that didn't involve finding dead bodies."

Abby's eyes narrowed. "It's not a test. And I'm wasting time worrying about why I can't see more than I do. I need to focus on helping you. Would you tell me what you saw?"

I scrubbed my face with my hands. This is the part I hated: reliving what I saw. It was gory enough seeing the murder in my head the first time; now I had to dissect the awful scene.

I winced at the memory. "I saw the body of an old man set on fire."

"Was he alive when the killer set him on fire?"

"No, thank God. I think he had a heart attack or something," I said, staring out the window. Looking back at Abby, I reached out and touched her arm. "I felt his fear, Abby. I smelled it."

"Did you recognize him?"

"No," I said, dropping my hand. "The killer's aura surrounded them, making it difficult to recognize anything."

I stared out the window again. What a great way to learn a new psychic skill. Watch a murder, see an aura. The thought made bile rise in my throat and I coughed to clear it.

"How was he dressed?"

"I don't know: Overalls, all the old men around here wear them."

Abby narrowed her eyes while she thought. "Do you remember the color of his hair, his eyes?"

"He was bald."

"Again, most of the old men around here are bald. Anything else?"

"The killer carved something on the man's forehead."

"Like Brian?"

"Yup, just like Brian. This murder is the work of the same killer."

"Did you sense anything from the killer?"

"Rage, hate." I chewed the inside of my lip. "Umm—a sick sense of satisfaction. He's accomplishing some sort of mission that only he understands. In his mind he has a reason for killing. Pretty twisted, huh?"

Abby arched her eyebrow. "Obviously. The killer is sick and twisted. Did you see his face?"

"No," I said, hitting my fist on the door in frustration. "In the vision he kept his back to me the whole time."

"What was he wearing?"

"Hard to say—the mist was thick—all black. Maybe a long coat and boots."

Abby frowned. "A lot of people wear black. What about the knife? Can you describe it?"

I closed my eyes and tried to recall the vision. "The knife was shiny, curved, but not a hunting knife. It was—" With my finger, I traced a pattern in the air. "The blade was wavy." I opened my eyes. "It's not a knife, it's a dagger. And on the metal piece above the hilt, I think it's called the *guard,* the dagger had two sharp points on either side of the blade. What a nasty weapon."

Abby thought for a moment. "Did it look old?"

"No, just sharp and wicked."

"The dagger sounds unusual." She glanced at me again. "You know you're going to have to tell Bill about the dagger, don't you?"

"If I do, don't you think he might want to know how I came across that piece of information? And I can't tell him, can I?"

"I'll think of something," she said, dismissing my words with a wave of her hand. "Did you hear any sounds?"

"Squawking chickens," I said, tracing a pattern on the window with my finger.

Abby slammed on the brakes and whirled toward me. I flung the door open and jumped out. Resting my hand on the side of the Jeep, I wretched until my stomach was empty. Abby stood behind me, rubbing my back. When I'd finished, I wiped a trembling hand across my mouth and turned to her. Silent tears ran down my face.

"He was going to kill Gus, wasn't he? But Gus died on him." I swiped the tears away. "He set the body on fire and left the body where he knew I'd stumble onto it."

Abby gathered me in her arms and patted my back, as though I was still a child. "Yes, dear, he did." She tightened her arms around me. "After five years, Brian's killer's found you."

Fourteen

I was hiding, hiding in my office to avoid the curious. Earlier, I had tried working at the counter, but the stares and whispers of the library's patrons had finally become too much to tolerate. I didn't blame them for their curiosity; it was the second time in less than six months a dead body had been found in Summerset. Both found by me. Six months ago, people were direct and questioned me relentlessly, wanting to know the "inside" story; but now they weren't as direct. Instead, they stood in tight little groups, whispering. And casting surreptitious glances my way. When I caught their eyes, they quickly looked away. It was almost as if they held me somehow responsible for the trouble the town was experiencing.

What would be next? Tar and feathers? Run out of town on a rail?

Scrubbing my face with my hands, I tried to get rid of my ridiculous thoughts. I jumped when a knock sounded at my office door. The door swung open and Sheriff Bill Wilson stood in the doorway.

"Sorry to bother you, Ophelia, but I have a few more questions," he said, shutting the door firmly. After walking to my desk, he pulled the extra chair closer to me and sat. He hunched over and absentmindedly twirled his hat in his hands before he spoke.

Bill stopped his twirling and looked right at me. I met his stare and tried to look innocent.

"Run it by me again. Why were you in the ditch?"

I picked up a paper clip and twisted it with my fingers. "I told you. I smelled something funny and I went down to investigate."

"And found the dead hog."

"Yeah."

"What happened next?"

I sighed. "It startled me and when I turned to run I tripped. It knocked the wind out of me. While I was lying there, I saw the material sticking out of the dirt."

"Why did you come and get me? Why didn't you push the dirt away to see what it was—if you were curious?"

Bending the paper clip back and forth in my hand, I tried to think of an answer to Bill's question. I couldn't tell him about feeling death, seeing a vision of a man being brutally murdered while I lay there.

"It seemed strange, that's all."

"Why did it seem strange? People dump stuff in ditches all the time. It could've been anything. It could've been an old shirt someone threw away."

"But it wasn't."

"How did you know, Ophelia?" he asked while his eyes drilled into mine.

"I *didn't* know. I saw the material sticking out and it looked as though something was buried there. I thought it was odd. I mean, why would someone bury a tarp or an old shirt in a ditch, for Pete's sake?" I paused a few beats while I stared back at him. "Are you accusing me of something, Bill?" I asked, frowning.

"No, I'm not, but it seems to me that you're getting yourself involved in some pretty weird stuff lately—"

"But—"

"No, let me finish. I know you weren't involved in any way with Adam Hoffman. You didn't have anything to do with the drugs and the murder of Hoffman's accomplice. You stumbled into that whole mess last fall. But what happened after Hoffman captured you and Delaney? Your story has so many holes in it that I can see right through it. And there's Benny's crazy statement about hexes, witches, and rats rushing at him and Jake."

"Please. Poor Benny is—and always has been—his brother's dupe. He was so scared that he would've said anything."

Bill twirled his hat again. "Okay. You're right. Benny wasn't the smartest guy in the world to start with. But the bottom line is that six months ago you involved yourself in an official investigation and almost got yourself killed." Bill stood and walked to the door. Turning, he gave me one last look. "Stay out of this investigation, Ophelia. I don't intend to be tripping over you this time."

Before he could open the door, it opened a crack and Darci stuck her head in.

"Excuse me. There's someone else here to see you, Ophelia," she said, opening the door wider.

Henry Comacho stood at her side.

"Hey, Jensen, thought I told you not to trip over any more dead bodies," he said, staring right at me.

Comacho sat in the chair Bill had vacated. We eyed each other in silence as if we were two opponents in some kind of serious card game, taking each other's measure.

Not a single expression flitted across his face and I hoped nothing showed in mine.

His dark brown eyes looked as hard as stones, shielding the thoughts that must be churning in his mind. His lips were held in a firm line, not a glimmer of a smile, a smirk, or a frown. In fact, his face was so lacking in humanity that it could've been carved from ice.

His frame sat in the chair easily, but I saw the tension in the lines of his body. If I uttered one word wrong, he'd strike.

"I know what you're trying to do," I said, finally breaking the silence.

He leaned forward, relaxing a little. "Really? What do you think I'm trying to do?"

"Get me blabbing. It makes people uncomfortable to be confronted with prolonged silence. They have a tendency to try to fill it any way they can, even if it means jabbering," I said, crossing my arms. "I watch *Cops*."

His face cracked into a smile. "Oh you do, do you? What else do you know about police investigation?"

I picked up the pencils lying scattered across my desk. "Not much. Oh, the 'bad cop, good cop' thing."

"Maybe Joe and I should've pulled that one on you when you were in Iowa City. Maybe we would've got more information from you."

"Look, Comacho, I don't have any information. Period," I said, opening a desk drawer and shoving the pencils I'd picked up inside the drawer.

I paused in the act of pushing the drawer shut. I didn't know anything about the murder, not really. Unless you counted the fact that I knew what the murder weapon—the dagger—looked like. I guess, strictly speaking, Comacho *would* count that. I chewed on the inside of my lip. Damn—how would I get that piece of information to him without telling him how I knew?

"You have something to tell me?" he asked while he studied my expression.

"Ahh no," I said, trying to settle my face into a mask while I closed the drawer.

His eyes didn't blink while he studied me. "You're sure?"

"Yes," I said, concentrating on not squirming in my seat.

"Okay, you want to tell me what you were doing in the ditch?"

"That's the same question Bill asked and I'll give you the same answer. I smelled a strange odor and thought I saw something. It's human nature to investigate," I said, leaning forward and crossing my legs.

"If it's your nature to investigate, why didn't you push the dirt back when you saw the corner of the buried tarp?"

"Another one of Bill's questions. Don't you guys ever compare notes? If you did, I wouldn't have to answer everything twice."

"Humor me."

"I thought it strange, someone taking the time to bury whatever it was in a ditch. Why not dump it and walk away? Why bury it?"

"Because they don't want it found."

"Exactly." I sat back in my chair, satisfied. "And maybe it was something illegal, so I asked Bill to take a look."

"You weren't afraid whatever someone wanted hidden might tie in to the demonstration and the vandalism that has occurred at the PP International facility?"

"What? Why would I think that? How could a dead

body be related to the situation with PP International?"

He shook his head. "I don't know. Finding a dead body in the ditch is causing them a lot of problems. There are investigators crawling all over the place. It's brought them unwanted publicity."

"Someone planted a body to inconvenience PP International? That's crazy."

"Maybe, maybe not. I've seen crazier reasons for murder." He cocked his head. "There's already been trouble at the facility. The manager had his tires flattened."

"Flat tires aren't the same thing as murder."

"No, they aren't, but in these situations, violence can escalate. We don't have an I.D. on the victim yet, but won't it be interesting if the victim is somehow tied to PP International?"

I bowed my head. The victim wasn't tied to PP International. Poor old Gus had nothing to do with them. If only I could let Bill know his John Doe was Gus, but I couldn't. Not without telling him how I knew. I raised my head and saw Comacho staring at me.

"Isn't your grandmother leading the group trying to stop them?" he asked thoughtfully.

I sat up straight in my chair and narrowed my eyes. "You keep Abby out of this."

"Her group will profit from any trouble caused to PP International, won't they?"

I shot out of my chair. "Are you accusing Abby of something?"

He looked up at me and gave a tiny shrug.

"Ha! You're blowing smoke, trying to tick me off. That way I'll tell you whatever it is you think I know. Are you that desperate for leads?"

Comacho stood. "You don't know what leads I have."

"You don't have anything," I said, my voice rising.

"Or you wouldn't be here bugging me. You said you don't even have an I.D. on the victim. You don't have motive and opportunity either. Necessary items before you can make accusations."

"Information you no doubt learned from watching *Cops*? Look, why don't you cut the crap, Jensen? And tell me what you're hiding."

"I'm not hiding anything."

"Okay. Maybe your grandmother can help me out."

My hands clenched tightly and I glared at Comacho. "I told you to leave Abby alone."

"You don't want people you care about questioned, do you, Jensen?"

"Damn straight I don't. Want to snoop around in my life, go right ahead. But stay away from Darci and my grandmother."

"Are you afraid of what they might tell me?"

"I'm not afraid because there's nothing to tell." I took a step forward. "*Leave them out of this or...*"

Comacho didn't budge an inch. "Or what? I've already told you it's against the law to threaten an officer."

I scrunched my eyes shut and took a deep breath, trying to calm down. Opening my eyes, I looked at Comacho, forcing my gaze not to waver.

"I'm not threatening you, but how do you feel about harassment charges?" I said, stepping back and leaning up against the corner of my desk.

"Not good. Guess I'll have to make sure I don't harass you, won't I?"

"Any more questions?" I asked, crossing my arms over my chest.

He gave another tiny shrug as he walked toward the door. "No, not right now. But I might later."

"Fine, but if you do, call and I'll come to Bill's office. You can ask your questions there."

"I'd prefer to keep it on a more informal level."

"Well, I wouldn't," I said, straightening and moving to behind my desk.

Turning, he said, "I'll look forward to talking to you again." With a slight nod, he left.

My knees gave out when he shut the door to my office and I sat on my chair with a *thump*. My right eyelid gave a nervous twitch and I pressed my finger against it. Dang! How was I going to get out of this one?

Fifteen

"Excuse me, Ophelia."

I looked up from the computer screen to see Claire standing in the doorway to my office. She had her glasses halfway down her nose and was peering at me over the top of them.

Oh no, I'm getting the look. *Must be trouble.*

"Hi, Claire." I smiled and waved her toward a chair. "What can I do for you?"

"Do you have a minute? I need to talk to you," she said, taking a step inside and shutting the door.

"Is this about finding the body? Look, I'm sorry. I know people in town are curious and it brings the wrong kind of attention to the library, but I can't change that. I—"

"No, what you found yesterday isn't the reason I need to talk to you," Claire said, holding up a hand, palm out, to stop me. She sat in the chair next to my desk and gave me a worried stare. "This is more serious than curious patrons hanging around bothering you."

"What?"

"You know I have nothing but the utmost respect for

you, don't you?" Claire asked as she picked a piece of lint off her lap.

"Of course. We've worked well together over the past four years."

"Well, I don't know how to broach this subject," she said, her eyes refusing to meet mine.

While I watched Claire continue to pluck imaginary lint off her lap, my mind scrambled, looking for a reason to explain her obvious distress. Was it the latest selection of books I'd bought? Had Mr. Carroll complained again? I did a mental inventory of everyone I might've ticked off in the last week and came up blank.

I reached over and lightly touched her hand. "Claire, tell me what's bothering you."

She stopped her plucking and looked at me. "Olive Martin is making allegations that you've mishandled library funds."

"What!" My jaw dropped.

Claire sighed and shook her head. "Yes. She's called several of the board members and wants a full audit of how you used the money left to the library by the Thompson estate."

"But you know how I spent the money." My fingers tensed around the arms of my chair. "It was used to repair the roof."

"I know, but the bill presented to the board was higher than estimated."

"And she thinks I'm skimming the money?" I asked, gripping the chair tighter. I couldn't believe what I was hearing.

"Yes."

I shoved myself out of my chair and began pacing the narrow space of my office. "Claire, you know that's not true. The bill was higher because the roof was in worse shape than we had originally thought."

Claire sighed again. "I know. And the rest of the board members know too. Olive is trying to cause you problems. That's all."

I stopped pacing and rolled my eyes to the ceiling. Peachy, like I don't have enough trouble? Now I would have to go before the board and explain the expenses to the roof. And drag all my records and receipts with me.

Glancing over at Claire, I said, "Why? Why would Olive want to cause me problems? I've never had any conflict with her. I barely know her."

"It's politics."

"Huh?"

"Think about it. Her husband is one of the biggest grain producers in the county and he strongly supports PP International's building project. PP International's hogs are a good market for his grain, but your grandmother wants to stop PP International. Olive is trying to get back at Abby through you."

I felt like jumping up and down and screaming, but I kept my tone even. "That's not fair. And it's petty."

Claire lifted one shoulder in a shrug. "I know, but that's the way a small town can be sometimes. Some people carry grudges and will do anything to get even. Olive thinks she'll hurt Abby by hurting you."

"She won't. I have all the receipts and can explain how the money was disbursed."

"I know, but I thought I'd better warn you about Olive." Claire stood and walked to the door. With her hand still on the doorknob, she turned and said, "You know it might be best if you keep a low profile for a while. At least, until this thing with PP International blows over."

* * *

My concentration was blown for the rest of the day. I tried, really tried to stay focused, but my mind kept bouncing, from the murder investigation to Olive Martin's accusations to the possibility of Comacho questioning Abby. At last the clock said 5 P.M. and I grabbed my backpack and left the library.

Charles Thornton waited for me at the bottom of the steps.

"Charles, I'm surprised to see you."

Charles crossed the distance separating us and handed me a small clear plastic container.

"I heard about what happened to you yesterday and I stopped by the florist and picked these up for you. I hope you enjoy them."

In the container, nestled in sparkling confetti, were two white orchids. Their petals were pale and fragile; I could see their delicate veining. The centers were a bright yellow that stood out in sharp contrast to the pristine petals.

"Oh, Charles, they're beautiful. It's sweet of you to give me flowers. Thank you," I said and gave him a big smile.

"You're welcome. My mama always said there's nothing like flowers to brighten a woman's day. I hope these brighten yours."

"They do, they do. The past twenty-four hours have been rotten. The flowers are the nicest thing that's happened to me."

My words pleased him. He rocked back and forth on his heels, grinning.

"After the demonstration, I didn't want to call and bother you."

"Were you there?" I asked.

"Yes, but I was late. I got there right after the medical examiner. Finding that body must've been terrible for you."

"Yes, it was. But it's under investigation now and hopefully the authorities will find the killer."

"But to think a killer's on the loose, here in Summerset. I'm sure people in the community are upset."

I nodded my head. "Yeah, it's like a wolf has been set among the sheep. I'm sure a lot of doors will be locked until the matter is settled."

"Well, I hope you're locking yours."

"Always."

"Hi, Ophelia," said a voice from behind me.

I whirled around to find myself staring into Fletcher Beasley's beady little eyes.

"Beasley." My nose wrinkled in disgust. "What are you doing in Summerset?"

"This little town's got a big story cooking." He took a long swig from the coffee cup he held in his hand. "Might be the work of our boy. You know, the one who killed your friend, Brian Mitchell?"

"I don't know anything. I'm not a part of the investigation," I replied coldly.

"Maybe you should be. From what I've been hearing today, you should be an expert on murder. It's what? The third one you've been involved with—Iowa City, last fall, and now this one," he said, sneering. "Make a good story, don't you think?"

I took one step toward him and shoved my finger at his chest. "Get out of Summerset and leave me alone."

"Hey, it's a free country. I can go anywhere I want."

"Oh yeah? Well—"

Charles took my arm, pulling me gently away from

Beasley, and stepped between us. "I think the lady's made it clear you're bothering her. I suggest you go."

"Who the hell are you?" Beasley asked.

"A friend and we have a dinner engagement."

With that Charles linked my arm through his and walked me to my car. Opening the door, he handed me inside. "Where do you want to go? I'll follow you."

"Umm—Joe's, I guess," I said, stunned at the way he had taken charge of the situation with Beasley.

"I'll meet you there." He shut my door and walked across the street to a car parked opposite mine.

When I pulled away from the curb, my eyes went to my rearview mirror, and I saw Beasley standing in the same spot. He held a notebook in one hand and with the other was scribbling in the notebook. His coffee cup sat on the ground at his feet.

I couldn't wait to see tomorrow's headlines.

Sixteen

I was still trying to get my bearings from my encounter with Beasley when I walked in the door at Joe's Café. Pausing to let my eyes adjust to the change in lighting, I noticed a sudden shift in the noise level inside the restaurant. It had become quiet. And as I gazed around the room, no one would meet my eye.

Joe himself hurried over to me. "Ophelia, nice to see you. Is anybody joining you? Do you want a booth?"

"Yes, there is and a booth would be good. Thanks, Joe," I said, smiling at his kindness.

"This way, this way," he said while he hustled me to a booth in the back. "How's this one? You can enjoy your meal without everyone's eyes boring a hole in the back of your head," he said with a wink and laid two menus on the table.

"Thanks again, Joe," I said, slinging my backpack onto the bench seat and sitting down.

"No problem." He put a hand on my shoulder and whispered in my ear. "Don't let these fools get to you. They're scared right now. It'll blow over soon enough."

"I won't," I said with a quick smile.

He gave my shoulder a small squeeze. "That'a girl."

After Joe left, placing my car keys on the table, I picked up a menu and held it in front of my face. I peered over the top, checking out who was here. I saw Mr. Carroll and Mrs. Simpson at the table by the door, locked in conversation. Over by the far wall sat Edna and Harley Walters.

Harley was going for the slicked-back look tonight. His hair was either plastered down with water or too much hair gel. And his face was shiny, as if he'd almost scrubbed it raw. A shirt with a button-down collar replaced his normal cut-off T-shirt and he kept tugging at the collar of the shirt. His shoulders were hunched forward and his eyes downcast.

Easy to see why—his grandmother was going at him like a fury. Once, Edna even shook her finger at him, followed by a quick look around to see if anyone had noticed. Her eyes met mine and she blushed. Quickly, she directed her attention back to Harley.

Lowering my eyes, I noticed my keys, still on the table. I scooped up the keys, opened the backpack, and dropped the keys inside. I was so intent on my task that I didn't notice Charles walk in. Suddenly there he was, sliding across the seat opposite me.

"Hi."

"Hi yourself. You know, Charles, you don't have to do this," I said, propping my arms on the table.

"What? Eat? Of course, I do, I'm hungry," he said and picked up a menu. "What do you recommend?"

"The roast beef is good."

"I don't suppose Joe has wine?"

I rolled my eyes and chuckled. "Sorry, no. But the food's good."

Within minutes Joe hustled over and took our orders. After ordering, Charles grinned at me. "Since Joe doesn't have wine, maybe we could have a glass later at your house?"

I pushed back against the booth and tilted my head. "Charles, are you flirting with me?"

"Maybe. Would you mind—if I were?" he said, his eyes twinkling.

Flustered, I folded my hands on top of the table to keep them still. "Hmm, well, ahh—"

"You don't get out much, do you, Ophelia?"

Feeling my cheeks grow pink, I stared at a spot over his shoulder. "Truthfully? No, I don't." Shifting my gaze toward him, I said, "My life changed five years ago when my best friend was murdered. It's only been within the past six months that I've started to feel I'm getting my life back."

He reached across the table and placed his hand on mine. "Poor Ophelia. I can empathize with you. I know how it feels to lose someone that you care for deeply. When my mother died, I didn't know if I could bear it."

"Was your loss recent?" I asked softly.

"No, it's been over fifteen years now. My mother was never strong and she suffered from heart-related seizures after I was born." Charles pulled his hand away, his body tensing. "My father's lifestyle placed a lot of demands on her. He expected her to entertain business associates, do charity work, keep up family appearances. It was a real strain on her. I don't know what we'd have done without my nurse."

My eyes widened. I'd never met anyone with that kind of lifestyle. "You had a nurse?"

"Yes." Charles smiled tightly. "A nurse was almost required in my parents' social circle."

"And where was that?"

His tight smile turned to a frown. "In Massachusetts.

My father was a captain of industry, as they say. His family had been prosperous mill owners for generations. But I was lucky, thanks to my mother and nurse, I was allowed to choose my own career instead of being forced to join the family business. In fact, even as a child, they tried to keep me as far away from the mill as possible. Most of my summers were spent at my uncle's vineyard in Long Island."

"You must've learned at a young age to appreciate wine," I said with a grin.

His face and whole body seemed to relax. "Yes, but I assure you the lessons in appreciation didn't begin until I was well into my teens. Cousin Lucy would've skinned both me and my uncle if I started drinking wine too young. She had very definite ideas about such things."

"Cousin Lucy?"

"Yes, my nurse, governess, second mother, whatever you want to call her. She basically raised me. Mother was too ill and my father was too busy at the mill and too occupied with his cronies." He gave me a sad smile. "One of my favorite memories is of Mother reading tales of King Arthur and Knights of the Round Table to me every night before I went to bed—when she was well enough to do so. Mother believed in the old virtue of chivalry." His smile faded. "How she ever married my father, I'll never know."

Now it was my turn to take his hand. "I'm sorry, Charles."

He smiled again. "It's all in the past now. I've created a life I think she'd be proud of and that's a comfort to me."

"She died from a seizure?" I asked gently.

Charles grimaced. "No, ironically, she didn't. She had a tumor the doctors didn't know about until it was too late. In her trachea. The tumor hemorrhaged and it killed her," he said, squeezing my hand tightly.

While I tried to think of something to say, I broke eye contact with Charles and looked up to see Ned standing by the booth.

"Ned," I said, surprised. Releasing Charles's hand, I quickly shoved both hands in my lap.

Too quickly. My elbow collided with my still-opened backpack. The bag and its contents clattered to the floor.

Before I could move, both men knelt and began picking up my scattered stuff and dropping the items into the bag. Embarrassed, I looked the other way.

Charles stood first and handed me the backpack.

"Thanks. Umm, Charles, I'd like you to meet Ned Thomas. He's the editor of our local paper."

Charles offered his hand to Ned. "My pleasure. I think I saw you at the demonstration yesterday," he said, shaking Ned's hand.

"Yes. The demonstration changed into something more than we anticipated. How are you holding up, Ophelia?"

"I'm okay," I said without looking at Ned.

I was uncomfortable with Ned meeting Charles. And I didn't understand the reason. Maybe it was the unwanted commotion I'd caused when I spilled my backpack. Maybe it was the way everyone had stared at me when I walked in. Whatever the reason, I squirmed in my seat.

"I met Charles at the meeting at the Methodist Church. He's in the area to photograph the covered bridges and he's interested in environmental issues. He might do a story on the situation with PP International."

Shut up, Ophelia, you're rambling, I thought.

Ned smiled down at me and patted my shoulder. "It's okay, Slugger. We'll talk later. Charles, nice to meet you."

After Ned left, Charles sat back down. "I take it he's someone important to you?"

"Yes, we're good friends."

"But Ned wants it to be more?"

"No. Like I said, we're friends."

Our dinner arrived, ending any further discussions. During our meal, Charles kept me amused with stories of his travels and his life. He had a wide range of interests and I found him witty and charming. The evening flew by quickly.

After dinner Charles walked me to my car. Tipping my head back, I looked at the sky. Clouds blocked the stars and I felt the ozone hanging in the air.

"A storm's coming," I said.

As if caused by my words, a low roar of thunder rumbled in the distance.

"You'd better get home before the storm hits," he said, opening my car door. "I enjoyed this evening, Ophelia."

"Thank you. I did too," I said and started to slide in. But before I could, Charles took my hand in his and raising it to his lips, placed a kiss as light as a snowflake on the back of my hand. The skin where his lips touched tingled.

And the thunder rumbled again.

On my way home lightning cut a jagged edge across the sky and the sound of thunder crept closer. With one hand tight on the steering wheel, I picked up my cell phone and dialed Ned's number. He answered on the first ring.

"Hi, Slugger."

"Ned, about Charles—"

"You don't owe me an explanation," he said, cutting in. "We're friends, remember?"

"I know." I tapped my finger on the steering wheel. "But for some reason it made me uncomfortable when you met Charles."

"Why?"

"I don't know. It just did." I tapped my finger faster.

"Do you like him?"

"I guess."

I heard his chuckle over the thunder. "Has he met Abby?"

"No, I don't know him well enough to introduce him to her yet."

"My advice as a friend," he said, stressing the word *friend,* "is to take your time. There's some strange things going on right now and you'd be wise to be cautious of any strangers."

"Good advice."

"That's what friends are for," he said, and I heard the smile in his voice. "Are you on your way home now?"

"Yeah. The way the storm's moving in, it's going to be nasty."

"The weather station has severe storm warnings on. When you get home, stay put. We'll talk tomorrow—if you have time. I want to hear more about Beasley. He's the reporter who gave you a bad time five years ago, isn't he?"

"Yes, he is. And I wish he hadn't shown up in Summerset."

"This murder's a big story. Lots of people will be knocking at your door, asking questions. Might be best to lay low for a while."

"I think so too. I've got some vacation time coming. I might take some of it now."

"Good idea. You'd better pay attention to the road, so I'll let you go. Remember, stay at home."

"I will. Thanks, Ned."

"No problem. Talk to you later."

I hit the END button on the phone and thought about what a great guy Ned was. Along with Darci, he was one of my closest friends. Wow, the thought stunned me. Who'd have thought six months ago that I'd have friends again? After Brian's death, I swore I'd never get close to anyone again, but now I had Abby, Darci, Ned, and Claire. My life was better and I'd be damned if I would let Henry Comacho or Fletcher Beasley take the security I'd found away from me.

Seventeen

My windshield wipers were beating a steady rhythm by the time I pulled into my driveway. Grabbing my backpack out of the seat next to me, I flung the car door open, jumped out, slammed the door shut, and flew up the walk to the porch. Standing there for a moment, I watched the rain come down in a heavy curtain. Over the noise of the thunder and falling rain, I heard a whimper from inside the house. Lady—she hated being alone during storms.

I unlocked the door and swung it wide. Immediately, Lady was at my side. She quivered so hard she could barely wag her tail. Her eyes stared up at me hopefully, as if to say: *Please make this go away.* I bent down and scratched her ear.

"Come on, girl, let's go inside."

She didn't need to be told twice and trotted in the door right at my side. In the dark I found the light switch and flicked it on, but nothing happened. I flicked it again and again till it hit me. *It's stupid to keep hitting the light switch. The power's out, dummy.*

Stumbling into the dining room, I grabbed the kerosene lamp from the sideboard and went into the living room. I felt around the top of the mantle, searching for the box of matches. Finally I found them and lit the lamp.

Crossing to the coffee table, I lit all my candles until the last of the gloom was chased away and the room was filled with a soft yellow glow.

"Kind of romantic isn't it, girl?" I said, surveying the room.

Lady, comfortable now that I was home, curled up on her rug near the fireplace. And from underneath the couch, Queenie peeked out, but another clap of thunder sent her scurrying back to her hiding place.

"Queenie, you are *such* a chicken," I said, laughing. "You're supposed to be a big bad predator."

Predator. A predator was stalking Summerset. I pulled my fingers through my wet hair. Well, now's as good a time as any to think about the murders. After all, dark stormy night, murder—the two fit together in a worn cliché. I hadn't tried the runes again since the night in Iowa City. Maybe they could give me some insight.

I'd brought my backpack into the living room with me and I rummaged around in it till I found the old leather pouch. While sitting crossed-legged on the floor and, holding the rune bag in my lap, I visualized peace and protection for all who dwell within these walls. Through my closed eyelids, I saw the light from the candles glow brighter and brighter until I felt the light expand and surround me in a safe bubble. Carefully I formed the question in my mind.

What must I do to find Brian's killer?

As I ran my fingers slowly through the bag, I asked that my hand would be guided and that I might know the truth. When my fingers tingled from the energy of one stone, I drew it out and placed it in front of me. I repeated the process two more times, until three stones were cast.

Opening my eyes, I looked at them. *Isa*—the situation at hand. *Hagalaz*—the advice the runes were giving me. *Berkana*—the outcome if I follow the advice.

Okay, hmm. What do the runes say? Isa is *murk-stave. That's not good,* I thought while I searched my backpack for the journal. Reading what was written in the journal, I saw *Isa* murk-stave wasn't a positive sign.

Isa (pronounced "ee-saw")—symbol for ice— frozen, static, unmoving, murk-stave—beneath the beautiful surface, hidden danger lies.

No kidding, things are static. I'm not any closer to finding Brian's killer than I was a week ago. But what could "hidden danger" mean? The killer hides from detection?

I moved on to the next one.

Hagalaz (pronounced "haw-gaw-laws")—symbol for hail—the destroyer—out of destruction comes change—crisis is at hand—be prepared.

Too bad the rune doesn't give me a clue as to how I could prepare.

I picked up the last one.

Berkano (pronounced "bear-kawn-oh")—birch trees—growth, physical and mental—new beginnings.

Well, at least the outcome wasn't too bad if I follow the rune's advice—Hagalaz. I picked up the stone and rolled it around in my hand. The advice was vague, but Abby had said to think outside of the box. *Okay, I'll think outside of the box.*

Crisis, transformation. I let my eyelids drift shut. *How will the crisis come?* I thought about crisis and preparation while I continued to roll the stone over and over in my left hand, the hand that absorbs energy. *Come on, talk to me.*

I felt myself drifting while the rune grew hot in my hand. Down and down, like a leaf caught in a whirlpool. Dark places. Evil faces. Blood. All the blood.

My eyes shot open and my heart pounded. Panting, I pressed my right hand to my heart as if to slow it down. *All right, Jensen, don't be a goof. You're in your own house, you're safe, and you're not going to be spooked by a little vision, are you?*

I let my eyes close again. From far away, I heard the peal of thunder and an animal whimper. In my mind I saw dark eyes boring into mine from a face blurred by darkness. Water dripped from the bill of a baseball cap that was pulled down, shading the rest of his face, and I couldn't see his features. But I could see the eyes. They burned from within with the fire of madness. I felt hands reach out, grabbing my arms and pulling me close. Close to the madness.

No, no. I wouldn't let it win. I fought to push the madness away from me. *Open your eyes, damn it, open your eyes,* my mind screamed.

Once again my eyes flew open and they darted around the room, taking in the familiar surroundings.

I saw Lady had crawled over to me and her head was in my lap next to the bag of runes. Silhouetted in the window, I saw the storm as it flashed and rumbled. The rune I still held tightly in my hand felt hot, so hot.

Gently moving Lady's head off my lap, I ran to the window while the rune vibrated in my fist. I looked out the window as a crack of lightning illuminated the street, casting objects in sharp relief, like a black-and-white photograph.

There, in the street, near the large elm tree. A figure, a man? I pressed my nose to the glass, searching the dark for what I thought I'd seen.

When the lightning cracked again, the rune, *Hagalaz*— the symbol for the destroyer, for the crisis at hand— slipped from my numb fingers. And all I saw was the empty street.

Eighteen

The next morning the first thing I did was call Claire and set up my vacation time. She agreed to it immediately. Along with Darci, the library board members would cover my absence. The second thing I did was make lots and lots of strong, dark coffee. I stood impatiently by the coffeemaker with my coffee cup in my hand, waiting.

"Oh come on, will you? Hurry up."

"Do you always talk to the coffeemaker?"

I jumped, almost dropping my cup. "Jeez, Abby. You startled me. What are you doing here so early?"

"I wanted to see how you weathered the storm last night. I hope you don't mind. I used my key to let myself in," she said, setting a grocery bag on the counter. "I had hoped to surprise you with breakfast, but since you're up, you can help me."

She emptied the sack, setting orange juice, eggs, and bacon out on the counter.

"Thanks, but I don't know if I can handle a big breakfast right now," I said and gave her a hug.

Maybe the hug was a little too tight or maybe she picked up on my distress. Either way she stepped back and, placing her hands on my shoulders, scanned my face.

"What happened?"

"I had an interesting rune reading," I said, taking my coffee and sitting down at the table.

"And?"

"The rune's advice was *Hagalaz*—hail, destruction, through crisis will come transformation. I'm to be prepared."

"A warning. What was the outcome?" Abby asked while she put away the groceries and filled her own cup with coffee.

"*Berkano*—growth, new beginnings."

"Well, the outcome's promising, at least," she said, joining me at the table.

I rubbed my eyes with the heels of my hands, trying to scrub away the images of last night. "Yeah, but 'Be prepared' doesn't tell me a whole heck of a lot, does it?" Taking a deep breath, I let it out slowly. "Umm—I don't want you to freak out, but I'm sure the killer was watching the house last night."

Abby didn't comment. Instead she clicked her nail on the side of her cup, thinking.

"You're not surprised, are you?"

"No," she said and took a drink of her coffee. "I was afraid this would happen. You had a connection to Gus and, as I told you, the killer knows who you are. Did you have any dreams last night?"

"Not a dream, but I saw something in my mind. The killer's eyes."

"But not the rest of his face?"

"No, just the eyes. In the vision I was staring into his eyes while he tried to pull me toward him." I shuddered, remembering the madness shining in those eyes. "The guy's seriously crazy, Abby."

"He'd have to be, dear, to do what he's done. How do you know he was watching the house?"

"After the vision, I ran to the window. When the lightning flashed, I thought I saw someone standing in the street, near the old elm tree. It was only for an instant. The next moment he was gone."

"Maybe it would be better if you came and stayed with me for a while."

"No, absolutely not. He could follow me and you'd be in danger too. I wish I could figure out some way to let Bill know what's happening. But I can't. Not without telling him how I know these things."

"I think the situation might come to that."

"No. I'm not going to tell Bill I'm psychic. He'd share the information with Comacho, and things are bad enough right now without that. Some people are treating me as if I'm a pariah. Last night at Joe's, I had dinner with Charles—"

"The photographer?"

"Yes. And when I walked in, the room got quiet. I don't need everyone in town knowing about my little talent. They'd think I'm nuts."

"I see your point, but—"

She was interrupted by a knock at the front door. I got up and went to the door. Opening it, I found Charles, with a sheepish grin on his face, standing on the porch. In his hand he held a box of doughnuts. Their sweet, yeasty smell set my empty stomach rumbling. Maybe it couldn't handle eggs and bacon right now, but baked goods were a different story.

"I'm sorry. I know it's early and I don't want to intrude, but I had such a good time with you last night." Charles picked nervously at the corner of the doughnut box. "I can't remember the last time I talked about my mother with anyone. It was, ah, ah, nice." He gave a little shrug. "I wanted to do something nice for you, so when I saw these at the bakery...Here," he said, shoving the box toward me, and turned to leave.

"No. Wait, Charles," I said, placing my hand on his arm and stopping him. I looked down at what I was wearing. Sweats and an old T-shirt. Not the best look for entertaining, but oh well. "Why don't you join us? I'm just having coffee with my grandmother."

"Are you sure I'm not interrupting?" he asked skeptically.

"Yeah, I'm sure," I said with a grin.

"Okay. I'd love to. Thank you."

Charles followed me into the kitchen where Abby still sat at the table.

"Abby, I'd like you to meet Charles Thornton. Charles, this is my grandmother, Abigail McDonald."

Charles shook Abby's hand. "It's nice to meet you, ma'am."

"Thank you. It's nice meeting you. Please sit down."

"Look, Abby, Charles brought doughnuts—fresh from the bakery," I said, setting the box in the middle of the table.

"How nice," she replied, ignoring the doughnuts.

I shrugged and picked out one from the box. The sugary dough seemed to melt in my mouth when I took a bite. "Delicious," I mumbled to Charles.

With a bob of his head, Charles acknowledged my remark while he pulled out a chair and sat down.

I poured him a cup of coffee and joined them at the table.

"Thanks, Ophelia." Turning away from me, he faced

Abby. "You know, Mrs. McDonald, you're something of a legend in Summerset."

"I don't know about that."

"Really, you are. I admire how you're taking a stand against PP International."

"I'm not the only one taking a stand."

"No, but you're the one leading the opposition. I've a feeling the group wouldn't be nearly as successful without you."

"No one is indispensable, Mr. Thornton," Abby said, swirling her coffee around in her cup.

This conversation isn't going well, I thought while I picked at the edge of the doughnut. For some reason, Abby seemed to resent Charles's presence.

"Please call me Charles. I've always been interested in environmental issues myself. I don't know if Ophelia told you, but I'm also a writer and I'd love to do a story on your group."

"I don't know if that would be possible, Mr. Thornton," Abby replied. "Everyone's distracted right now, and I don't know who would have the time to give you an interview."

What? Abby turning down free publicity for her cause? What's up with that? I gave her a perplexed look.

She met my look with a slight shake of her head.

Charles squirmed uncomfortably in his chair. "I'd hoped you would have the time, Mrs. McDonald."

"I'm sorry I don't. I also own a greenhouse and my busy season is beginning."

"I understand. Well, I must be going," Charles said, standing. "Thank you for the coffee, Ophelia. Mrs. McDonald, again, it was nice to meet you."

"You too, Mr. Thornton," Abby said, looking down at her cup.

"I'll walk you to the door, Charles," I said and stood.

At the door Charles said in a slight whisper, "I don't think your grandmother likes me."

"It's not that, Charles," I responded, shaking my head. "She has a lot on her mind right now. The murder has upset her and she's worried about PP International. Don't take her attitude personally."

"If you're sure?"

"I'm sure. Thank you for the box of doughnuts. It was very thoughtful of you."

He took my hand in his. "My pleasure. I'd really like to see you again, Ophelia. May I call you later?"

"I think I'd like that, Charles," I said, nodding my head.

While I stood in the doorway and watched Charles pull away in his car, I thought about the way Abby had acted. What was the matter with her? I'd never seen her treat someone as coldly as she had Charles. Shutting the door, I marched back into the kitchen.

"Hey, what's up with the way you treated Charles? He thinks you don't like him."

"I don't know him well enough to make that kind of a judgment," Abby said, picking up her cup and walking to the sink with it.

"You know what I mean. I've never seen you be so distant with someone. You weren't very gracious."

Abby relaxed against the counter. "Did you see that young man's aura?"

"No, I didn't look at his aura. You said not to do that without the person's permission. You said it was rude. And what's his aura got to do with anything?"

"It has *holes* in it."

"So? Didn't you tell me holes can indicate someone's upset? And I'm sure he was upset. You weren't very friendly. Anyway, doesn't an aura change from day to day?"

"Yes."

"Well, maybe something else is bothering him. Something we don't know about."

"Are you going to continue to see him?"

Before I answered her, I heard another knock at the front door.

"God, doesn't anyone around here ever look at a clock?" I said, striding to the door. Fuming, I looked out the window to see Edna Walters standing on the porch.

Her eyes darted back and forth while she gripped her purse tightly in her hand.

I opened the door as she was raising one hand to knock again.

"Ophelia, I was driving by and saw Abby's truck. Is she here? I need to talk to her," Edna said and walked through the door, her eyes searching for Abby.

I stood to the side with my hand still on the door. "Come right in, Edna," I said to her retreating back.

From the doorway to the kitchen, I watched while Edna crumpled onto a chair and began to sob. What now?

"I don't know what to do, Abby. I'm afraid Harley's done it this time," she said, her voice catching as she spoke.

Abby stood next to Edna's chair, patting her shoulder and making comforting sounds.

"Okay," I said, walking into the kitchen, "what *has* Harley done?"

Edna lifted her tear-stained face and looked at me. "Last night the storm knocked out the electricity."

"Yes, I know, Edna."

"It did at PP International's farrowing operation too. Gladys Simpson called me this morning to tell me." Edna spoke rapidly, making her false teeth click.

"Tell you what, Edna?" I asked.

"That someone had monkeyed around with PP International's emergency generator. It's supposed to kick on when the power's out, so the ventilation system stays in operation. But it didn't 'cause someone fiddled with it."

"And you think that someone is Harley?"

"Y-y-yes," she stuttered. "That many animals in a confined space without ventilation, they started dying right off. Gladys said she heard PP International's lost as many as twenty sows."

"Doesn't Bill still have a deputy stationed at PP International?" I asked.

"Yes, but Gladys said the generator could've been tampered with days ago, before you found the body, Ophelia. And whoever did it was waiting for a storm to knock out the power. I know they'll blame Harley. Oh, I don't know what to do, I don't know what to do," she said, wringing her hands. "They'll put him in jail for sure."

"Edna, calm down," Abby said, rubbing between her shoulders.

Edna grabbed Abby's other hand. "Would you please talk to him? He might listen to you."

"No, she won't."

They both looked at me, surprised.

"I'll go."

I walked out of the kitchen to go change. If I was going to have a showdown with a redneck, I might as well dress the part.

Nineteen

Harley Walter's farm was located about three miles from Abby's, not far from the proposed PP International building site. I understood why Harley didn't want eight thousand pigs for neighbors, but the dope was going about it the wrong way. And Edna was right to be afraid for him. Bill had already warned him once.

As I pulled into Harley's driveway, I tugged my baseball cap lower on my head and pushed my sunglasses higher up my nose. The sunglasses had been a last-minute thought. Comacho hid behind his in order to intimidate me, why couldn't I do the same to Harley?

Getting out of my car, I noticed two abandoned cars. Their wheels had been removed and they were setting on concrete blocks. An old green truck was parked next to them. Its hood was off and made the truck look as if it had been scalped. The windshield was a spiderweb of cracks and weeds hid the tires from sight. The whole place had a junkyard look.

Harley puttered around in the garage, working on yet another old truck. He stopped and watched me.

"What do you want? Your witch of a grandmother

send you?" he called to me as I strolled up the weed-in-fested yard.

Witch? Why witch? I was sure he meant the remark as an insult. I felt a flutter of irritation, but tamped it down. My job was to reason with Harley, and I couldn't do it if I were angry.

A tight smile stretched my lips. "Your grandmother asked me to talk to you. She's worried about you, Harley. Thinks maybe you're taking this PP International thing too far."

"Ha. The old biddy. I told her to keep her nose out of my business. She doesn't understand." He whirled around, putting his back to me. "She thinks by saying, 'Please, oh, please, Mr. Kyle, don't build your building,'" he said, wiggling his head and mincing his words, "Kyle will stop. Well, they won't, not until somebody stands up to them. Make them feel a little pain."

He slammed his hands down on the hood of the truck, startling me. Man, did this guy have a lot of rage inside of him. I felt sorry for Edna.

"Look, Harley," I said, trying to calm him down. "I know you're upset, but violence never solves anything."

He spun to face me, glaring. "You don't know nothing. Sometimes it takes extreme measures to solve a problem. Kyle and his buddies have to be hurt where it counts, in their pockets. They lose enough money, they'll pull up stakes and go. And it takes a man to make that happen, not a bunch of little old ladies who ought to be in some nursing home instead of running the show."

He'd already tried to insult Abby by calling her a witch. And now he said she should be in a nursing home? I felt my blood pressure do a steady rise.

"Listen, buster, one of those little old ladies happens to be *my* grandmother." I whipped my sunglasses off.

"You've shot your mouth off about Abby twice. Don't try it again. You may not respect yours, but you'll bloody well show respect to mine. You got that?"

"Yeah, I got it," he said, his voice carrying a sneer.

"Good," I said, standing with my hands on my hips and giving him what I hoped was my toughest look. "Your grandmother, for some strange reason, wants to keep your sorry butt out of jail and she sent me out here. You'd better straighten up or I'll help them put you in jail myself."

Harley smirked. "I'm not going to jail. I haven't done nothing."

"You might want to practice saying that, Harley, because I imagine the next person you're going to be talking to will be Bill. And he'll cut right through your load of crap."

"Maybe. But he can't prove anything. Anyway, my cause is just."

"You're willing to go to jail for your cause; be a martyr?"

I saw his eyes gleam while he thought of all the attention that would bring him.

"If I have to," he said and picked up a spray can. He started to walk over to the truck. As he did, he snapped some kind of mask over his mouth and nose. After shaking the can a couple of times, he sprayed the contents of the can on the engine.

"Jeez, what is that stuff? It stinks," I said, holding my nose.

He pulled the mask down. "Ether. And if you don't want to pass out, I suggest you get out of here," he said and pushed the mask back over his mouth.

When I reached my car, I looked back toward the garage. Harley stood by the truck with the can of ether in one hand. And even with twenty feet between us, I felt the anger in his eyes, staring at me from underneath the bill of his baseball cap.

I decided to drive to Abby's and give her an update on my conversation with Harley, but when I rounded the corner of her lane, I saw Bill's patrol car parked by the greenhouse. My heart jumped and I skidded the car to a halt.

"What is it? What's happened?" I said, running inside.

Abby and Bill were standing by some of Abby's plants. I detected a strange odor in the air.

"What's that smell?" I said, wrinkling my nose.

"Herbicide. Someone gave Abby's plants a good dose of it last night."

My eyes scanned the greenhouse. All of Abby's plants looked brown, as if they'd been burned. Glancing over my shoulder, I saw her maidenhair fern. Its fronds were drooping and the floor beneath the fern was covered with its leaves.

"Oh, Abby, your fern. They got it too?"

"Yes, they did," she said, her eyes filling with tears.

Abby's fern had been a wedding gift from her mother. She had carted it all the way from Appalachia when she married my grandfather and settled in Iowa. In the spring, when the temperature warmed, the fern was moved from the house to the greenhouse. The fern had sat proudly on its stand behind Abby's old-fashioned cash register every spring and summer since I was a child.

"Abby, I'm sorry," I said and gave her a hug.

She sniffed. "It's all right, dear. Everything has its season. I hate the poor old thing had to go this way. It would've been easier if the fern had died on its own, in its own time."

"Got any ideas, Bill?" I asked.

"Not really, but somebody sure was busy last night. I imagine poisoning Abby's plants is related to the incident at PP International. We think the hogs are being poisoned too."

"You're kidding," I said. "I thought they were dying because of the lack of ventilation last night?"

"Yeah, we did too. But when the manager checked the feed bins this morning, he noticed one of the lids was on cockeyed. He thinks something's been dumped in the feed. They've sent samples to the lab, but we won't know till later on this afternoon."

"But wouldn't the manager have seen or heard a noise?" I asked.

"No. His trailer is on the other side of the property and the bins are behind the hog buildings." Bill scratched his head and snapped his notebook shut. "Guess I'd better go talk to Harley. Kyle's fit to be tied—the big boys are coming in from Chicago and he's going to want answers to give them. Maybe I can shake Harley up."

"What big boys from Chicago?"

"From PP International's corporate office."

"Wait a second, Bill. I—" I was interrupted by my cell phone ringing. I answered it.

"Hello."

"Hi, Ophelia."

"Charles." I walked over to the corner of the greenhouse, away from Bill and Abby.

"I know this is kind of sudden, but I just read in the paper there's a wine tasting at a café in Des Moines tonight. Would you like to attend?"

"Gosh, Charles, I can't. It sounds like fun, but now

isn't a good time. Abby's greenhouse was vandalized last night."

"I'm sorry. Is there anything I can do to help?"

"No, but I do have to go. I'll call you later. Bye." I disconnected and looked over to see Abby watching me.

"What?" I said defensively.

"Charles?" she asked, arching an eyebrow.

"Who's Charles?" Bill butted in.

"Never mind him, Bill. Forget Charles. I wanted to ask you how the murder investigation is going."

"You know I can't talk about it, Ophelia."

"I know. Umm, is Comacho still hanging around?"

"Yes, he is." Bill chuckled. "I don't know what you said to him. But from the way he was acting, you sure dusted the seat of his pants. You did, didn't you?"

"I don't know what you mean, Bill. I answered his questions as politely as I could, under the circumstances."

Bill chuckled again. "Yeah. Right, 'under the circumstances.' That's a good one."

After Bill left, Abby and I looked over her fern.

"I didn't want to ask you in front of Bill, but is there anything you can do for the fern, any way you can bring it back?"

Abby shook her head sadly. "No, it's beyond any special magick I possess."

"Do you think someone from PP International is responsible?"

"Maybe. Gladys called earlier and told me the manager of the farrowing unit was bragging about bringing in 'protection' from Chicago."

"I thought the men coming were from PP International's corporate office."

"Oh, I'm sure they *are* from the corporate office. I'm also sure they're very large men with broken noses."

"You don't sound too worried about Kyle bringing in muscle."

"I learned a long time ago even magick can't control everything. Nevertheless, I was upset when I received the certified letter from their attorneys today."

"What? What certified letter?"

"PP International's attorneys are threatening a lawsuit charging defamation of character. Everyone in the group received one."

"Abby, that's awful."

She patted my shoulder while her eyes surveyed her damaged greenhouse. "Don't worry. We'll hire an attorney to settle the matter."

"Not to change the subject, but Bill said Comacho is still in town. He hasn't been here, has he?"

"Why, yes, as a matter of fact, he has."

"Damn him!" I stomped my foot. "I told him he'd better not harass you. And why didn't you tell me?"

"First of all, he didn't harass me. He was polite and respectful while he questioned me about the group's activities. He didn't cross any lines. It was routine, Ophelia," she said sternly. "I didn't tell you because you were upset this morning. And it wouldn't have been appropriate to tell you in front of Charles." She settled a disapproving look on me.

"You know I don't understand this. You don't approve of Charles, but Comacho doesn't bother you. I don't get it."

"Charles has holes in his aura."

"What about Comacho? I'd imagine he's got plenty of holes."

"No, he doesn't. He has a pleasant aura. A healthy one with a lot of orange and red, indicating passion and vitality."

"You read him? That's the second time you've read someone without their permission."

"I've heard so much about him from you, I wanted to see what kind of a man he is."

"The red should've told you about his anger."

"Red can also indicate a zest for life and a man of strong convictions. He also had a nice bit of green and indigo in his aura. Green shows his compassion and the indigo means he's highly intuitive. With the amount of indigo he had, it wouldn't surprise me if he's a touch psychic."

My mouth fell open and I made a choking sound. *Give me a break. Comacho, psychic?*

Abby continued, not noticing my expression. "His aura was a little muddy around the throat *chakra.* The color indicates he has trouble communicating his feelings."

"Yeah? Well, what color indicates he's a jerk?"

"Ophelia!"

"He is," I said and began to pace back and forth in the greenhouse. "I don't believe you. You're sticking up for Comacho—after everything he's done to me—"

"Ophelia, listen to me—"

"No. I won't listen. You're defending Comacho and don't tell me you're not," I said, stopping to point my finger at her. "But when a nice man like Charles comes into my life, you don't approve!" I started pacing again. "What's the deal? Are you jealous of Charles? Is that why you don't want him hanging around?"

Abby bristled. "What are you talking about? What jealousy? I'd never be jealous of a man who treated you well."

"What if he came between you and me?"

"How could Charles come between us?"

"If I became involved with him, I might ignore my training. You wouldn't want that."

"That *is* a nasty remark, Ophelia Jensen, and quite beneath you. I have never wanted anything other than your happiness, but you don't even know this man. And you're talking about a romance? What *are* you thinking?"

"I don't know what I'm thinking about Charles, but I did expect more from you than 'He has holes in his aura.'"

"That's enough, Ophelia. I think you'd better go before you say something you might regret. We'll talk again when you can discuss this matter rationally," Abby said, pivoted on her heel, and walked out of the greenhouse, leaving me alone.

Damn, my grandmother had kicked me out.

Twenty

Moping around the house for the rest of the afternoon, I thought about my argument with Abby. I hated arguing with her, but she was wrong about Comacho. Compassionate, a zest for life, psychic—ha. Should've told her his nickname was Iceman. Couldn't be too sympathetic if he'd earned a nickname like that.

Instead of worrying about my argument with Abby, I should be worrying about the Harvester stalking me. My house was secure; I'd checked all the windows and doors when I got home. And I hadn't sensed any strange vibes. While I was driving home, I had watched in the rearview mirror to see if anyone followed, but nothing suspicious. Just normal, everyday traffic, and I recognized most of the vehicles. Advantage of living in a small town.

Advantage of living in a small town? I thought about it. *Everyone knows their neighbors and a stranger in town generates talk. How could a serial killer, a stranger, slip into town without anyone commenting on the new face in town?* I chewed the inside of my mouth. *Of course, until last night, I didn't know he was in Summerset. Maybe he showed up at night. Summerset is close to Des Moines. He could be staying there or in one of the other small towns nearby.*

What about all the publicity the murder had generated? Yesterday a lot of strangers had been in town. Maybe one was the killer? I wonder if he had the audacity to stay in Summerset? I could ask Georgia, the owner of the local bed-and-breakfast, about any new guests, or Darci could ask her. Georgia was not only one of Darci's closest friends, she was one of the biggest gossips in town and she told Darci everything.

While I was standing in the kitchen pondering, Lady zipped by me, headed for the front door. Someone must be here. I followed her and saw Darci's car parked in my drive.

Darci got out of her car. She carried a pizza box in one hand and a six-pack of beer in the other. *Is that a friend or what?*

"Hey, Darci," I said, opening the door.

"Hi. I didn't know if you wanted company, but I knew you wouldn't turn me away if I brought pizza," she said and walked in.

"I never refuse pizza. Do you want to eat in the kitchen or the living room?"

"Let's eat in the living room."

"I'll grab plates and forks from the kitchen," I said and headed down the hallway while Darci set our meal out on the coffee table.

"Hey, do you want a glass for your beer?" I called from the kitchen.

"Nope, out of the bottle's fine."

"This is great, Darci," I said, as I joined her in the living room.

"I figured you'd enjoy it. We can stuff our faces till our blue jeans pop," she said and dug into the pizza.

"How was it at the library today?" I asked between bites.

"The usual, I guess. Claire and I manned the counter and we didn't have much traffic till the afternoon. Everyone's talking about PP International and the dead hogs."

"Bill said they expected lab results back this afternoon. Did you hear if the feed was tampered with?"

"Yup, sure was—insecticide. Naturally, everyone thinks Harley did it. If Bill can prove it, Harley won't be causing any more problems. He'll be sitting in jail."

"Anything about the murder?"

"Nope. Dead hogs replaced the dead body as the main topic of conversation," she said, licking pizza sauce off her thumb. "Oh, some little man did stop by asking for you."

"Did he look like a ferret?"

She giggled. "Yeah, he did."

"Must've been Fletcher Beasley," I said and frowned.

"The reporter?"

"Yeah. I ran into him yesterday. I'd hoped he left town, but no such luck." I shook my head in disgust. "He can't get to me here, at least. I don't think he'd have the guts to come to my house."

"Olive Martin was in too, but Claire and I ignored her. Golly, I think it stinks what she's trying to do to you." Darci picked up her beer and took a long drink.

"Don't worry about Olive. She can't cause me trouble."

"I did hear Olive talking about the guys from Chicago."

"I heard about them. Gladys called Abby and told her. Has anyone seen them?"

"Not yet. But I bet they're big, bad, and mean. Do you think they're mob?"

"I don't know, but Harley had better watch it. If he tries any more of his tricks, he'll wind up getting the crap kicked out of him."

I thought for a moment, spinning my beer bottle around. What would be the best way to broach the subject with Darci? I needed her help, but I didn't want her running off to investigate Harley.

"Ahh, Darci, speaking of Harley, what do you know about him?"

"Just what I told you the other day." Her eyes took on a gleam and she sat up straight. "Say, are you starting to think Harley could be the killer?"

Taking a drink of my beer, I didn't answer her.

"You are, I know you are. I can see it on your face," she said, her excitement rising. "What do we do now? Go toss his place? Find the evidence?"

"Whoa—stop right there. *We're* not doing anything. Especially 'toss' his place. God, Darci, you sound like *you're* in the mob."

She made a little pout. "Well, what *are* we going to do?"

"First you're going to tell me what you know about serial killers."

"Okay." She settled back on the couch. "Of course, there are always exceptions, but most are men, between the ages of eighteen and forty-five. Usually, they are the same race as their victims. They're manipulative and into self-gratification at any cost. They get angry easily, they enjoy the publicity their murders generate, and often they will taunt the police investigating the murders. Some killers develop an almost personal relationship with the investigators. Has that happened to Bill?"

"Not that I know of? He's not talking."

"Too bad." She sipped her beer before she continued.

"Cruelty excites them. Symptoms of their psychosis are shown even in childhood. Experts call the symptoms the *triad*: torturing small animals, setting fires to cause damage, and bed-wetting into adolescence. But the most important thing about a serial killer," she said, setting her beer down and looking at me, "they enjoy killing. They enjoy it. They enjoy the total control over another human being. In fact, the high they get from that control drives them and it must be maintained."

I watched Darci as she talked. She was amazing. I knew some people in town blew her off as a mental lightweight, but they were wrong. A bright and cagey mind hid beneath all that hair. A mind that soaked up information like the ground soaks up water after a rain.

"Did you hear me, Ophelia?"

"What? I'm sorry, I was thinking about something else. What did you say?"

"I asked you if any of the information I rattled off sounds like Harley?"

"The anger does."

"And the control part. You know he's jealous of Abby, don't you?"

"Yeah, kind of figured it out after talking to him today. He thinks he should be in charge, not an old woman, which is what he called Abby."

Darci choked on her beer. "He called Abby an old lady? He wouldn't call her that to her face. She'd take his head off." She pursed her lips. "Too bad we don't know if he showed any of the *triad*'s symptoms." Her faced brightened. "Let's call Edna and ask her."

"Oh sure." I held my hand up to my ear as if I were holding a phone receiver. " 'Hello, Edna. Would you mind telling me if Harley tortured small animals and set fires as a child? Oh, and by the way, did he pee the bed when he was a teenager?' "

Darci smiled broadly. "Okay, maybe we can't call Edna. You won't let me burgle Harley's." She must have noticed my face go white. "Silly, I'm teasing. I've read enough about these killers to know I don't want to get caught by one." Leaning forward, her face became serious. "What are we going to do?"

"You're an expert at worming information out of people. I want you to find out what route Harley took when he drove a semitruck. Find out what states he visited and what towns. We'll match up what you find with where the murders occurred. If there's a match, we'll turn all the information over to Bill and let him handle it."

"What are you going to do?"

"Umm, well," I said, looking down and picking at the fringe on the rug.

"You've been leaving information out, haven't you?"

I looked over at her. "Yeah. I was afraid you'd go charging off and get hurt. I know whose body was in the ditch."

"But how? Who?" Darci's eyes widened. "Sure, a vision. I keep forgetting you can do that. Did you see the killer's face too?"

"No," I said while I felt the tears gather at the thought of Gus. "The body in the ditch—it's Gus Pike."

Darci gasped and covered her mouth with her hand. "Oh my God, no. Gus was a harmless old man."

A tear slipped down my cheek. "I know. But Gus cheated the murderer out of his kill. He actually died of a heart attack, I think." I wiped away the tear. "And I feel guilty that I can't tell Bill who it is without explaining how I know."

Darci stared thoughtfully at the now-cold pizza. Lifting her eyes, she looked at me. "Don't worry about it. I'll go out to Gus's place tomorrow and I'll report to Bill that Gus is missing. He'll have to put two and two together and figure out the body's Gus."

"I also saw the killer's weapon."

Darci pulled her hand through her hair. "What a mess. Bill needs to know about Gus and about the murder weapon. But you can't talk to him without giving away how you know all this stuff."

"I know. I was going to write an anonymous note, describing the weapon. Yeah, I know, pretty lame, but I couldn't think of any other way."

"Hey, a note isn't a bad idea. Let's see," she said, tapping her cheek with her finger. "You'll need a piece of generic paper, one that can't be traced. Same with the pen. No, that's too complicated." She snapped her fingers. "I know, type the note on a computer. But not the library's or yours: It could lead back to you somehow." Darci grabbed her purse and pulled out a piece of paper and a pen. "Here," she said, handing them to me. "Write your note. I'll type it and get it to Bill."

"But if using my computer could lead to me, yours might lead back to you," I said, writing my note.

She waved away my concerns. "Don't worry about it—I'm not going to use mine or the library's. I know just the right person. I'll use hers."

"Who?" I asked, looking up.

Darci's face glowed with an evil grin. "Olive Martin's."

Twenty-One

I'd watched Darci drive away to make sure no one was lurking in the shadows, spying on her. Before I went to bed, I once again checked all the doors and windows. And to be safe, I left the front porch light on to discourage unwanted visitors.

Once in bed, thoughts of my argument weighed heavily on my heart. If it weren't so late, I'd call and apologize. But now it would have to wait until morning. My last thought before sleep claimed me: *Please, no dreams tonight.*

I didn't get my request.

Once again I stood on Abby's front porch, watching Grandpa and Henry Comacho swing back and forth on the swing. This time I saw Comacho's aura. It glowed in swirls of red, orange, green, and indigo, like Abby had described it. But Grandpa's aura shone with pure white light, the color of cosmic energy. The color made sense. Grandpa had crossed over and his aura reflected his spirit.

Their heads were bent close together, and this time, Comacho was doing all the talking while Grandpa listened closely to what Comacho was saying. Was he telling my grandfather what a pain in the butt his granddaughter was?

I knew the dream would shift and I waited patiently for the next scene to unfold.

When the scene changed, I found myself on a dark street. I was present, but not present. Somehow I wasn't part of the scene. I was an observer, floating in time and space, watching events beyond my control happen.

But a new element had been added to the vision—music. To my ears, it sounded like a song played on an old player piano. Strangely, the song I heard was "Pop Goes the Weasel." It played repeatedly in my head, but when the music reached the "Pop goes the weasel!" the note for "pop" was flat, discordant, harsh. Off-tune. Why?

A man walked the empty streets alone. He sensed someone followed. Stopping, he peered over his shoulder and listened for echoing footsteps. Hearing nothing, he walked on, in and out of the streetlights. He was anxious to get home. He'd had a long day. When his steps quickened, so did the killer's.

The killer felt his victim's fear and it delighted him. In his excitement his black aura curled around him. Fear made the chase more thrilling. He'd planned it all so carefully. He'd watched his victim for days. He knew all of the man's habits, routines. Soon the victim would be at the capture point. The white van the killer would use to transport his victim to the killing place was parked a block from the man's house.

The killer crossed the street, traveling away from his victim, and cut through the alley. He arrived at the van shortly before the victim. Crouching next to the van, he waited, the damp rag clutched tightly in his gloved hand.

The man passed the rear of the van and the killer sprang, grabbing the man from behind with one arm.

With his other hand, he held the damp rag over the man's nose and mouth. The victim struggled, but the fight soon left him and he slumped forward.

Balancing the nearly unconscious man with one arm, the killer wrenched the back door open and wrestled the man inside. He crawled in next to his victim and pulled the door shut. Opening the bag he'd placed near the back, he grabbed the duct tape and wound it around the man's wrists and ankles. The last piece he placed over the man's mouth. He would listen to his victim's screams later.

It took the killer a long time to reach his special place. Once there, he drove the van into the barn. Opening the door, he saw the victim was awake. *Good, it's more fun when they're conscious,* he thought.

The man tried to struggle while the killer hauled him out of the van, but he was still weak from the effects of the chemical the killer had used to render him senseless. His eyes, wide with fear, searched for an escape. When he didn't find one, a sense of doom spread through his mind. He was helpless as the killer half-dragged, half-carried him to a small room in the back of the barn.

The killer pushed the man on to a small cot, where manacles were attached to the cot's frame. Using his knee to hold the man down, he cut the duct tape and attached the manacles to the man's wrists and ankles.

Once the victim was secured, he crossed the room and lit the candles. The entire room—walls and floor— was covered with heavy plastic. But from underneath the plastic, picture glass reflected the candlelight. Walking back to the cot, he stood over his victim, admiring his work, relishing the fear in the man's face. He reached down, toward the man's face, grabbed a corner of the duct tape, and...

I shot up in bed. *Ringing,* I heard ringing. What in the hell was ringing? The phone—the phone was ringing.

"Hello," I said, fumbling with the receiver.

"Ophelia, this is Arthur."

"Who?"

"Arthur. I have some bad news—I'm at the hospital with Abby. She's been hurt."

The last thing I heard was Arthur's voice coming from the receiver dangling off the nightstand as I rushed out the door.

"Hello? Hello? Ophelia, are you there?"

They tried to force me to go home, but I wouldn't do it. I did manage to persuade Arthur to go home. He moved sadly out of Abby's hospital room, taking one last look through his thick glasses at her lying motionless in her bed.

From this day forward, I would be in his debt for finding Abby. He had tried calling her several times during the evening. When she didn't answer, he'd driven to her house to check on her. The light was on in the greenhouse, so he stopped there first. He'd found her lying on the floor unconscious and immediately called 911. Once they arrived at the hospital, he not only called me, but also my mother. Another debt I owed him.

The doctors said Abby had suffered a blow to the back of her head. It appeared Abby had been working in the greenhouse, trying to save some of her plants, no doubt, when an intruder knocked her out. Her brain scans were normal, but she was in a coma. The danger they said would come from posttrauma swelling of the brain. The next few days were critical.

Even though her condition was critical, the doctors gave me permission to stay in her room. I spent the night curled up in a chair near her bed, watching a parade of nurses come in and out, checking her vitals. Sleep was impossible. Memories of Abby and guilt crowded it from my mind.

Why did I argue with her? Will I have the opportunity to say I was sorry? Why didn't I feel her danger? Has my gift let me down once again as it had with Brian? I hugged my knees to my chest. *Who did this to her? Harley, out of jealousy? PP International's imported goons? Was it the same person who had poisoned her plants?* Wiping the tears from my face, I stared out the window at the rising sun and tried to think what I should do next, but without Abby's guidance I was lost. Lost and afraid.

Hours ticked by and the sun climbed higher in the sky while I sat there in misery. Suddenly the door to Abby's room softly whooshed open and my mother breezed in. She glanced at me, giving me a small smile, and went straight to the bed. Bending down, she gently brushed Abby's hair back from her forehead.

"What have you got yourself into now, Mother?" she whispered. Straightening, she wiped a tear from her face and looked at me, sitting in the chair, still curled up in a tight ball.

"You look awful, dear."

I gave her a watery smile. "Thanks, Mom."

She crossed the room and knelt in front of me. Placing her arms around me, she hugged me tight.

All the fear and pain I'd felt over the last few hours erupted from me in gasping sobs. I clutched my mother's shoulders and buried my face in her soft warmth while my body shook. Finally, the sobbing subsided and I raised my head.

"Better?" she asked.

I took a depth breath and blew it out. "Yeah," I said,

smoothing the last of the tears away. I picked up my backpack and rummaged around for a tissue and my brush. I found the tissue, but no brush. Oh well, instead I grabbed a scrunchie out of the bag and twisted it around my tangled hair.

Mother still knelt in front of me and eyed me speculatively. Little lines of worry wrinkled her forehead and her lips were pursed. It was a look I'd seen before—when I was a teenager—and she had suspected I'd been up to no good. Mother supposedly didn't have any psychic talent, but she'd always seemed to instinctively know when I was in trouble. Her scrutiny made me squirm in my chair.

"How's Dad?" I asked, stalling for time while I tried to decide how much information to give her.

If I told her too much, she'd call in the cavalry—namely my dad. And he'd be on me like stink. He'd be so determined to protect me that he wouldn't let me out of his sight. I couldn't find the killer and the person responsible for hurting Abby if that happened.

But if I didn't give her enough information, she could blunder into the middle of what was going on and be hurt like Abby. I loved my mother too much to let that happen.

"Did you hear me, Ophelia?" she asked, rising and pulling up a chair next to me.

"What?" I shook my head to clear it. "Sorry, I tuned out for a moment. What did you say?"

"I said your father was concerned about Mother, but otherwise fine. He sends his love, of course. All the flights out of Key West were later, so he drove me to Miami to catch an earlier flight." Reaching in her bag, she drew out her needlepoint and set to work. "Are you going to tell me what happened?"

I made my decision—I told her everything. About the serial killer, Abby's fight with PP International, my visions, my dreams. It all came pouring out of me.

When I'd finished, she put down her needlepoint and took her glasses off.

"Well, you and Mother have been busy, haven't you?"

"I guess," I answered, my voice full of guilt.

"My first thought is to pack the both of you up and take you back to Florida with me." She gazed at Abby. "Obviously, I can't do that. And even if I could, neither one of you would agree to come with me. Or I could call your father."

I groaned.

She gave me an arched look. "Right, I agree. Your father loves Mother as much as I do, but he's never really understood the gifts you two possess." She stopped for a moment and picked her needlepoint up. "All righty, then. What are you going to do?"

" 'Do'? I don't know what to do, Mom," I said, rubbing my eyes with the heel of my hand. "I'm beat without Abby, without her guidance."

"Nonsense, I'm sure Mother has taught you well. You have gifts, Ophelia. Gifts most people don't." She shook her head sadly. "You know I've envied you those gifts. And regretted I wasn't one of the chosen, like you and Mother. I've always felt left out. Great confession for a mother to make, isn't it?"

I patted her arm. "The gift isn't much of a blessing at times, Mom."

"I suppose so, but still..," she said, smoothing her needlepoint and thinking. "Oh well, what is, is. Everyone has their own path to follow. Now you must follow yours and without Mother leading you. This is your time, Ophelia."

I slunk down in my chair. "But I don't know how."

"Sure you do. But I think you're afraid."

"I am not."

"Oh, yes, you are, dear." She put her needlepoint down and stared at me. "You're afraid of your gift, afraid to use it, afraid of what people might think if you do. But you can't afford to surrender to the fear, Ophelia. You can't sit back, wringing your hands, questioning your gift. Use what's been given you."

At her words I felt a spark of energy glow inside me. Like a twig suddenly catching fire. Was Mother right? Had fear been blocking my talent? The fire inside burned hotter. A killer had taken Brian's life and almost ruined mine. It was the killer and what he did, not Comacho that had sent me over the edge five years ago. And he was out there somewhere, watching me, playing with me. I sat up straight in my chair while the fire spread through me.

Standing, I crossed the room to where Abby lay in her bed. She looked fragile and helpless and, for the first time, looked all of her seventy-four years. She was the kindest, gentlest person I knew and never in her life had she hurt anyone. She didn't deserve to be treated so cruelly. My anger fueled the fire while I stood staring down at her.

The fire throbbed deep in my soul. It kindled each cell, each nerve, till I felt as if I'd burst into flames.

Use my gift? Oh, I'd use my gift, all right! With one last look at Abby, I whirled around and ran from the room.

Twenty-Two

On the hilltop behind Abby's house I created my circle of salt as she had taught me. The air around me felt thick with ozone. Another storm approached, but I didn't care. My anger, my rage put me past caring. The fire kindled at the hospital burned hot, hotter than before. It consumed me from the inside out.

My cowled robe clung to my legs in the still-quiet world while I prepared myself for what I was about to do. Uttering a silent prayer that my magick be guided, I stepped to the north. I paused and it seemed the world waited for me to act.

Bending down, I scooped a handful of dirt and called to the element of Earth. Still holding it tightly in my hand, I closed my eyes and felt as if I'd been transported deep into the rich black soil. My skin tingled with the soil's energy of rebirth and my hand throbbed. I opened my eyes and my hand and with one quick move cast the soil in the air. Falling back on me, it showered me with tiny pinpricks of energy as the earth undulated beneath my feet.

Walking to the east, I called the element of Air. Lifting my arms, I tilted my head back and watched the clouds begin to swirl above me. They formed a rotating whirlpool of energy reaching down to surround me. The wind, created by the energy, tugged at my hair and plastered my robe against my body.

I walked against the wind to the south and called the element of Fire. Stretching out my arm, I pointed to the sky and traced a jagged line with my finger. Lightning flashed across the sky and the air around me felt scorched.

Stopping first to pull fresh air into my lungs, I walked around the circle to the west. Lifting my arms again, I called the element of Water. The clouds wrenched apart and torrents of rain poured down on me. Each raindrop sparkled and gleamed with power, drenching me in it.

Walking slowly to the center of the circle, I felt the power of the four elements rage around me—Earth, Air, Fire, and Water. Each different, with a different energy, but all joined, joined with me in my purpose. Opening both arms, I gathered the energy inside me. I felt the seductive power run through my blood, increasing in force, making my fire burn brighter.

In my mind I saw Abby lying still and lifeless. Put there by some unknown hand. I saw Brian ripped apart by a killer who thrived on pain and terror. The power inside me grew and grew till I thought I'd burst—fueled by my hate of those who sought to harm and my need for revenge. I struggled to keep it chained until I was ready.

Opening my arms farther still, I kept the vision of Abby and Brian in my mind. I would slip the chains and set my power free, free to seek out those who would hurt the innocent.

Suddenly a voice soft as a breeze whispered in my ear.

The power doesn't belong to you.

I lowered my arms. "Abby?"

You can't bend the world to suit your will, the voice whispered again.

I wiped away the tears that ran down my face, mingling with the rain. "Abby."

Your gift. Use it wisely. Follow the pattern.

"Oh, Abby," I said, sinking to my knees.

On the hilltop in my circle of salt, the energy I had called forth slowly faded. The earth no longer vibrated beneath me, clouds no longer swirled overhead, and lightning no longer flashed across the sky. And the rain fell in a cool, soothing shower on my bent head while I wept.

Wiping my face, I sat in the wet grass and stared out through the rain. *Follow the pattern,* Abby's voice had said. But what pattern? The murderer killed Brian with a knife and would've killed Gus the same way, but Gus beat him to it by dying of a heart attack. He'd marked both bodies after death—did Gus have a star on his forehead too? The bodies had been dumped differently: Brian's had been placed in a Dumpster and Gus's had been buried in the ditch. Gus had been set on fire, Brian hadn't. No pattern there.

Abby put a lot of stock in auras. I thought about the dreams I'd had, chasing the killer through the park, Gus's death and the dream I'd had last night. I shook my head, throwing droplets of water from my wet hair. No aura around the killer when I'd chased him. At Gus's place, the killer's aura had been a dark red. In the dream last night it had been black.

And the music—I'd never heard that before. Off-tune, false. The song hadn't rung true.

I smacked myself on the forehead. Jumping to my feet, I took off down the hill, slipping and sliding in the wet grass. I knew what to do. Like the runes had fore-told, it would require I sacrifice, sacrifice my pride, something dear to me, as Abby had pointed out. I'd have to ask for help from someone I disliked. And if I couldn't convince him I was right, I might wind up in jail.

A killer was here in Summerset, stalking me, for whatever reason, and he *was* the one responsible for the deaths of both Brian and Gus.

Comacho thought so too. He thought he was on the trail of the Harvester, who'd plagued the Midwest. His questions about PP International, Abby, and Darci were a smoke screen, a way to badger information out of me, to figure out what connection I might have with the Harvester.

The killer I'd dreamed of last night.

But last night the song I'd heard didn't ring true and the killer didn't ring true. Different aura, different killer. Comacho was looking for the wrong man—not the Harvester, but someone who killed for a personal reason.

A reason tied to me.

After calling the hospital and checking on Abby, I called Bill's office and asked the dispatcher to contact Henry Comacho and requested Henry call me on my cell phone. It didn't take long to get a response. I'd told him to meet me at Abby's. After changing into jeans and a sweat-shirt—didn't want Comacho to see me in my cowled robe—I waited by the greenhouse. He showed up about twenty minutes later.

"You must've read my mind—"

"What?" I asked, surprised.

"Hey, it's just an expression," he said, looking puzzled. "I'd planned on calling you. Seems the body you found in the ditch was another one of your friends, Gus

Pike. Care to explain here or do you want to accompany me to Bill's office?"

I scanned his face before I answered and felt nervous perspiration soak my shirt. *Well, at least he doesn't have his mirrored sunglasses on. Good. I need to see his eyes.*

"Here. I'll explain here. Let's go inside," I said, moving toward the greenhouse.

Comacho followed me into the greenhouse. Shoving my hands in my back pockets to keep from fidgeting, my eyes traveled over Abby's dead plants while I tried to think of a way to begin.

He scuffed the floor with his toe. "Bill told me about the break-in and gave me an update on her condition. I'm sorry. She's a nice lady."

"Yes, she is. It's for her sake I've decided to confide in you. Things are spinning out of control and it has to stop. It's too late to save Gus. But before someone else gets hurt…" I trailed off, letting my gaze travel over Comacho's face. Taking my hands out of my pockets, I continued. "I'm going to ask you not to say anything till I'm finished, okay?"

"Okay," he answered, perplexed.

God, this is going to be hard. Taking a deep breath, I stared directly into Comacho's eyes. "I'm a psychic."

"What?" His eyes widened in surprise.

I glared at him. "I asked you not to say anything. Talking about my talent isn't the easiest thing in the world for me. And I need you to listen."

"Sorry."

Breathing deeply, I started again. "Five years ago, when I came to the police station to report Brian missing, I knew he was already dead. I'd seen the murder. I'd hoped I was wrong, but…" I felt the tears start to gather in the corner of my eyes and I squeezed the bridge of my nose. "Anyway, I felt so guilty that I hadn't been able to save him, hadn't had the vision in time to help. The guilt sent me over the edge and I had my breakdown." The words came out in a rush. "I rejected my gift until last fall when Rick Delaney came to Summerset, investigating the drug ring. I was pulled into the situation, kicking and screaming all the way. It was my gift that led me to make the connection between Adam Hoffman and the drug lab. And I used my gift to give Rick and me time to escape."

"I won't ask you how right now. You can explain later. What does your 'gift' have to do with this situation?"

"It wasn't the smell that drew me to the ditch. I felt death. I did trip when I found the bloated pig. While I was lying there, I saw what happened to Gus."

"Really?"

"You don't believe me, do you?"

He shook his head. "It's hard to swallow. I deal in facts, not 'visions.'"

"You want facts? The killer dresses all in black, he's dark, dark hair, dark eyes. He carved a five-pointed star on Brian's forehead—and Gus's. Did they find the star on Gus's forehead or was the body too badly burned?"

He looked surprised. "How did you...Never mind, go on."

"He uses an unusual weapon. It's a dagger. I could draw it for you," I said, folding my arms.

Comacho stared at me, not answering.

This isn't going well. I searched my mind to come up with something to convince him I was telling the truth.

"Okay, still don't believe me." I took a deep breath. "The Harvester captures his victim and takes him to a special place, a barn."

"Did you 'see' where this barn is?"

"No, but the walls and floor are lined with plastic. Makes the cleanup easier. He keeps his victim chained to a cot with manacles. Did any of the bodies found in other states have bruising around the wrists?"

"How about residue from duct tape around the wrists and ankles? It prevents them from struggling."

He tossed his head. "You could be guessing."

"Okay. He subdues the victims by using a rag with some chemical sprayed on it."

"How did you know about the rag?"

I had his attention now.

"I told you, I'm a psychic."

"Oh yeah? How do you do at Lotto numbers?"

His sarcasm made me angry. "You don't get it, do you, Comacho? I'm trying to help you."

"Even if you are a psychic, nothing you've told me so far is much help."

Time to drop the bomb.

"Brian wasn't killed by the Harvester, the killer operating in the Midwest."

"Okay, that's it," he said, taking an angry step toward me. "You're going with me to Bill's office. You obviously know something, but what you're feeding me now is the biggest load of BS I've ever heard in my life."

I watched, my palms sweating, while Comacho pulled a pair of handcuffs out of his pocket and purposefully strode toward me.

Crap! He was going to arrest me.

Twenty-Three

"Wait," I said, holding up my hand to stop him. "Did Brian have tape residue around his wrists? Did the bodies in other states have the five-pointed star on their foreheads?"

Comacho stopped, listening.

Encouraged, I continued. "Gus died before the killer could murder him. I think, of a heart attack—"

"No smoke in the lungs," Comacho mumbled.

"What?"

"Keep talking."

"He was angry at being cheated. He got something from the house, drenched the body, and set it on fire."

"Okay," he said, nodding his head. "I'll play along. If Brian and Gus weren't victims of the Harvester, who killed them—and why? Can you answer that one, Ms. Psychic?"

"No," I answered softly.

"What? I didn't hear you?"

I kicked a broken pot lying by my foot and sent it spinning across the floor. "I said 'no.' Don't you think if I did, I'd tell you? All I know is the reason has something to do with me." I sighed deeply. "And I'm scared,

Comacho. I don't want anyone else close to me to die."

God, it took a lot to admit to him how scared I was. I hate being weak, hate being vulnerable. So much for my pride. It hung about me in shreds now.

Comacho must've believed I was scared. He looked a little sympathetic.

"Look," he said and looked down at the handcuffs in his hand. "What you're telling me is hard to swallow. Brian Mitchell's death fit the M.O. of the Harvester—"

"Not quite," I interrupted. "The other bodies didn't have a star on them, did they?"

"Well, no."

"You didn't find any tape residue, did you?"

"No."

I pressed my advantage. "You've got to believe me. It's another killer. I don't know what his motive is and I don't know what it has to do with me—yet. But I do know he's still in Summerset."

"How do you know that?" he asked, staring at me.

Not answering, I met his stare with confidence.

"Okay, okay, let me suspend my doubts for a minute and rephrase that remark. How or where did you see him? In a vision? Or did you actually see him in person?"

"Both."

"Both?" His eyebrows shot up.

"Look, explaining how I saw him is kind of hard without sounding crazy at the same time."

"Like what you've told me so far doesn't sound crazy?" he scoffed.

I gave him a steely look. "You know, I didn't have to tell you anything. I could've sat back and let you muddle through this investigation on your own."

"I take exception to the word *muddle*."

"What else would you call it? It's been five years since Brian was killed? And you *still* haven't caught his killer. I'd think you'd be grateful for new information."

"Give me information I can use to catch him and I will be," he said. "Nothing you've told me does that."

"I don't have any more information, but I will. I seem to have this weird mental connection with him. He's in my dreams, but I haven't seen his face. I think I am able to sense him, though. The other night, during the thunderstorm, I caught a glimpse of someone standing across the street from my house. I know it was him."

"He's watching you?"

"Yes. And I sense he's getting ready to make some kind of contact with me. There's a reason he's picked me and it's the reason Brian and Gus died."

"Yeah, I came to that conclusion too."

"Do you know why he's focused on me?"

"No. I don't know if I believe we have two different killers, but it doesn't matter how many there are." He stared off into space, thinking. "You're some sort of link to a killer. Right now the only link. And whether or not you're psychic..." His voice trailed off, and he tossed his hand in the air.

"Does that mean you'll let me help you find him?"

"No, I don't work with civilians."

"But you said I'm a link?"

"That doesn't mean I'm going to let you interfere with the investigation. It means we'll monitor you, watch your house, watch who approaches you," he said, slipping the handcuffs back in his pocket.

"You'll have me tailed?"

"Yeah."

"That's not acceptable. I refuse to cooperate," I said stubbornly.

He made a derisive sound. "Did I indicate you had a choice?"

I glared at him. "There are always choices, Comacho. You have me tailed and I'll figure out a way to lose them. You watch my house and I'll disappear."

"Oh, not only are you psychic, but you're a magician too, huh?"

"Ahh, well not exactly," I said, looking away.

"What do you mean, 'not exactly'?" he asked.

I looked back over at him. "Umm—let's just call it a certain sensitivity to the world around me, okay?"

"What in the hell is that supposed to mean?"

"Never mind, if I find out you need to know, I'll explain."

"The same way you've explained about being a psychic?"

"You still don't believe me, do you?"

"No."

"Give me your hand."

"What?"

I crossed the distance between us and stood right in front of him. Holding out my hand, I repeated, "Give me your hand."

Reluctantly he extended his hand.

"No, your right hand."

He switched hands.

Taking his right hand in my left, I placed my right hand over our joined hands while my eyelids drifted shut.

I felt Comacho's energy seeping through the cracks in the wall around his mind. *Wow, reading him won't be easy. He has a lot of resistance.* I went deeper in my mind, strengthening the link between us.

Incomplete images of his life and his thoughts floated

through the wall like pictures moving at a rapid pace across a movie screen. Comacho questioning me five years ago. A soldier in a hot desert. A little dark-haired girl, chasing a red balloon across the park. A young Comacho, in a shiny blue uniform, facing down a man holding a gun. A woman saying good-bye.

I released his hand quickly. His thoughts of the woman were too private for me to intrude. Shaking my head to clear the vision, I looked up at Comacho.

His face wore a stunned expression.

Comacho's appearance didn't surprise me—reading someone always scrambles their brain a little. I gave him a moment to collect himself before I spoke.

"There's a young girl you're fond of, a close relative, daughter, maybe. She's about four and she was chasing a red balloon across the park. You watched, laughing."

"My niece—last Sunday—I took her to the park. Her balloon got away from her. How did you know?"

"I read your thoughts. By the way, you have quite a wall up around your mind and you're hard to read. But do you believe me now?"

He ran his fingers through his hair. "I don't know. This is strange." Comacho's mouth tightened and he exhaled a long breath. "Okay, I'll think about what you've told me."

"You'll let me help?"

"I didn't say *help;* I said I'd think about it." He squinted and looked at me sternly. "But if you get yourself killed, don't blame me," he said.

"I won't, I promise," I said, relief bubbling inside me.

Yes. He agreed. He wasn't going to lock me up or put a call in to the nearest psych ward. And I was, at last, taking some action to find the killer. Joining forces with Comacho would work, it had to work.

"Right now, I'm going back to the hospital to check on Abby, but may I call you later? There's something I want to try. It might help me see the killer more clearly," I said.

Comacho rolled his eyes toward the ceiling. "If I weren't desperate to find this guy, I'd..." He looked back at me and shook his head. Reaching in his pocket, he handed me his card. "Yeah, call me. My cell number's on this."

"Umm. I'd appreciate if you didn't share this information with Bill," I said, taking the card. "It would be sure to leak out somehow and I don't want the whole town to know I'm psychic. I have enough problems without that."

"Oh, don't worry. I'm not telling anyone about *you*."

As I walked away, I looked over my shoulder at him.

"One last thing. About what I saw in your mind—I think you have a nice butt too, Comacho."

Twenty-Four

After leaving Comacho, I went to the hospital to check on Abby. The room was empty, except for Abby lying quietly in the bed.

I stood over the bed and looked down at her while I took her hand in mine. The hand felt frail and lifeless as I smoothed the skin over fragile bones.

"You're still in there, aren't you, Abby?" I asked, staring at her and stroking her hand. "I felt you. I heard your voice. I almost did it. Almost went against everything you've taught me."

I stopped talking and, closing my eyes, I remembered the power I'd felt there on the hilltop. My hand holding Abby's tingled with the memory.

"I've never felt anything like it. The energy was like a beast pulling at its chain. It would've been so easy to slip that chain, Abby. Set the beast loose to find the evil. Find justice for you and Brian. But it would've been wrong. I would have been using my gift for my own purpose." A tear snaked down my cheek. "Thank you for stopping me."

Suddenly I felt a slight pressure from her fingers. She was trying to squeeze my hand.

Before I reacted, the door swung wide and a nurse walked into the room.

"She's waking up," I said, whirling away from the bed toward the nurse. "She tried to squeeze my hand."

"I'll get a doctor," she said and hurried from the room, her rubber soles squeaking on the polished tile.

Moments later she was back, accompanied by Abby's doctor.

I stepped aside when the doctor approached the bed.

"She squeezed my hand," I said, not able to keep the excitement out of my voice.

"Well, let's take a look," he said, putting his stethoscope in his ears. "It could've been an involuntary response, but we'll see."

I stood silently while he examined Abby.

"Vitals are good," he said and took Abby's hand in his. "Abby can you hear me? Abby, squeeze my hand."

Nothing. No movement at all.

The doctor leaned closer. "Abby, squeeze my hand."

My fingers curled in tight fists while I waited and watched. No response and the disappointment rushed through me.

The doctor shook his head slowly. "Sorry," he said. "But her heart's strong and her lungs are clear, which is good. We'll continue to keep a close eye on her condition."

I numbly watched Abby, while the doctor moved toward the door of the silent room.

A moan broke the silence, a moan that came from Abby.

The doctor heard the sound, too, and returned to Abby's bedside. "Abby, can you hear me?" he asked in a voice that echoed in the quiet.

Abby's eyes shot open, as if startled, but they quickly shut again.

"Great. She's showing response to loud noises," he said, smiling. Picking up Abby's hand, he pinched the end of her finger.

Her hand jerked back and the doctor's smile grew wider.

"Good motor response." He turned to the nurse. "Her level of responsiveness is increasing."

I almost fell to my knees in relief, but his next words brought me out of it.

"She's not out of danger yet. And we have no idea how much brain damage there might be. But the signs indicate she's waking up."

"But the prognosis is good?" I asked desperately.

The doctor gave me a kind look. "The prognosis is positive."

The door glided open and my mother walked in.

"Mom," I said and hurried over to her. "Abby squeezed my hand and opened her eyes for a second."

My mother wrapped her arms around me in a big hug. "Thank God." Releasing me, she patted my face and smiled.

"Now, Mrs. Jensen," the doctor said, holding up his hand, "as I explained to your daughter, her responses are a good indication she's waking up, but until she does—"

"I understand, Doctor," Mother broke in, "but her condition is better than it was twenty-four hours ago?"

"Yes."

"Well, we'll focus on that for now."

"I don't want you to expect too much or have any false hopes," he said cautiously.

"We won't."

The doctor pursed his lips and nodded while he moved toward the door. "Good."

The nurse followed him, but stopped at the door. Reaching in her pocket, she pulled out an ivory envelope and held it out to me. "I found this laying on the floor near the door while you were both out. I imagine one of the aides dropped it when she brought your grandmother's flowers in."

"Thank you," I said, taking the envelope.

Mother had crossed to Abby's bed and was silently stroking Abby's hand.

When I joined her, she gazed over at me. "Did you find your answers?"

"Part of them." I hesitated. "Gus and Brian were killed because of their relationship to me."

"You don't know that," she replied, shocked.

I let out a long sigh. "Yes, I do, Mom."

"But I thought a serial killer murdered Brian?"

"Everyone did. It's probably what he wanted us to think. It's not the same killer; I've seen both of them. Took me a while to figure it out, but I'm positive I'm right." I sighed again. "Now I have to convince Henry Comacho."

"You talked to him? Did you tell him how you knew?"

"I had to."

Mother squeezed Abby's hand and, pulling up a chair, sat. I moved to the one next to her and flopped down.

"Well. Well..." Her eyes moved around the room while she tried to think of something to say.

In spite of the seriousness of our conversation, I chuckled. For the first time in my life, I'd rendered my mother speechless.

"You're surprised?"

"Yes. It took a lot of courage for you to do that."

"I don't know about courage, but I came this close," I

said, holding my thumb and forefinger up, an inch apart, "to being led away in handcuffs."

My mother grinned. "I would've posted bail."

"Thanks," I said, returning her grin.

My grin faded while I thought about how to ask her my next question. "Mom, what's the deal with Harley Walters?" Reaching out, I placed my hand on her leg. "And please don't say, 'It's not my story to tell.' Harley could've been the one responsible for hurting Abby."

"I know," she said, staring at Abby's still form. "All right. Ten years ago I helped Harley's wife leave him."

"What?"

"He was drinking—a lot. And when he was drunk, he was abusive. It was the summer you went with your father to Mexico to help him with his research on the Aztecs. I was in Summerset, visiting Mother." She picked up her needlepoint and slowly followed the pattern with her fingertips. "For some reason, Elaine came to me. Maybe because I'd been a good friend of her older sister—"

"Elizabeth, right?"

"Yes, Elizabeth. Do you remember her?"

I nodded. "Sure I do. She came to Iowa City a couple of times when I was a kid. She died, didn't she?"

A look of sadness crossed my mother's face. "Yes, cancer." She took a deep breath. "Their parents were dead too. I guess Elaine felt alone, with no one to help her, so she came to me."

A look of disgust quickly replaced the sadness on her face. "She had bruises up and down her arms. And one eye was starting to turn black. She had their two little boys with her," she said, her voice cold. "I wanted her to go to the sheriff, but Elaine wouldn't, she was ashamed." My mother snorted. "In my opinion, the shame wasn't hers, it was Harley's. I thought about asking Mother to put a hex on him, I was so angry, but I knew she wouldn't." She paused and frowned. "We left that day for Iowa City. I found her a job at the university and a place for her and the boys to live. Harley's never forgiven me for helping her."

"Abby knew the story?" I asked.

"Yes."

"Wow. What happened to Elaine?"

"She went to counseling, eventually remarried, and had two more children."

"The story has a happy ending."

Mother made a face. "For Elaine it did. Not Harley. He was a jerk ten years ago and he's a jerk now."

I stood and walked to the window. Gazing out the window at nothing in particular, I thought about Elaine's story.

"Mom," I said, turning around. "Does Harley hate us enough to commit murder?"

"Oh, he hates us and he's a bully," she scoffed. "I can see him hurting Abby, trashing her greenhouse, but murder?" She chewed her bottom lip. "I don't know," she said finally. "I don't know."

I turned back to the window. Somebody better figure out if Harley's hate was great enough to kill for. Maybe I could talk Comacho into investigating Harley? Reaching in my pocket for my cell phone, I found the envelope the nurse had given me. I'd forgotten about it.

"Hey, here's the envelope the nurse handed me," I said, waving it in front of me.

"Let me see it," Mother said, holding out her hand.

She took it from me and flipped it over. "Hmm, it doesn't have a name on it. Do you suppose we should open it?"

"I guess. The nurse said she found the envelope in here. If it's not for Abby, we'll give it back."

"Okay," Mother said and tore the envelope open. "It's not a card." She pulled out the contents. "It's a newspaper clipping." Her eyebrows arched in surprise while she read it. "The clipping's from *The Hawkeye,* the university's student paper. You're mentioned in the article."

"What?" I asked, taking the clipping from her.

My eyes quickly scanned the article. It had been written five years ago, before Brian's death, when I still worked at the university's library. The clipping related how a girl, a student, had suffered a grand mal seizure while studying at the library.

"I remember this," I said with a quick glance at Mother. "A student went into convulsions. I was working that day and was the first one to assist her. I held her head while someone called 911. Later, she learned from the doctors the convulsion had been brought on by the medication she was taking for an infection. Why would anyone send this?" I flipped the clipping over. "Oh my God."

On the back, in big red letters, was one word:

WITCH!

Twenty-Five

Mother took the clipping from my numb fingers. Frowning, she looked at the word written on the back.

"I thought you and Mother had been more careful than this."

"We have been. We are," I exclaimed. Jumping up, I paced the room. "I don't understand this. Who would have this clipping? How did they get it?"

"Someone who was in Iowa City five years ago," she said in a matter-of-fact tone.

I skidded to a stop. "Maybe Harley. Maybe the killer," I exclaimed, my eyes darting to Abby's bed.

"Shh, keep your voice down. You're in a hospital. Do you want the nurses running in here to see what the commotion is?" she said sternly.

Ignoring her, I flipped my cell phone open and punched in some numbers, numbers I knew by heart after the past few months.

"Yes," I said when the voice answered, "this is Ophelia Jensen. May I please speak to the sheriff?"

Raking my hand through my hair, I waited for the call to be transferred to Bill.

"Sheriff Wilson," his gruff voice answered.

"Bill, Ophelia. I can't explain now, but I think you need to have a guard posted on Abby's room."

"What? What's happened now?"

"I told you I can't explain, but if you could send someone over," I said in a rush, "my mother will fill them in." I snapped the phone shut. Pivoting on my heel, I headed for the door.

"Wait right there, young lady," my mother commanded. "What am I supposed to say when Bill shows up?"

I stopped midstep and raised a shoulder. "I don't know—make something up. You're creative. But don't tell them about the clipping." I ran back to her, grabbed the clipping, and gave her a peck on the cheek. While I moved toward the door, I looked back over my shoulder at my mother. "I'm stopping by the cafeteria for coffee and I want Comacho to meet me at the spot where I found Gus."

While I waited for the elevator, I dialed Comacho. He answered on the fourth ring and I turned my face to the wall, speaking softly into the phone.

"Will you meet me at the spot I found Gus?"

"Now?"

He sounded irritated.

"Yes, now. Why? Are you tied up?" I asked.

"I'm fishing."

"What?"

My voiced echoed down the hall.

"I said 'fishing.'"

"'Fishing'?" I hissed. "You're supposed to be finding the killer."

"Hey, it's my day off. I'm trying a couple of the spots Bill's been bragging about. This is the second time today you've interrupted me."

"I don't believe it. A killer's running loose and you're"—my voice raised a notch—"FISHING!"

Okay, maybe more than a notch. I lowered my cell phone and saw two nurses at the station, watching me. Lucky for me the elevator door opened at that instant. Calmly smiling at the nurses, I moved inside the elevator and hit the DOWN button.

I put my cell phone back to my ear in time to hear Comacho say.

"...nothing wrong with that. I do my best thinking fishing. It's quiet. I don't have to listen to crazy people."

I think he meant me. If he did, too bad for him. I had more crazy stuff I intended to tell him.

"Look," I said impatiently, "meet me at the ditch." Not waiting for him to say "no," I rushed ahead. "How long will it take you to get there?"

A long sigh answered me.

"Forty-five minutes," he said, resigned. "And Jensen, this better be good."

Oh, it was, I thought while I strode down the hall to the cafeteria. I checked my watch. Plenty of time to grab a coffee and meet Comacho.

The cafeteria was full of the late lunch crowd. I hesitated at the door and scanned the room. My eyes darted back to the man standing by the condiments.

Fletcher Beasley, dumping sugar in his coffee. Like he didn't have enough—the counter next to him was littered with empty sugar wrappers.

I made a move to go, but I was too late. He spotted me and came toward me at a jog, spilling coffee all over the floor.

"Jensen, Jensen," he hollered.

I turned around and walked away from him.

"Heard your grandmother was here. Tough break."

His voice followed. "But you've had several tough breaks lately, haven't you?"

"Go away, Beasley," I said with a quick look over my shoulder.

He was right behind me.

Beasley scooted along until his steps matched mine. "Can I get a statement from your grandmother?" he asked.

"No," I said, increasing my pace.

"How 'bout you? Want to tell me about your new boy-friend?" he asked, bouncing along next to me.

"He's a friend," I said without slowing my steps.

"You got yourself a big catch there. Only kid, mother was sickly, father too busy. Wound up being raised by a governess, a poor relation. Doesn't your heart just ache for him?" he asked snidely before continuing to run his mouth. "Has money up the wazoo. Family's a big deal in Massachusetts."

"You're slime, Beasley."

I had to think of a way to ditch this guy. I didn't want him following me.

"Just doing my job," he panted.

"Do your job somewhere else," I said while I turned the corner in the hallway.

Glancing at my watch again, I saw that I had thirty minutes before I met Comacho. Maybe I could lose him once I reached my car? If he tried following me, I'd drive around the country roads till he was dizzy. The thought made me smile.

"Maybe you don't want to talk about your new boy-friend 'cause you're worried he might turn up dead too? Or maybe your grandmother?"

I jerked to a stop, accidentally hitting Beasley's coffee

cup. The cup flew, flinging coffee all over him, the wall, and the floor.

"Whoops," I said with a grin.

Big wet spots of coffee covered Beasley's cheap suit. He wrenched a handkerchief from his pocket and tried to pat the spots dry. Raising his head, his face wore an expression of fury.

"You'd better listen to me. You think I won't find anything out, don't you? Don't you?" he yelled. "I've known from the start there's something weird about you. And I'm going to dig and dig until I know what it is. You're my ticket out of the minors, sister." His hard brown eyes glazed over. "With the story I'm going to do on you, I'll hit the big time. I'll have the respect I deserve."

"You're nuts," I said, making a move away from him.

Before I took a step, his hand shot out and grasped my arm, pulling me around to face him.

"By the time I'm finished with you, I'll know more about you than your own mother," he said, shaking my arm for emphasis. "You're going to be sorry you ever met me."

"I already am," I said and jerked my arm out of his grasp. I took a step forward. Beasley retreated, but I was still right in his face. "You're an annoying little twit. And a second-rate journalist. It would take more than a story on me for *you* to hit the big time."

His face flushed a dark red. "You'll see how second-rate I am. Your name's going to be plastered in every newspaper in the state. Everyone's going to know what a spook you are."

"Ha. You don't have that much clout, Beasley." I took another step forward till we were eye to eye. "You're not going to badger me the same way you did five years ago. This time you mess with me and you'll be sorry."

Furious, I pivoted sharply on my heel and walked out the door to the parking lot. On the way I noticed the hospital staff quickly looked the other way. I didn't care. If that little jerk didn't back off, I'd slap a restraining order on him so fast. And I'd call his editor and complain. By the time I'd finished with him, he'd not only be out of Summerset, he'd be out of a job.

Twenty-Six

I leaned up against the side of my car, my arms crossed at my chest and my legs at the ankles, while I watched Comacho's car pull to a stop behind mine.

He got out of his car. Dressed in the same jeans he'd worn this morning, he'd changed into a T-shirt and wore a baseball cap pulled low on his forehead. And the aroma of dead fish hung around him like cheap cologne.

"Jeez, Comacho," I said, wrinkling my nose, "you smell like a bait house."

"I was fishing. When you're fishing, you smell like fish," he said defensively as he approached me. "This better be important."

I handed him the note I carried in my pocket and watched while he examined the envelope.

"Pretty fancy," he said, flipping it over and looking for a name. "Where'd you find it?"

"Abby's room. A nurse found it on the floor while we were gone. She thought it had fallen from the flowers Arthur had sent Abby. But I don't think Arthur sent it," I said and stood straight.

He pulled the clipping from the envelope and, turning it over, saw the word WITCH written on the back. A puzzled look crossed his face. He opened the clipping and read the article.

Finished, he looked up at me. "Any idea why whoever left this article about you wrote *witch* on the back?"

"They have a fascination with witches?" I asked not meeting his eyes.

"But why would they pick an article about you?"

"'Cause I am," I said, still not looking at him.

"Are what?" he asked, puzzled.

I looked straight into Comacho's eyes. "A witch."

"Je..." He choked the word back and stomped to the front of my car. He stomped back to where I stood. Shaking his finger in my face, his brown eyes drilled into mine. "You *are* pushing your luck, Jensen. First you expected me to swallow that psychic BS and now this. Next you're going to tell me you worship the devil and fly on a broomstick."

Insulted, I closed the distance till we were only inches apart. "We do not worship the devil, we *fight* evil," I said, poking my finger at his chest. "We don't fly on broomsticks." I took a step back and folded my arms. "And one other thing, we don't wear pointy hats either. We wear cowled robes."

"'We'?"

"Abby and me."

"You're kidding, right?" he asked, throwing back his head and laughing.

His laughter stopped when he saw my face.

"You're not kidding." His jaw clenched and he took a step forward. "I should've locked you up when I had the chance. You are nuts. But hey, maybe it's not too late." He reached behind him for his cuffs.

I scooted away, putting my car between us. "Wait. Let me explain. The women in my family, Abby's family,

were healers; granny women, in the mountains of Appalachia. We have the talent of tapping into energy—"

"And shoot fireballs from your fingertips, I suppose,"
he interrupted.

"No, that's crazy—"

"Like you're not?" he interrupted again.

"Shooting fireballs, making people disappear, that
stuff's only on TV. It's not real."

"Real?" he scoffed. "Okay prove it."

*Prove it? How can I prove something that can only be
felt, not seen?*

I kicked the tire of my car in frustration. "This isn't to
be used for parlor tricks. You have to have a need."

"Oh, you have a need," he said, nodding his head.
"Either prove it or I'm taking you back to town for some
serious questioning. I stopped and stared up at the blue
sky, where a hawk circled.

Earlier today, I had called the elements, but now, the
angry passion I'd felt was gone. Without the passion, I
didn't know if I could call them again. My need wasn't
great enough. And how stupid would that look, standing
in the ditch, my arms stretched above me and have nothing happen? He'd arrest me for sure.

I looked back up at the hawk. Last fall I'd used energy to
set pigeons flying and rats scurrying. But I didn't see any
rats or pigeons—only the hawk. Suddenly I had an idea.

"Okay, you want proof," I called over my shoulder to
Comacho. "Stay where you are and don't move till I do."

I'd never tried this before, but Abby had explained it
to me when I was a child. I only hoped I remembered all
she'd said.

With a deep breath, I emptied my mind and imagined
a circle, above and below me, protecting me. Tilting my
head back and with arms opened wide, I focused on the

sky and called to the spirit of the hawk, wheeling on the currents above me. Inside the circle, I heard the breeze stir the weeds and felt it lift my hair. I watched the hawk dip lower and lower till I could almost see the feathers on his wing.

I shut my eyes and imagined the strength of those wings. The muscles as they moved the wings down in a graceful arc. The heart as it pumped blood to power the muscles. I saw, I felt, the freedom the hawk had always known. I envied him.

All at once, I was with him, one with his spirit, and together we rode the air currents high above the earth. We swooped and dipped, without effort, through the clouds, across the sky in a graceful dance.

We spiraled lower and lower, and again I stood in my circle. I heard the breeze stir the weeds. I felt it lift my hair. Looking up, I saw the hawk moving away in the distance.

Mentally, I withdrew my circle and the breeze died. Turning, I looked at Comacho.

He was where I'd left him, but his expression had changed. His sunglasses hung from his limp fingers and his jaw had dropped. With an effort, he closed his mouth and shook his head, as if to clear his mind.

"Well?" I asked, moving toward him.

"That was the damnedest thing I've ever seen," he said, shaking his head again. "How did you get the hawk to land on your arm?"

"He landed on my arm?" I asked, frowning.

He grabbed my wrist and pulled my arm out in front of me. "See, on your coat sleeve, you can still see the marks of his talons. Don't you remember?"

"Not exactly," I said, pulling my arm back.

"The hawk came down and landed on your outstretched

arm. He perched there for a couple of minutes while you stared into the hawk's eyes."

"Ah, must've been when I thought I was flying," I said softly while I moved down the ditch.

"What did you say?"

"Nothing. You wouldn't believe me," I said over my shoulder.

Comacho caught up with me. "I do believe anyone seeing you pull a trick like that—"

"It wasn't a trick," I broke in.

"Whatever it was," he said with a wave of his hand. "Might've freaked someone out bad enough to think you're a witch." He hesitated, twirling his sunglasses in his hand. "Any suspects?"

"Not really. Abby and I don't do *tricks* and I can't think of anyone who would fear us. The only enemy I can think of is Harley Walters. He hates my family and it's possible he was in Iowa City five years ago. It's where his boys live with his ex-wife."

"I'll check into it," he said, settling his sunglasses back on his face.

The breath I didn't know I'd been holding escaped in a long sigh. Finally Comacho was beginning to believe me. I decided to make the most of his cooperation and tell him why I wanted him to meet me here.

"I want to take a look around—if you don't mind?"

"Why?"

"I want to see if I can pick anything up. Maybe my fear the day of the demonstration prevented me from seeing the whole thing."

"You want to..." He stopped and hung his head. "Oh well, what the hell. Like I said, right now you're the only game in town, Jensen." Shoving his hands in his jacket pockets, he faced me. "What do you want me to do?"

"I don't know. I've never done this before. Walk with me, I guess. If I feel anything, I'll let you know."

"Okay."

We tromped slowly through the weeds to the spot where I'd found Gus. While we did, the air around me hummed, getting louder when we reached the section where Gus had been buried.

I paused, trying to see the killer's face. No good. The energy I'd felt the day of the demonstration was only a faint whisper now. Too many people had been here, leaving remnants of their energy behind, diluting what had been.

I moved on, in a way, relieved. I hadn't looked forward to repeating my experience. But the killer. I clenched my fists. I had to find him, had to protect the people I cared about.

A different sound caught my attention and I walked toward it, Comacho following behind me. The sound became louder as I walked.

Then it hit me: the energy I'd felt at Abby's meeting. Striking against me with such force that I staggered and would've fallen, but Comacho reached out and steadied me.

"What's wrong?" he asked, his voice concerned.

Shaking my head and not speaking, I pointed toward a spot thirty yards away.

Comacho left me, taking careful steps through the weeds. But he veered too far to his left.

"No," I called out in a shaky voice. "To your right."

He moved to the left.

"No, your other right."

He stopped and fisted his hands on his hips. "What are we doing? Playing hot and cold?"

"Just follow my directions."

"Give me directions I can follow. How far to my right?"

"About five feet," I called out again.

"There, right there," I yelled when he moved five feet away.

Comacho squatted and brushed back the weeds. Shaking his head, he grabbed a rag from his pocket. Using the rag, he reached down and picked something up. Standing, he walked back toward me. He carried what looked to be an old wine bottle.

With every step he took, the force assaulting me got stronger and stronger. I couldn't get near whatever was in that wine bottle without getting the psychic crap knocked out of me. I hustled back.

"Wait," I said, holding up my hand to stop him. "Give me a minute."

I had an idea. I removed the talisman, which was made from a fire agate that I'd worn for five years, from around my neck. Holding it in my left hand, I let the stone's protection wrap around me. As it did, the force hitting me subsided. Satisfied I was safe, I waved Comacho forward.

"I'm not even going to ask what that was all about," he said, holding the dirty bottle away from him.

Comacho shook the bottle gently from side to side and I heard liquid sloshing. I also heard something rattling against the glass.

Removing the cork with the edge of the rag, Comacho took a sniff. His face puckered and his eyes watered. "My God," he said in disgust.

"What is it?"

"Urine, I think. What do you think?" he asked, holding the bottle toward me.

I took a step back, waving my hands. "Ah, no thanks. I'll take your word for it."

He corked the bottle. "I bet some kids, out drinking, chucked this in the ditch. Too lazy to get out of the car, they used what was handy."

"But what's rattling?"

"Don't know—don't care," he said and made a move to toss it.

"No," I yelled.

Comacho dropped his arm, holding the bottle.

"You can't throw it away," I said in a rush. "It's from a crime scene."

"The team from the crime lab didn't think the bottle was important. They would've taken it if they did."

"Maybe they didn't see it."

"I doubt it. Those guys don't miss a thing."

"Please," I pleaded, "take the bottle to the lab and have it tested."

Comacho looked at the bottle, thinking. Finally he made his decision. "What the hell. We don't have any other evidence to test. Might as well waste the taxpayers' money on this."

"It won't be a waste," I said, walking toward our cars.

When we reached the cars, Comacho opened his back door and wrapping the bottle in a towel, put it on the floor. "This sucker better not spill on the way to Des Moines. Or you're cleaning out my car."

"Can the lab test the bottle right away?"

"Why is this bottle so important to you?"

Turning, I narrowed my eyes at him. "I don't care if you believe me or not, Comacho, but I'm telling you, without a doubt, this bottle is a message from the killer. You have to figure out what the message says."

Twenty-Seven

My weary steps faltered at the door to Abby's room.
Mother and Arthur sat by Abby's bedside, quietly talking. She took one look at me and insisted I go home. She
assured me she was more than capable of handling anything that might come up. Hadn't I left her to deal with
Bill? Hadn't she convinced him to post a guard without
giving out too much information? She had, indeed, so
after one final check on Abby, I headed home.

Kicking my shoes off by the door, I went to the kitchen
and made sure Lady and Queenie were fed and watered. I
struggled up the stairs and into my bedroom. My unmade
bed looked so inviting that I fell, still dressed, across it.

When I opened my eyes again, the early morning sunshine was spilling through the window onto the bedroom floor. Rubbing my gritty eyes, I looked at the clock:
7 A.M. I'd slept for over twelve hours. I rolled over and
thought about yesterday.

I'd had two major psychic experiences and been almost arrested twice. Not bad for one day, but too many
more like it would probably kill me. I needed a shower,
coffee, and to make a call to the hospital before I tried to
figure out yesterday's events.

After my shower, I dressed in comfortable sweats and piled my wet hair on top of my head. Securing it with a clip, I made the call to the hospital on the phone in my bedroom and talked to my mother.

Abby's condition was much the same, except she was moving more. Her brain scans were normal and the doctors were optimistic. Mother pointed out my time would be better put to use trying to help Comacho.

I thought about calling him to find out if the contents of the wine bottle had been tested. A quick look at the clock told me the lab wouldn't have had enough time to complete the test.

Too early to call Comacho. Not needed at the hospital. Hmm, what next? I thought while I walked down the stairs. *Oh yeah, coffee. And a lot of it.*

I drummed my fingers on the kitchen counter while I waited for the coffeemaker to finish. Too anxious to wait, I pulled the pot and poured what was brewed in a mug.

Well, half a cup's better than none. I'll fill my mug once the coffeemaker finishes.

Lady and Queenie followed while I padded on bare feet to the living room. The aroma of the steaming coffee almost made me salivate. I swirled it around in my mug, enjoying the anticipation of the first sip. Lifting the cup to my lips, I closed my eyes and started to take a cautious drink, but I stopped before the coffee hit my lips. I wrinkled my nose. There was another scent in the room—cloying, almost overpowering. Opening my eyes, I scanned the living room and saw a huge vase of red and white roses.

They were beautiful. The red was so dark that it was almost burgundy. The difference in colors was such a contrast, the white roses seemed to glow. Yes, they *were* beautiful, but for some reason, they also made a slow chill creep up my spine. Why?

My thoughts were interrupted by a knock on my front door. From the window I saw Darci's car in my driveway.

"Who sent the flowers?" I said without preamble when I opened the door.

"Good morning to you too," she said. "I wondered what you'd think when you saw them."

"They're lovely, but..." I paused, rubbing my arm. "They kind of creep me out for some reason." I shook my head. "I guess I just don't like red and white flowers together. Do you want coffee?" I asked, changing the subject.

"No thanks," she said as she walked past me to the kitchen. She stopped and took a deep breath. "Whew, the smell's strong, isn't it?"

"Yeah. It's nice out. Let's go out back and sit in the sun."

"Good idea," she said, moving through the kitchen and out the back door.

Grabbing my cell phone in case the hospital called, I joined her.

Once outside, we sat in my lawn chairs. The warm April sun felt good on my face. I took a deep breath of the clean fresh air while I watched Queenie stalk an unsuspecting bird and Lady roll in the grass.

Darci laughed, watching her. "I bet she's trying to get rid of the smell of those flowers."

"No doubt. I wish I could join her," I replied.

She laughed again.

"Okay, who sent them?" I asked.

"Who do you think?" Darci gave me a quizzical look.

"Charles?"

"Yup. And I took the liberty to read the poem he sent too. You must've made quite an impression on him."

I rolled my eyes. "He's just lonely and I'm someone he can talk to. But how did the florist deliver them? I was gone all day?"

"She called the library. I was coming over here to take care of Lady and Queenie anyway—"

I patted her arm, interrupting her. "By the way, thanks."

"No problem," she said with a wave of her hand. "I unlocked the house with the key you gave me and let her in."

I tucked a strand of wet hair behind my ear. "Darci, do you think the roses and the poem are a little over the top? I've been out with the man once."

"I don't know," she replied with a slight shrug. "Like you said, he's lonely and you're someone he relates to. Maybe he treats every woman he's interested in this way. Who knows?"

"That's the problem. I don't know," I said thoughtfully. "I just met him, but it's like he's *courting* me."

Darci laughed. "I guess you have to decide if you *want* to be courted."

Frowning, I took my cell phone from my pocket and scrolled down through the received calls.

"I don't think I do. He's going too fast for me and I need to tell him that."

Finding the phone number I wanted, I hit SEND. It rang twice before he answered.

"Hello." Charles sounded sleepy.

"I'm sorry, did I wake you, Charles?" I asked.

"No. I'm feeling a little under the weather."

"You're sick?"

Dang, now I couldn't tell him to cool all the attention. I had to be nice.

"Yes, I think I have a mild case of food poisoning, but it's passing. I heard about your grandmother. Did you get my flowers?"

"Umm, yes I did. Umm, very thoughtful of you," I said, stumbling over my words. "But we'll talk about them later, when you're over the food poisoning. Hope you're feeling better soon." Without waiting for his good-bye, I hit the END button.

"Well, that was smooth," Darci remarked sarcastically.

"He's sick. You can't tell someone to back off when they're sick." I hesitated, then sighed. "I can't worry about Charles now. I've got too many other things to think about."

"I wouldn't be too hasty about writing off Charles. You did enjoy your date and he is a successful man. A very respected writer. Maybe later, when everything's resolved, you can take your time to get to know him better."

"Hey, how do you know Charles is successful?" I asked suspiciously.

Darci shrugged. "I looked him up on the Internet."

"You checked up on him?"

She nodded her head firmly. "You bet I did. This guy blows into town, starts putting the rush on you. I wanted to know as much about him as I could." She hesitated. "He's rich, old money. His family owns factories in Massachusetts."

"I know. Charles mentioned his family and so did Beasley."

"You talked to Beasley?" she exclaimed.

I scowled. "Yeah, unfortunately."

Drinking the last of my coffee in one gulp, I took a deep breath and told her everything that had happened the day before.

When I finished, Darci's face wore a stunned expression.

"Oh my gosh," she whispered. "Oh my gosh," she whispered again. "Oh my—"

I broke in, "Darci, you've said 'Oh my gosh' twice now."

"I know, but...oh my gosh," she said her voice hushed.

I shook my head back. "I had hoped for something a little more helpful than that."

"Yeah, yeah." Darci drummed the arms of her chair. "I know. Let me think a minute."

Patiently I waited while a parade of expressions crossed Darci's face. Finally, her lips tightened in a determined line, she looked at me.

"When you felt the negative energy attacking you in the ditch, you held your talisman and it helped?"

"Yes. It's a fire agate."

"What does that mean?"

I lifted my eyebrows, thinking. "Abby gave it to me after Brian's death five years ago. A fire agate is for protection. Its energy helps insulate the wearer—like a shield. In fact, Abby says any ill wishing bounces off the shield and back at the one who wished you harm."

"The person seeking to harm gets a dose of what they wanted for you?"

"Sort of. But at the meeting, I don't think it was directed at me. Maybe Gus? He was standing near me when I felt it. Or even Charles. I'm sure he was close to me too, but I hadn't noticed him yet." I thought about what I'd felt at the end of the meeting. "It did seem to follow Charles out the door."

"What about when you found Gus's body and when Comacho picked up the bottle? Was the energy directed at you?"

I nodded vigorously. "Oh yeah."

"Hmm," she said, tapping her chin, "I don't understand why there'd be a difference, but I'll think about it. Now back to Brian."

There's a leap in conversation. We hadn't talked about Brian, but I didn't point it out to her.

"Brian was alive when the incident with the student happened in the library?" Darci asked.

"Yes," I answered.

"How soon after the incident was he killed?"

"I think about two weeks later. Why?" I asked, not understanding where she was headed with her questions.

"Were there a lot of people in the library when the girl went into convulsions?"

"Yes. Quite a crowd gathered, I think. I was too busy trying to help the girl to notice."

"You were the one closest to her when the convulsions started?"

"Yes." I squinted, trying to remember. "She was standing at the counter, trying to check out a book for a research assignment. I remember now," I said. "We were having an argument. The book she wanted wasn't allowed out of the library and she didn't think it was fair. She'd started to raise her voice, when all of a sudden her eyes rolled back in her head and she collapsed in a grand mal seizure. I rushed to the other side of the counter to help her while someone called the paramedics."

Darci nodded her head wisely.

"What?" I asked.

"Don't you know any of the superstitions concerning witches?"

I heard the exasperation in her voice, but I didn't understand why.

I threw my hands in the air. "What's a girl getting sick have to do with superstition?"

Darci rolled her eyes at my ignorance. "At one time, people believed seizures, or fits, were caused by the victim being possessed."

"So?"

"By a *witch*," she said with emphasis on the word *witch*.

I stood and walked over to the edge of my patio. "You're saying someone thought I'd hexed that girl?"

Darci came to stand beside me. "Yes. You were arguing with her and she fell down in a fit."

"Okay, someone thought I was a witch and caused the girl to get sick. But it doesn't explain why someone killed Brian, why they did what they did to him. The wounds, the star carved on his forehead—"

Darci grabbed my arm, stopping me. "What star?"

I took the clip out of my hair and smoothed it flat. "A five-pointed star. The police have never released that piece of information, but I saw the star in my vision."

"Can you show me?"

"Sure, it's just a star." I bent down, and with a stick, drew the star I'd seen in my dreams in the dirt. Throwing the stick away, I stood and looked at Darci.

Her eyes were wide and her hand covered her mouth. Slowly she lowered her hand and turned to me. As she did, her eyes filled with tears.

"That's not only a star, it's a pentagram."

My god, she was right! We'd all been so sure Brian

had been killed by a serial killer that I'd never made the connection between the marks on his body and my heritage. The pentagram—the mark of the witch. I suddenly felt like I was standing in a pit and the walls were closing in. And from the pit, I watched the tears trickle down Darci's face, while her voice sounded very far away.

"I don't think the killer intended to kill Brian. You—he wanted to kill you."

Twenty-Eight

The sun was getting higher in the sky and clouds were building in the west. *There'll be rain before nightfall,* I thought from where I sat on the cold concrete.

Birds flew over the trees that circled my backyard. *Is one of them my hawk,* I wondered? *I wish I was with him now.*

Queenie lay in the grass near me, watching a robin hop around, hunting for worms. Her predator eyes gleamed and the tip of her tail twitched slowly back and forth. She'd never catch him if she pounced. The robin was too far away.

Lady was on the ground next to me, her head in my lap. When I'd sank to the patio, my legs no longer able to support my weight, she'd plopped down near me. With a whimper, she'd snuggled close.

Darci sat at my other side, slowly rubbing my back while I stared at nothing in particular.

Everything looked so *normal.*

I made a derisive snort. *Normal? Nothing is normal, especially me. And because of my oddity, because of who and what I am, my best friend Brian had been killed.*

And what about Gus? A low groan came from deep in my throat. *Am I responsible for Gus too?*

I looked at Darci, questioning, "Gus? Do you think Gus was killed because of me too?"

Darci shook my arm in irritation. "Gus and Brian weren't killed because of you. They were killed because some sicko believes in old superstitions."

"But if Gus hadn't spoken to me at the meeting, maybe the killer wouldn't have tied him to me."

She shook my arm again. "Snap out of the guilt trip," she said sternly. "You said you didn't know if the energy you felt was directed at you. Maybe it was at Gus. Maybe the killer went to the meeting to find you, but then zeroed in on Gus."

"But why Gus?"

"He had a squint," she said, her eyes focused on Queenie as she made a mighty leap and missed the robin completely.

Her words soaked through my misery. "'A squint'? I don't understand."

"You really need to read more about witches," she said patting my leg. "A squint is the mark of the evil eye."

"A squint means the person can curse someone simply by looking at them? That's crazy."

"The killer's sane?"

"I get your point," I mumbled. "But he's going to kill people because they squint?"

"He might"—she trailed off—"if you and Comacho don't stop him. Listen, he thinks he's a witch hunter and he's hunting *you*. If you don't quit feeling guilty, you could screw up and he might get lucky and kill you. Then Abby could be next."

I scrambled to my feet and whipped out my cell phone. I quickly punched in the number for Abby's room.

"Hello," Mother answered.

"Is everything okay?"

"Yes. Arthur is still here and we were talking about going down to the cafeteria. Why?"

"I think it would be better if you went one at a time."

"You don't want your grandmother left alone. Is that it?"

"Yeah. I know there's a guard, but I'd feel better knowing either you or Arthur were with her too. I'll explain later."

"All right, dear," she said and hung up.

I jumped when my cell phone rang as I was putting it back in my pocket. Opening it, I answered, "Hello."

"You were right. Something's weird about the bottle," Comacho said without preamble.

I couldn't see the expression on his face, naturally, but I bet he about choked on the words "You were right." I tried not to gloat.

"Hey, you still there? Did you hear me?" he asked.

"Yes." I moved over to the side of the house and leaned against the siding. "What did the lab find?"

"The bottle did contain urine, but it had been wiped clean, no fingerprints at all."

"Teenagers wouldn't have bothered to wipe off the prints before they chucked the bottle in the ditch," I speculated.

"That's what I think too."

"What rattled in the bottle?"

I felt Comacho weighing his words before answering my question.

"Nine bent nails. And get this. The urine had human hair in it." He hesitated. "Since you're supposed to be a witch—"

"What did you say?" I interrupted.

"You heard me," he growled. "Is the stuff in the bottle a spell—or what?"

"Does the question mean you believe me?"

"No." His voice sounded positive. "It means I'm a cop and it's my job to examine all the angles, even if I think they're wacky."

"I see. Sorry, Abby's the spell expert not me."

"But don't you guys write this stuff down? Don't you have some recipe?"

"You mean like 'eye of newt, hair of toad. Bubble, bubble; toil and trouble'?" I asked.

Comacho missed the sarcasm. "Yeah."

"Don't be ridiculous," I said, my tone derisive.

I wasn't the only one who needed to read up on witches. Comacho's only frame of reference was obviously TV shows. I intended to set him straight.

"There are books, journals, handed down from mother to daughter, and I know Abby has them," I explained. "But I've already told you: What we do isn't about charms and curses. Our magick is about using the energy around us to heal and help. Whatever was in that bottle was meant to hurt; Abby wouldn't have anything like that written in her journal. Even to write the words, the spell, used in that bottle would give off enough bad vibes to hurt someone."

"Would you at least look?"

"Yes."

"Good," he said, satisfied. "One more thing, tomorrow I'm going to check out the stores in Des Moines that sell this particular wine, see if anyone remembers someone buying it recently. Do you want to go with me?"

Shocked, I almost dropped my phone.

"Sure," I said.

Wait a second. This was too easy. Comacho had fought

my involvement in his investigation from the start. Why the sudden change?

"Why do want me to go with you?" I asked, trying to keep the suspicion out of my voice.

"'Cause if you're with me, you won't be getting into any more trouble."

The line went dead.

Clicking the phone shut, I walked over to Darci.

"That was Comacho. The bottle we found had nine bent nails, human hair, and urine in it. Since you've been doing so much reading, any idea what the bottle could mean?" I asked.

Darci pursed her lips. "Hmm," she said, thinking. "No, but I'll see what I can find out."

I placed my hand on her shoulder. "Listen to me carefully, Darci. I only want you to do research. No going off on your own, snooping around, okay?"

Her eyes slid over to the circle of trees. "Okay."

I gave her shoulder a little squeeze. "I mean it, Darci."

"I thought I heard voices back here," said a voice coming around the corner of the house.

We both jumped at the same time.

"Gosh, Bill, you startled me," I said.

"Sorry. I knocked, but no one answered. I saw Darci's car and I figured you might be out here." He looked up at the sky. "Nice day, isn't it?"

"Yes, but I think there'll be rain before tonight."

He sniffed the air. "Maybe."

"I know you're not here to talk about the weather. What's up?"

"First, I hear Abby's better?"

"Yes. Thank you for posting the guard on her room. We appreciate it."

"No problem. What with her greenhouse getting trashed and someone attacking her, it makes sense they might try something foolish again. We've got a car going by the house every so often too."

"That's good to know."

"Ahh..." Bill twirled his hat in his hand. "Henry said you know Gus Pike's dead."

"Yes," I answered sadly.

"Know anything about an anonymous tip we got on the weapon the killer used to mark Gus?" he asked, suddenly catching me off-guard.

"No."

"Didn't think so. At first, we thought the tip came from Olive Martin, but now we know it was a setup. Someone's idea of a joke," he said, looking squarely at Darci.

She smiled, twisting a strand of hair with her finger. "Was Olive upset?"

"A little," he said, giving Darci a stern look.

She smiled back at him, not saying anything.

He turned the look to me. "We've got a killer on the loose and I intend to catch him. Last fall you almost got yourself killed 'cause you stuck your nose in the wrong person's business."

I knew where he was going with this. I held up my hand, stopping him.

"I know what you're going to say, Bill. 'Stay out of it.'"

"Right, I am. Trust Henry and me to do our jobs."

I looked up at the clouds blowing in, not meeting Bill's eyes. "I will."

He made a small noise in his throat as if he didn't believe me.

"Well, I warned you," he muttered softly.

"Do you have any idea who attacked Abby?" I asked, changing the subject.

"No. I questioned Harley. Wanted to talk to Kyle, but he's gone, of course. We're tracking him down."

"Wait a second. Kyle's gone?" I asked, surprised.

"Yeah, didn't you hear? PP International pulled out sometime in the middle of the night. Wednesday, the night Abby was hurt. Packed up all those hogs and took off. All that's left are empty buildings and a lagoon full of crap the county's going to have to take care of."

Shocked, I glanced at Darci. She shrugged and shook her head.

"Comacho never said anything about PP International leaving," I said.

"He didn't find out about it till last night," Bill replied.

"Does that mean those goons they brought in might've been responsible for the attack on Abby? They're guilty and now they're running?"

Bill scratched his head. "I doubt it, but I'm checking. I think the atmosphere became too uncomfortable for them. They didn't care for all the attention they were getting after Gus's body was found right across the road from their building." Bill settled his hat back on his head. "It'll be good news for Abby when she wakes up, won't it?"

"Yes. Yes, very good news," I said, pondering what this latest development might mean.

"Got to go. I wanted to stop by and have a chat." He looked first at Darci, then at me. "You girls remember what I said about trusting the law," he said, shaking his finger in our direction.

"We will," we said simultaneously.

But I had my fingers crossed.

Twenty-Nine

After Darci left, I changed into jeans and a sweatshirt. One last disgusted look at all the flowers and I headed to Abby's.

I'd been in the greenhouse yesterday with Comacho, but I hadn't gone in the house. I walked up to the wide porch and unlocked the door.

It had been less than a week since I'd been inside the house, but much had changed. Gus Pike was dead, Abby in the hospital. The familiar walls were no more than a shell, a body without a spirit, without Abby's presence to make the house a home.

I felt a growing tightness in my chest and a thickness in my throat made it hard for me to swallow. Not wanting to linger, I walked with my head down through the kitchen and out the back door toward Abby's summerhouse.

Taking the key from Abby's hiding place, I unlocked the door and let it swing wide. The faint smell of Abby's special candles reached out of the darkened room and drew me in. Lighting several of them, I scanned the room for Abby's journals.

Moving quickly to the bookshelves, I withdrew several

of them and carried them to a chair by the window where the light was sufficient to read. Sitting, I carefully placed the top journal on my lap. With a rag from my pocket, I gently wiped the dust from the cover and opened it. I recognized at once the spidery handwriting of Abby's grandmother, the first owner of my runes.

Tracing the handwriting with my finger, I sensed the woman who'd written these words. I saw her as she toiled by candlelight writing down each spell, each healing. What she'd used, how successful it was. A woman similar to Abby. A strong woman, gentle, but not willing to suffer fools gladly. A woman accustomed to hard work. A woman who spoke her mind and, when she did, expected people to listen.

While I carefully turned over each page, I noticed the handwriting change as she aged. The handwriting became harder and harder to read as I looked further into the book. I knew these yellowed pages represented her life's work and had only been set aside when her eyes could no longer see well enough to write.

This is my heritage, part of who I am, I thought, my hand gliding over the smooth surface. Whether I accepted it or not, I carried a fragment of this woman's spirit inside me. I wondered what she'd think of me.

Settling back in the chair, I read how to make a wand for witching water and how to cure horses of poll-evil, whatever that was. She wrote of destroying warts by using roasted chicken feet.

Yuck. I skipped reading the details for that spell.

She had a tonic recipe for babies with colic. The recipe called for "good" rye whiskey and tobacco smoke.

I shook my head, chuckling. Of course, any baby forced to drink rye whiskey would sleep better.

For weakness of the limbs, she recommended a tea

made from white oak. Cotton soaked in camphor oil was good for both an earache and a toothache.

One spell prevented fires in the home. Chicken heads and a piece of cloth, worn by a virgin, were necessary items.

I skipped that one too.

I read about dyeing cloth, using juice from plants I'd never heard of; rendering lard; brewing beer; keeping weevils out of the flour bin.

Not once did I read any spell that required a bottle containing urine, nails, and human hair.

I looked down at the other books on the floor by the chair. I knew I wouldn't find a spell in them either.

Closing the journal, I picked up the rest of the books and walked over to the shelf. After placing them one by one on the shelf, I stroked the spine of the book I'd read; written by a woman whose name I didn't even know. Her book had held the spells she used to heal her neighbors, cure their livestock, and make their lives easier.

Whatever had been used to create the energy in the wine bottle wouldn't be in her book.

That spell was created out of evil.

On the drive home I thought about the killer. I knew he'd left the bottle in the ditch, but for what purpose? And where was he now? I hadn't dreamed about him since Abby had been hurt. Did the lack of dreams mean he'd left Summerset? No, the clipping proved he was still around. Was he watching, waiting to catch me off-guard?

A shiver slid down my back.

What about Harley? Could he have been in Iowa City five years ago and witnessed the girl's seizure? Harley in a library? The thought stretched my imagination.

Shaking the image away, I concentrated again on Harley as a suspect. How superstitious was he? Enough to kill? Did he *hate* enough to kill?

The images of Brian and Gus floated in my mind and I felt a twinge of guilt spring to life. I extinguished it. Darci had been right. Guilt could cloud my thoughts and I couldn't afford to let that happen.

Once home, I changed into my sweats again and checked with Mother on Abby's condition. No change. I prowled the house, but avoided the living room.

I had to do something about those flowers.

Maybe I should go to the hospital. Anything would be better than this feeling of being at loose ends. I stopped and looked out the window. No. What if the killer, the witch hunter, came after me there? It would put Abby and Mother in danger.

Staring out the window, I felt the sudden change in air pressure and smelled the ozone. A storm was coming. Might as well curl up in bed and watch an old movie.

After checking all the windows and door, I climbed the stairs to my room. Queenie ran ahead, but Lady stayed close to my side.

"It's okay," I said, scratching her ear. "We'll watch *The Thin Man*. You like that one. I know Asta's your hero."

I popped the movie in the DVD/VCR and crawled into bed. Searching for the remote that had somehow gotten buried under the pillows, my hand fell on the bag of runes. I pulled them out and weighed the old leather pouch in my hand.

Hmm, I haven't worked with them since the night I thought I saw the killer across the street. Maybe I should tonight?

I lit a candle and shut off the lights. I sat cross-legged

on the bed and, breathing deeply, thought of my question.

How can I find the killer?

I reached into the pouch and drew a rune. After placing it facedown on the bed, I repeated the process two more times. Slowly I turned each one over.

I said each name aloud enunciating each syllable. *Laguz. law-gooze. Thurisaz. Thoor-ee-saw.*

Dang, not him again. The one with the brambles.

Wunjo. Woon-yo.

I grabbed the journal on my nightstand and looked each one up.

Laguz—represents water; calm surface with hidden mystery lying beneath; secrets; stormy sea: possible loss.

Laguz described the situation as it stood now. A mystery definitely lay hidden beneath the surface. Or did it mean the killer hid beneath a calm appearance?

Thurisaz—giant, troll, demon, torturer of women, said to be used to evoke those from the underworld. The hammer of Thor. A rune indicating challenges, tests.

Well, I was facing a challenge all right. *Thurisaz* didn't tell me anything that I didn't already know.

Wunjo—peace; prosperity; a hard battle well fought and won; partnership flourishes.

Wunjo was the result if I followed the advice of the rune *Thurisaz.* But what was the rune's advice?

Abby had told me I needed to think outside the box.

Picking up the three runes, I closed my eyes and thought about them.

In my mind I walked past the fires burning in the Viking longhouse. The air was filled with smoke and the smell of roasting meat. I heard men laughing while their women served them. From the dark corners came another sound, the sound of growling dogs as they fought over scraps of food. Without a word, I moved through the door and out into the clear cold night.

A thousand stars glittered in the black sky and the light of the full moon guided my way into the woods. Soon I found myself next to a pool, the sky reflected in its still waters. Kneeling, I touched the smooth surface with my fingertips and the moon and stars danced upon the ripples.

Amazed, my eyes followed the ripples across the pool to where they washed against the feet of a dark warrior, staring at me from the other side of the pool. My gaze flew to his face, but it was masked by shadows. He was dressed in black and his dark hair gleamed in the moonlight. I watched while he stepped around the edge of the pool, his soft leather boots silent on the rocky rim. I felt no fear.

Without speaking, he knelt next to me and took my wrist with his gloved hand. I gasped when he plunged both of our hands into the cold water. Guided by his hand, my fingers trailed over the moss-covered rocks beneath the pool's shallow surface until they rested on a piece of wood. His hand curled my fingers around the thick wood. And releasing my hand, he placed his hand above mine and together we lifted the piece of wood.

With a *whoosh*, the wood came out of the water,

pulling us to our feet. We stood side by side, our arms extended as we held the wood aloft.

Droplets of water rained down on me and the air sizzled with steam. I tilted my head back to see what it was we held above us.

The iron head attached to the rough wooden handle burned red-hot against the night sky. It was a Norse war hammer.

It was *Mjolnir*—the hammer of Thor.

Thirty

The next morning Comacho called to inform me he'd pick me up at eleven. A quick glance at the clock told me I'd have time to pop by the hospital and check on Abby. Throwing on a pair of jeans and a sweater, I hurried over to the hospital.

Her condition was the same, except she grew more restless. Abby would respond to loud noises and occasionally open her eyes for a second. The doctor indicated the restlessness was a good sign. Mother and Arthur continued their vigil. Satisfied, I returned home to wait for Comacho.

While I waited, I used the time productively; I dumped all the flowers in the living room and stacked Charles's notes on my desk. I'd read them later.

The living room clock was still chiming eleven o'clock when Comacho pulled in the drive. Grabbing my bag, I rushed out the door, remembering to lock it as I went.

Comacho wore jeans, a dark red sweater, and his mirrored sunglasses. I caught a whiff of his cologne while I buckled my seat belt.

"I hope you don't mind, but I promised to stop by my

sister's. She's having a birthday party for my niece," he said, backing the car out of my drive. "A bunch of little girls. Isabella wants me to meet them."

He said the name gently and with an accent. I noticed how the hard lines in his face softened as he did. Was it the same little girl I'd seen in his mind? I was dying to ask, but didn't think it wise to open a conversation about psychics and witches yet.

"I don't mind," I said, adjusting the strap on my seat belt.

I'd never paid much attention to Comacho's face before; I'd never looked past the disapproval reflected on his face whenever he looked at me. But now, out of the corner of my eye, I watched him while he drove.

He had a strong profile—a firm jaw, high cheekbones, and narrow lips. His nose jutted out from his forehead and, though a little on the large side, it fit his face perfectly, adding character. He appeared to be a man in complete control, and it was hard to imagine him at a child's party.

"You like kids?" he asked suddenly.

"I haven't had too much experience with them, except for babysitting as a teenager. I'm an only child. No nieces and nephews. What about you?" I asked, trying to keep the conversation going.

He grinned. "Yeah, I've had plenty of experience. My dad died when I was twelve and I had to help my mom with my sisters."

"Where did you grow up?"

"Chicago."

"It must've been tough."

He gave a slight shrug. "Sometimes. We made out okay."

Finished with personal confessions, he reached over

and switched on the radio. The sound of the Beatles filled the car.

Unwilling to share any more information myself, I turned my attention to looking out the window while I thought about the rune reading.

Should I mention the reading to Comacho? Nope, he'd reach for his handcuffs and haul me off to the nearest psych ward for evaluation. Glancing at him, I wondered if he had them tucked in his belt. *What about his gun? Is he wearing it?* I squinted to see if I detected any lumps under his sweater.

"What are you doing?" His face wore a perplexed look.

Startled, I jumped. "Umm," I muttered, feeling my face get hot. "I was trying to figure out if you had your gun and your handcuffs with you."

"Why? Think I'll need them?"

I shrugged. "You like to pull out the handcuffs whenever you're around me. I wondered if you brought them, just in case."

He chuckled. "No, I don't think I'll arrest you today." He put emphasis on the word *today.*

Does that mean he might tomorrow?

He reached over and turned the radio down. "Lonely?"

"Huh?" I asked, puzzled.

"Were you lonely? You said you were an only child."

"Some of the time, I suppose." I tugged at my seat belt. "I spent a lot of time with Abby and my grandfather. I was never lonely with them."

"I know your mother's here now, what about her?" He frowned. "Is she, you know, a—"

"Witch?" I said, supplying the word for him.

His frown deepened. "No. Don't even go there," he said, glancing at me, my smiling reflection caught for a moment in his mirrored sunglasses. "I'm having a hard enough time with the idea of psychics, let alone witches."

"Oh, you wanted to know if my mother's one of them...psychic, I mean," I said, smiling broadly.

"Yeah," he answered in a disgruntled tone.

I decided to quit teasing him. Anyway, it isn't a good idea to tease someone with a gun.

"No," I answered. "The gift can skip a generation."

"Did you always know?"

"Yes, but from a young age, I was taught not to talk about it. Believe it or not, some people might think you're crazy if you tell them about the gift," I said, smirking.

"You know, you're kind of a smartass, Jensen," he said, glancing at me again. "Five years ago, I never would've suspected you have such a smart mouth."

"Five years ago, I was too scared."

"You're not scared now?"

I snorted. "Of course I am. Spitless."

Comacho drummed his fingers on the steering wheel. "What can you do? Read minds?"

"My particular talent is precognitive images," I replied, thinking about my gift. "And I seem to be good at finding things."

Comacho made a choking sound before he spoke. "Bodies, you mean."

I glared at him. "I don't understand why people have a hard time accepting what a psychic can do. Cops use dogs to find things: drugs, search, and rescue—"

"They're dogs, not people," he said, interrupting me. "They have a heightened sense of smell."

"Well," I huffed, "I have a heightened sense too. It's located in my brain, not my nose."

The set of his jaw told me that he was pondering my analogy.

"Lack of understanding, is that why you haven't married?" he asked, cocking his head.

Getting pretty personal, Comacho, but I decided to answer him.

"Put it this way: The gift isn't the easiest thing to live with—for me or for someone who cares about me. I was engaged once," I said, turning and staring out the window.

"He didn't understand your gift?"

"You might say that. I think it embarrassed him and, deep down, scared him."

"Did he know about, you know," he said, waving his hand, "the other thing?"

I arched my eyebrow. "You mean the 'witch' thing?"

"Yeah," he said, gripping the steering wheel, "that thing."

"No. You're one of the few people in my life who's ever learned about 'that thing.' "

I saw him pull on his bottom lip and I think his eyes narrowed. Hard to tell with the sunglasses on.

"Did Brian Mitchell know?"

"Yes and I'm ahead of you on this one, Comacho. He was killed because of his knowledge."

"Okay. Why Gus? Gus know?"

I didn't answer right away. I was trying to decide if I should tell Comacho of my suspicions. While I thought about it, I noticed we'd turned down a street into a residential neighborhood. The houses were well kept with neatly trimmed yards. Bicycles and tricycles sat in many of the driveways and every backyard had a swing set.

Comacho whipped into one of the driveways. We'd arrived at his sister's.

I looked at Comacho quickly, my decision made. "Gus didn't know, I think he suspected. But I think Gus was killed because the killer thought he was a witch too. Gus had a squint." The words came out in a rush. "The star on Brian's and Gus's foreheads? I'm sure it's a pentagram, Darci figured it out. And—"

Comacho held up his hand, stopping me. "Okay. Okay. Sounds like you've been doing a lot of thinking. You can tell me all about it later." He got out of the car, opened the back door, and grabbed a present from the backseat. He stuck his head back in the car.

"Want to come in?"

"If you'd be more comfortable with me waiting in the car, I will."

"No, it's okay if you come in." He paused, thinking. "But don't let my sister pump you, okay?"

He walked around the car and opened my door for me.

Getting out, I looked up at him. "You didn't tell me I was crazy this time."

Before he replied, a little girl flew out the front door and flung herself at his legs.

"Uncle Henry," she squealed.

Balancing the gift under his arm, Comacho reached down and scooped the little girl into his other arm while an older replica of the girl stood in the doorway, watching.

His sister and niece.

His niece pulled his sunglasses off and, placing her small hands on his shoulders, planted wet, smacking kisses all over his face.

Comacho responded by burying his face in her soft hair and growled like a bear.

She giggled, her brown eyes sparkling. Those brown eyes slid down to the present, wrapped in Barbie paper and bright pink ribbon.

Comacho lifted his head and looked at her.

"Is the present for me?" she asked in hushed tones.

"Isabella," called the woman from the doorway, "don't be asking your uncle about presents."

He leaned in close to the little girl's ear. "Yes," he whispered.

Her eyes widened and she looked down at the present again. Looking past Comacho, she noticed me standing on the walk.

"Who's that?" she asked and pointed a little finger at me.

"Don't point, Chica. It's rude," he said, his voice kind.

She rested her head on his shoulder and watched me, her eyes never leaving my face.

"This is Ophelia," Comacho said to the little girl. "Ophelia, my niece, Isabella."

"Hello, Isabella. Happy birthday," I said, smiling.

Isabella gave me a shy smile and a tiny wave from the safety of her uncle's arms.

"What do you say?" He gave her a slight jiggle while we moved up the walk.

"Thank you," she said, giggling. "It's nice to meet you."

At the door his sister threw her arms around her brother and daughter, hugging them both.

"*Ki-kay*. You made it," she said, patting his arm.

Ki-kay? Comacho's sister called the Iceman, *Ki-kay*? Wouldn't his fellow officers love to hear that one? I tried to hide my smile, but he caught it.

He tilted his head slightly and gave me a look that said: *Don't you dare say a word.*

Grinning, I diverted my attention back to his sister.

"Isabella has been watching for you. *And* ignoring her guests," she said, shaking her finger playfully at the little girl.

"Sorry, Mama."

"Well, he's here now, so go play. You can open your presents later," she said and turned to me.

Comacho put Isabella down and she took off down the hallway.

"Belinda," he said to his sister, "I'd like you to meet Ophelia Jensen."

Belinda took my hand and shook it warmly while she sized me up.

I could see the questions running through her mind. Who is this woman? And why is she with my brother?

"Nice to meet you, Belinda," I replied, meeting her frank gaze with one of my own.

She nodded slightly and smiled, releasing my hand. "This way," she said, motioning down the hall.

We walked down the hallway where it opened to the family room and kitchen. Windows covered the back wall and I saw several children playing in the backyard. Looking to my left, I noticed their mothers sitting at the kitchen table.

Isabella ran back inside and grabbed her uncle's hand. "Please, come outside," she asked, tugging on his hand.

"Go on, *Ki-kay*," Belinda said. "Isabella wants to show you off to her friends."

Laughing, Comacho allowed his small niece to pull him out the door and into the backyard, where he was immediately the center of attention.

"Please." Belinda waved me toward the kitchen. "Sit down. I'll get you some coffee." She stopped. "Or would you care for something else."

"No, coffee's fine," I said, sitting down with the other women.

I heard Belinda behind me as she opened and shut cupboard doors.

"You're a friend of my brother's?" she asked.

I almost said, "I guess—if you don't count the number of times he's tried to arrest me." I clamped my mouth shut and nodded.

"How long have you known each other?"

He wasn't kidding about his sister pumping me. The talent must run in the family.

I cleared my throat. "About five years."

Not a lie—I *had* met him five years ago when he wanted to charge me with Brian's murder.

"Funny, he's never mentioned you," she said, placing the coffee in front of me.

"Oh," I stumbled over my words. "I meant I was introduced to him five years ago. We only recently ran into each other again."

The conversation was not going well. I grabbed my cup and took a big sip and the hot liquid scalded my tongue. I spluttered and coughed while Belinda pounded my back.

"Sorry," I said and wiped away the coffee dribbling off my chin with my napkin.

I noticed the raised eyebrows of the other women, the sly glances they exchanged. *Boy, oh boy, am I making a good impression or what?*

Belinda moved to the other side of the table and sat.

While the silence stretched on, I struggled to think of something to say. Clearing my throat, I looked at Belinda. "Isabella is charming."

"Thank you," she said, watching her daughter and her friends in the backyard. "She adores Enrique."

My eyes followed hers and I saw the little girls swarming all over him like a jungle gym. I was pleasantly surprised to see that Comacho was good with children. *Go figure,* I thought. My next words just seemed to slip out on their own. "And he's always seemed like such a hard-ass."

I slapped my hand over my mouth. *Oh God, I didn't say that aloud, did I?*

Yes, I did.

A stunned silence hung over the room and I felt the red creep into my face as I saw the other women staring at me.

Belinda broke the silence.

"You think?" she said and chuckled.

She smiled at the shocked look on my face.

"Try having him for an older brother," she said and laughed. The other women laughed too.

Leaning forward in her chair, she placed her arms on the table. "'Hardass'?" she said and rolled her eyes. "You should've seen him with my boyfriends. It's a wonder I ever got married."

Turning back to the window, I noticed something had changed. The little girls no longer climbed all over Comacho. He stood near a tree with his cell phone to his ear. Snapping it shut, he put on his sunglasses and, after giving Isabella a quick hug, he marched to the house.

"Come on, Ophelia, we've got to go," he said abruptly. Leaning down, he kissed Belinda on the top of her head. "Sorry, something's come up." Pivoting on his heel, he walked out.

I scrambled out of my chair to follow. "Nice meeting you," I said over my shoulder and ran to catch up with him.

He was standing by the driver's side of the car when I reached him.

"What's going on?" I asked, out of breath.

He rested his arms on the roof of the car, his mouth in a tight line. "Why didn't you tell me you threatened Beasley at the hospital?"

"I didn't threaten him." I stopped and shoved my hands in my back pockets. "Well, yeah," I said, remembering my conversation with him. "I told him he'd better not mess with me. But what I meant was I'd complain and file a restraining order if he didn't leave me alone."

"But that's not what you said, was it?" he questioned, his face grim.

"No," I said my voice sullen.

"Get in the car," he said, throwing his body into the driver's seat.

Acknowledging now was not a good time to argue, I did what he said and shut the door.

The car was in motion before I got my seat belt buckled. We peeled out of the driveway and down the street.

"Hey," I said to his angry profile. "What's happened?"

"Bill called. They found a body dumped in the sewage lagoon at PP International. Still had the I.D. in the pocket." His jaw clenched. "It's Fletcher Beasley. Someone killed him and threw him in the hog shit." He glared at me, his face cold. "You wouldn't know anything about it, would you?"

Thirty-One

Comacho's hand hit the rim of the steering wheel with a *thud*.

"You really had me going, you know? I almost believed the psychic BS." He gave me an ugly sneer. "I was even beginning to wonder about the 'witch' thing."

He said the word *witch* as if it were a bad word.

"How do you know Beasley was murdered? He could've been snooping around, fell in, and drowned."

His hand gripped the steering wheel. "Right. Not even Beasley was dumb enough to do that. I was the dumb one—for thinking even part of what you told me was the truth."

I slumped down in my seat. "I did tell you the truth."

"Bullshit!" His anger expanded till it filled the car. "You've lied to me since the first day I met you."

"You think I killed Brian?" I asked, sitting up.

"No, the Harvester killed Mitchell. But I think you liked the attention it brought you. Liked the attention you got last fall when you found the dead body in the woods. Maybe you missed the attention, missed playing the hero."

"What?" I couldn't keep the shock out of my voice.

"Yeah," Comacho said, warming to the subject. "You found Gus dead and saw the opportunity to play the hero again. Set fire to his body and buried it where you could conveniently find it." He nodded his head. "And it gave you the chance to annoy PP International and bring attention to your grandmother's group."

"That's nuts," I said, staring straight ahead.

"Well, lady, so are you. Five years ago, they must've locked you in the psych ward for a reason."

The cruelty in his tone made my head spin and I felt the pain building from deep inside me. A storm of guilt swept through me.

No! I hit the seat next to me. *I will not allow it. Comacho's words are not going to send me back to that dark place inside me. The dark place I lived in five years ago after Brian's death. I will not cry in front of him.*

"Why would I kill Beasley?" I asked, struggling to keep my voice calm.

"He found out what you were doing and threatened to expose you."

"The bottle?"

"You planted it." A humorless smile stretched his lips. "It will be interesting to see whose hair is in the bottle. We'll want a sample of yours, by the way."

"The envelope in Abby's room?"

"Planted that too."

"Okay, if you think everything I've told you has been a lie. How do you explain what happened with the hawk."

He made a derisive sound. "For all I know, it's a pet you trained. As far as I'm concerned, all that psychic and witch stuff was nothing more than smoke and mirrors. I deal with facts."

I stared out the window in misery. Everything he said sounded logical. The events could've happened the way he described them—if I were crazy.

But I'm not crazy. Problem was—how could I convince Comacho? Not enough magick in the world to accomplish that task.

I shifted in my seat toward Comacho. His body was rigid and I felt waves of freezing energy surrounding him. I had to break through.

"Henry," I said, touching his sleeve, "I've told you the truth about everything."

He glanced over at me and I saw his face soften for an instant. I saw the glimmer of the man I'd watched play with children, but only for a moment.

His face frosted over and the Iceman was back.

Well, I thought while I stared at Comacho backing out of my driveway, *at least he didn't pull out his handcuffs.* He had insisted I give him a lock of my hair. For DNA testing.

He'd given me the standard "Don't leave town" line and told me Bill would want to talk with me. Hopefully, Bill would be easier to convince of my innocence than Comacho.

Grabbing my keys, I drove to the hospital. I needed to see Abby—even if she couldn't help me. I still needed to go to her.

When I walked in her room, I saw Arthur sleeping in the chair. His shiny bald head hung till his chin rested on his chest. His glasses had slid down his nose and a soft snore came from his chest.

I looked toward the bed and Abby held her finger on her lips, a silent signal for me not to wake him.

I did a double take. *Abby is awake!*

My shriek woke poor Arthur. "What? What?" he said, his head jerking up and his owl eyes peering around the room.

"She's awake," I said, crossing quickly to steady him, before he tumbled off his chair. "She's awake," I repeated, the excitement in my voice rising.

After giving Arthur's shoulder a quick squeeze, I ran across the room to Abby's bedside. "Are you okay? Are you really okay?" I asked, my hands stroking her face.

A lovely smile lit up her face. "Yes, dear, I'm really okay. A little groggy still. But I think I have all my wits about me."

"Does your head hurt? What do you remember? Do you want anything? A glass of water? Something to eat?" I asked, the questions tumbling out of my mouth.

She patted my hand. "Water would be nice."

I grabbed the pitcher and began pouring the water, but my hands trembled and I spilled most of it on the floor. While I held the glass close to her lips, using the straw, she took a small sip.

Arthur had joined me at Abby's bedside and stood wiping his eyes under the thick glasses with an ancient handkerchief. "You gave us a scare, Abby," he said with a sniff.

Abby looked at him with a soft smile. "I'm sorry you were worried, Arthur."

He lifted her hand to his lips and gave it a light kiss.

Her smile widened.

A sudden thought penetrated my excitement. Abby and Arthur's relationship went beyond friendship. *Deah-duh,* I did a mental head slap. *They're having a romance. How did I miss it?*

"Mom," I said, my mind shifting away from Abby and Arthur, "where's Mom?"

"She went to the cafeteria," Arthur said, his eyes not leaving Abby's face.

"I've got to find her," I said, pivoting. "Oh, and a doctor. I've got to find a doctor. Don't leave her alone."

"Don't worry, I won't," he said, still staring at Abby.

I ran from the room. Scanning the hall, I saw Abby's doctor standing at the nurses' station. "She's awake," I said, rushing over to him.

The doctor hurried toward Abby's room while I ran toward the elevator. I hit the DOWN button. Shifting from one foot to the other, I hit it again. "Come on," I said, watching the numbers above the door change as the elevator made its slow progress downward.

When the door slid open, I took one quick step forward and almost knocked my mother down.

She grabbed my arms to regain her balance. "What's wrong?"

"Nothing. Abby's awake."

We wrapped our arms around each other, oblivious to the stares of those getting off the elevator, and hugged each other in relief. After a moment my mother took a step back and then, with our arms linked, we walked to Abby's room.

The doctor had finished examining Abby when we walked in.

Removing his stethoscope, he made notes on Abby's chart while we waited for his verdict.

"Well?" asked Mother, her voice impatient.

"Everything checks out okay," he said, snapping Abby's chart shut. "Her lungs sound clear. Heart's steady. A little weakness in her left hand, but other than that, she's doing well. Better than I would've expected for a woman her age."

I watched Abby's eyebrows arch at the "woman her age" remark.

Yup, I thought, satisfied. *Abby is going to be okay.*

After the doctor left Abby insisted Mother and Arthur go home. The tension of the past few days over, they both wilted before my eyes. Without arguing, they did what Abby insisted and left.

Alone with Abby, I pulled a chair close to her bed and sat. She didn't waste any time.

"What's been going on?" she asked.

"We'll talk about it later. You need to get some rest," I said with a weak smile.

"We'll talk about it now, young lady. I've been resting for what?" she asked, her eyes meeting mine.

I silently held up three fingers.

"Three days," she said, frowning. "The last thing I want right now is sleep. Tell me what's happened?"

Her statement was all the encouragement I needed.

About an hour later and a gallon of tears—mine—Abby knew everything.

"See," I said, my throat tight. "I've made a mess of things."

"No, you haven't." She stared thoughtfully at the ceiling. "Interesting what happened with the hawk."

"Has that ever happened to you?"

She shook her head. "No. You have talents we didn't know about. We'll have to explore what they are once this is all over."

Oh great, I thought. At that moment I wasn't too happy about the talents I knew about. The way I saw it, they'd done nothing but land me in a world of trouble.

"Your last experience with the runes—did you really see the hammer of Thor?" Abby asked, her eyes bright.

"Yeah. I think so. I've never read much about *Mjolnir,* the hammer of Thor, but somehow in the vision, I knew that's what we held."

"Ah yes, the dark warrior," she said with a grin.

"Hey, I know what you're thinking. And you're wrong. Comacho is *not* the dark warrior. He is *not* going to help me find the answer. But he *is* going to arrest me."

"Nonsense." She waved away my concern. "We simply won't let him."

"Ha," I said, rolling my eyes. "Pretty big talk from a woman in a hospital bed."

Abby scooted up in bed. "I've no intention of being here much longer."

"Abby, may I point out, you've been unconscious for three days and you just woke up. Do you think they're going to let you out just like that?" I said, snapping my fingers.

She looked at me surprised. "Why, yes, I do."

I shook my head. Maybe she was right. Abby was good at persuading people to do what she wanted. Too bad she couldn't persuade Comacho to believe me.

Unable to sit still any longer, I began to pace the room. "I don't know what to do. I've done everything I can to get Comacho to believe me," I said, stopping at the end of her bed. "But if he arrests me, I won't be able to find the witch hunter, as Darci calls him. I'm afraid if I'm out of the way, he'll come after you. Maybe he already has."

"In the greenhouse?"

"Yes." I resumed my pacing. "I thought maybe Harley or the goons from PP International were responsible, but now I'm not sure."

"I'm sorry, but I can't help you. The last thing I re-member is working in the greenhouse and hearing a noise behind me. The rest is a blank."

"Nothing else, no feeling, no sense of who's responsi-ble?" I asked while I paced.

"No."

"Dang." I felt like pounding my head on the wall. "I don't know where to go from here."

"Beasley's room at the motel," she said in a pragmatic voice. "See what you sense."

I came to a sudden stop. "What?" I tugged at my hair in frustration. "Bill or Comacho won't let me within a hundred yards of Beasley's room."

"Give them a reason to."

"What reason? I've tried telling the truth. It didn't work."

My sweet, gentle grandmother looked at me with a sly grin and uttered one word.

"Lie."

Thirty-Two

I felt safe leaving Abby alone. The deputy was still posted at her door and I knew Mother and Arthur would be back soon. My mother required little sleep; she'd want to get back to the hospital as soon as possible so she could start bossing the doctors and nurses around.

While I drove to the motel, my brain scrambled for an excuse to be in Beasley's room, but I drew a blank. I'd have to wing it. When I pulled into the parking lot, I noticed Comacho's car parked next to Bill's patrol car.

Wonderful. I'd hoped to find Bill alone. I had a feeling that Bill would be more sympathetic—if Comacho and his ice-cold presence weren't there. Steeling myself for the inevitable, I got out of the car and walked into the motel.

As I wandered down the hall, it wasn't hard to find Beasley's room; it was the one with CRIME SCENE tape covering the door. And had Deputy Alan Bauer standing at attention, looking official. Maybe Alan didn't know I was a suspect and I could talk him into letting me in the room.

"Hi, Alan," I said, keeping my voice light.

"Ophelia, what are you doing here?" A frown puckered his brow.

So much for talking Alan into anything.

"Is Bill in there?"

"Yes." His eyes narrowed.

"May I go in and talk to him?"

"No."

"Please?"

"No."

The conversation wasn't going well. I wondered if Alan would let me in if I told him I was here to make a confession.

Frustrated, I shoved my hands in my back pockets. Rubbing the toe of my shoe across the carpet, I tried to think of a way around Alan. My attention shifted from the carpet to the door when it swung open. Alan lifted the tape and the crime scene team walked out carrying their equipment.

No one made an effort to shut the door, but Alan stood blocking the doorway. I stood on my tiptoes and peered around him, trying to get a glimpse inside.

I didn't see Bill or Comacho. *Are they in there? Can I make an end run around Alan? Nope. Alan is bigger than me.*

Abruptly Bill and Comacho appeared by the window in Beasley's room. I caught Bill's eye with what I hoped was a friendly wave. His brow puckered just like Alan's had. Comacho, his eyes following Bill's, glared.

Gee, no one seems glad to see me today.

"Bill," I called out, "can I come in?"

Wiping his bald head, Bill looked at Alan and nodded. "Let her in, Alan."

Alan stepped to the side and I moved past him.

"What are you doing here, Ophelia?" Bill asked.

I didn't answer right away. I was busy searching the

room with my psychic radar, trying to pick up some-thing—anything.

The walls were a putty beige with a piece of motel art hanging over the bed. The bed itself was bare. The team had stripped it of the bedspread and sheets. The surfaces of the fake wood dresser and nightstand were covered with a fine powder from the team lifting prints.

I sensed energy in the room, but I couldn't focus on it. The frigid waves coming off Comacho kept blocking the other energy in the room. I needed to concentrate, but I was running out of time.

"I asked you what you were doing here, Ophelia?" Bill's voice sounded sharp.

Time's up. Nothing. I ground my teeth in irritation. *Dang Comacho and his Iceman attitude.*

"Ahh, Abby's awake."

Boy, did that sound lame. I didn't dare look at Coma-cho, but I felt the room temperature drop a notch.

"I know. The deputy at the hospital called," Bill said.

"Oh," I chewed on my lip. "I never thought of that."

The temperature dropped again.

"Umm, are there any questions you want to ask me?" I asked while I tried scanning the room again.

The room was getting so cold that I almost shivered.

"One right now—where were you Thursday night?"

I pursed my lips, thinking. Ever since Abby had been hurt, the days blended together. *Thursday? Playing with the runes?* Better not tell him that. *No, the rune reading was last night. Friday night. Thursday night I fell asleep as soon as I arrived home.*

"Home asleep?" I didn't mean to make my answer sound like a question.

"Anyone talk to you, stop by?" Bill asked.

I shook my head.

"Well," Bill scratched his head. "I'll have more later, but I think it would be better if you came to the office for those."

My eyes flew to Comacho's face. He was staring at a spot on the wall above my head.

My anger simmered below the surface. I'd told him more about myself, my gifts, than I'd ever shared with anyone in my life and he didn't even have the guts to look at me. I'd never felt so betrayed. *This is what I get for being honest? Arrested for murder. Damn you, Comacho, look at me!*

When his eyes finally met mine, I thought I saw a spark of regret before the wall of ice came slamming down. Defeated, I turned, without speaking, and left the room.

My steps were heavy as I walked down the hall. All I could think about was how I'd blown it. I hadn't been able to shut Comacho out long enough to learn anything.

A door opening to my left startled me.

Charles Thornton.

"Ophelia, I was headed over to your house in hopes of finding you," he said, grabbing my hand and pulling me into the room before I responded.

I took a fast look over my shoulder. At least he left the door opened.

His room was exactly like Beasley's. Same putty beige walls, same cheap picture, but the dresser and nightstand were clean. The nightstand drew my attention again.

Charles's books lay there.

Trying to read upside down, I studied the books. All I read on one was the name of the author—Cotton Mather. The other book's title was in Latin. I craned my neck to read it better. *Malleus Maleficarum.*

Amazed, I looked over at Charles. "You read Latin?"

He quickly walked to the nightstand and, after opening the drawer, picked up the books and dropped them in.

"Yes," he replied, shutting the drawer with a *bang*.

"Hey, no need to be embarrassed, Charles. I'm impressed you read Latin."

"My nurse taught me. She liked the classics." He turned around and smiled. "I'm glad you're here. I wanted to—"

"Wait a second," I said, breaking in. "I appreciate the flowers and all, but I'm afraid I've misled you."

"I know all about you. How could you mislead me?" he asked, frowning.

"I have. I think." I paused. I might as well get right to the point. "I don't want a relationship, Charles. It's not you," I said, rushing on. "I'm not interested in that with anyone."

"You're rejecting me?" he asked in a shocked voice.

"Charles, how can I reject you when I don't even know you?" I asked, surprised at his reaction.

"You could get to know me," he said with a pout.

"No, Charles, I don't think so," I said quietly.

He stuck out his bottom lip. "You're like the others, after all. I thought, after I'd met you, that you had some goodness in you. I was wrong."

What an odd thing to say.

I eyed the distance between the door and me. I took a careful step in that direction.

"I'm sorry if you've been hurt by other people, but I can't be involved with anyone right now."

Charles's reaction made me uncomfortable. His blue eyes glinted while he watched me.

I edged myself backward toward the door, and as I did, I made a snap decision.

Time to get the hell out of here.

I pivoted on my heel and ran, not slowing till I reached my car.

Driving home, I couldn't get over Charles's strange behavior. We'd talked maybe three times, but he acted like we were involved. Was he that crazy?

I peeked at the clock on my dashboard. It was close to nine o'clock. I made a fast call to check on Abby and talked to my mother. Abby was fine, Mother was fine. Dad, who she'd called before returning to the hospital, was fine. Everybody was fine. Except me. Comacho was getting ready to arrest me.

A sense of unease pricked at me. I tried to trap its source, but it slid away. I drummed my fingers on the steering column. If I got arrested, the killer, the witch hunter, might win.

Yanking the steering wheel around, I made a fast U-turn in the middle of the street. Darci had said I needed to learn more about the history of witches, so I would. I headed to the library.

At the top of the steps, I fished my keys out of my backpack and unlocked the door. Hitting the light switches on my way, I headed to the reference section. I found the books I wanted right away. After pulling them off the shelf, I went down the stairs to my office.

I hesitated at the door to my office and looked around.

The pictures of Abby and my parents stared at me from my desk. My chair was pushed in just like I always left it at the end of the day. The clutter on the desk was in its normal spot.

Boy, do I miss this place. I have to find the killer so my life can go back to normal. Well, at least normal for a witch and a psychic.

Settling down at my desk, I opened the first book and started reading about the Salem Witch Trials.

An hour and half later, I'd finished.

I propped my feet on my desk and thought about what I'd read.

What had started out as a game of fortune-telling between a group of girls in the winter of 1692 soon became something more sinister.

The girls began to suffer from fits, convulsions. Finding no physical reason, the doctor diagnosed they were bewitched. Charges of witchcraft were brought against the girls by clergyman Samuel Parris. When questioned, at first the girls resisted naming names, but soon, they named a slave, Tituba, then Sarah Osborne and Sarah Good. More names were to come, and, by the time the last witch trial was held in January of 1693, over twenty people had been executed and their property seized. Many of the convictions were based on the testimony of one of the girls, twelve-year-old Anne Putnam. Terror reigned and anyone who spoke out against the trials was at risk of being accused themselves.

I flipped back through the pages and looked at the names of those executed, in most cases, by hanging. One man, Giles Corey, was pressed to death after he refused to answer the court's questions during his trial. He was bound and taken to a field where, each time he refused to answer, his tormentors piled more rocks on his body. It took him two days to die. He was eighty years old.

I'd heard about pressing before, but when? Suddenly it came to me—Darci on the way to Iowa City had been telling me about an article she'd read.

I ran upstairs to the magazine rack and found the article. Taking it with me, I went back to my office and skimmed through it.

Exactly as Darci had told me. An old woman, thought odd by her neighbors, had disappeared from her cabin. Fifteen years later, her bones were found under a pile of rocks in the middle of the woods. It happened in Massachusetts.

Had someone tried to get the old woman to confess to witchcraft? What could've happened to make someone suspect her of being a witch? Did she have a squint, too, like Gus? I looked at a photo of her in the magazine; it didn't appear she had a squint. Had she been a witch?

I rubbed my eyes and took a deep breath. What about the people in Salem? Were they witches? One woman had cursed a judge as she stood on the gallows. She'd said, "May God give you blood to drink, for taking my life." Twenty-five years later, the judge died from a hemorrhage in the throat, literally drowning on his own blood. Coincidence?

Tired, I was getting nowhere. I rubbed my eyes again. Did the book mention the name of the judge? I was so exhausted, I couldn't remember. I'd look one more time and go home.

My finger skimmed down the page, looking for the judge's name, I didn't find it. But another name jumped out at me. A name I'd seen recently.

Oh my God! Follow the pattern Abby had told me and here it was: the pattern. How could I have missed it?

I grabbed the other book and searched until I found what I was looking for.

I read the word out loud. *"Malleus Maleficarum."*

"That's right, Ophelia," said a voice from the doorway, *"The Hammer of Witches.* An excellent guide on how to seek out witches and destroy them."

Charles.

Thirty-Three

Charles Thornton leaned carelessly against the door-jamb, one hand in his pocket. In his other he held a very shiny, very nasty knife. The one I'd seen the day I'd found Gus's body. If I'd had any doubts, they were gone at the sight of the knife.

The runes had told the truth. A hammer lying beneath a calm surface. Only it wasn't *Mjolnir,* the hammer of Thor, I sought. It was *The Hammer of Witches* and finding it would lead me to a killer beneath the calm surface of an ordinary man.

Too bad I was a little late figuring it out. I stared at the knife. Why couldn't the runes have given me his initials or something? Instead of clues couched in mystery.

Charles noticed my eyes fixed on the knife. He held it up in front of his face, turning it this way and that. "Like it? It's a replica of a medieval dagger. The knights carried them." He smiled, watching the way the fluorescent light flashed on the silver blade. "My mother told me stories of the men who carried daggers similar to this one." He pointed the knife toward me. "I used it to kill your friend, you know."

"You bastard!" I cried, springing to my feet.

He motioned, with the knife, for me to sit down. "Now, now," he said. "I'm not ready to end this yet, but if you don't behave, I will." He pursed his lips in a pout. "I have something special planned for you, but I want us to talk first."

"Okay," I said, sitting down and picking up a pen. The longer we talked, the longer I lived. I drew a doodle of a hammer on a piece of paper. "What do you want to talk about?"

"I didn't mean to kill your friend." He stopped and sighed. "I've always felt bad about him. It *was* his fault, though. He shouldn't have chased me."

"Brian chased you? When?" I asked, perplexed.

He pushed away from the door and took a step inside my office. "That night at your apartment. I was there, you know. In back. On the porch. I'd been watching you through the window." He smiled at the memory. "I'd watched you so many nights, Ophelia. Watched and waited for the perfect moment. And when the moment came, he spoiled it for me."

"How?"

"Oh, my foot hit a pop can when I was sneaking off your porch. He heard it and came running around the side of the house." Charles frowned. "He chased me all the way back to the van I'd stolen. We fought; he fell against the bumper and was knocked out. After that it was easy."

Charles walked over to the pictures of Abby and my parents. Picking them up, he looked the pictures over.

Yuck, he's touching my things. My lip curled in disgust. If I lived through this, I'd have to disinfect everything in here.

He set the picture frames down in the same spot.

Studying their positions, he moved Abby's over a touch. Satisfied, he strolled back toward my desk.

"You said, 'After that it was easy'?" I reminded him.

"Oh yes," he said, remembering. "I threw him in the van, took him out in the woods, and killed him. I drove back to town and disposed of the body in the Dumpster. I was angry, though, and got carried away."

Carried away? He'd butchered Brian.

Running his finger down the side of the blade, he kept talking. "I thought the pentagram on his forehead was a nice touch." He threw his hands wide. "You see, if he hadn't chased me, he'd be alive today. You'd be dead, but your friend would've lived."

"Why me, Charles? I've done you no harm."

"No, but your kind harms everyone. Like the girl in the library. I saw what you did to her."

"I tried to help her—"

"No," he interrupted. "You made her have that fit, like that woman did to my mother. I know what witches do. Cousin Lucy told me all about witches, from the time I was a small child."

"But you said your mother had a heart problem?"

"That was a lie my father told to cover up what was happening to my mother. Cousin Lucy said he wanted her dead, so he let the witch curse her." He looked down at the knife in his hand. "I tried to help my mother, but my father beat me every time I did."

Peachy, I'm trapped in a room with a guy who'd had a sociopath for a nurse and a father who abused him.

"My father won in the end. The witch cursed her and she drowned in her own blood, like our ancestor. The one my father forbade Cousin Lucy to talk about," he said, pouting again.

Ancestor?

"Ah, this ancestor, he wouldn't have happened to have been a judge at the Salem Witch Trials, would he?"

"Yes," he said, his face brightening. "Have you heard of him? Judge Thorntun, spelled with a *u*. Cousin Lucy said my great-great-grandfather changed the spelling of our last name because he was ashamed." Charles shook his head in disbelief. "Can you imagine? Ashamed of a man who fought evil. Cousin Lucy said we should be proud of the judge."

I was beginning *not* to like this Cousin Lucy.

I looked down at the paper and noticed I'd drawn "frowny" faces all over it. Charles gazed at the paper and smiled.

When he raised his eyes to my face, he looked sad. "I'd hoped you were different, that maybe I could convince you to forsake your evil ways." Charles shook his head slowly. "I saw you crying at the hospital. And when the witch bottle didn't kill you—"

I broke in. "What are you talking about? Crying and a witch bottle?"

"Witches can't cry. You know that." Charles rolled his eyes as if he were talking to an idiot. "You must've faked it somehow. *The Hammer of Witches* cautions to be alert for trickery when you see a witch cry."

"The witch bottle?"

"Oh, a bottle with nine nails, urine, and hair from the witch you want to kill. I know you found it; I went back to the ditch and looked for it. When you didn't die, I thought maybe it was a sign you could be saved. I even tried to warn you to abandon your ways by sending you the flowers. Red and white flowers are a sign of death, you know," Charles said in a rambling voice. "I thought maybe receiving them would scare you. Scare you enough to change, but I was wrong."

"Whoa, forget the flowers and back up a second—hair of the witch? That bottle Comacho and I found had my hair in it?" I was astonished. "How did you get any of my hair?"

"From your hairbrush. I picked it up when you spilled your bag at the restaurant."

I shut my eyes. The lab would come back with a positive DNA match when they compared my hair sample to what they found in the bottle. Comacho would see the report as proof I lied to him. By then, I'd be dead, but...I shook my head and opened my eyes.

Charles looked over his shoulder at the clock. "It's time to go," he said sadly.

I picked up the pen and doodled again. "Where are we going, Charles?" I asked. My voice sounded calm, but inside I was shaking.

"I told you I have something special for you. I thought about burning. I'd planned burning for the old man, the witch I buried in the ditch, but he died first." Charles lifted one shoulder. "But I remembered the judge hanged witches." His eyes lit up with excitement. "We're going back to where you dumped poor Beasley. Oh, don't look surprised," he chided.

I ignored him and continued to doodle.

"People in small towns talk. Your fight with him was all over town, and I know the sheriff suspects you killed him." He licked his lips in satisfaction. "You're going to hang yourself out of remorse. They're going to find your dead body swinging from the rafters."

I put the pencil down. "I didn't kill Beasley."

Charles smiled. "I know. I did."

* * *

Charles walked me out the back door of the library to where he'd parked his car in the alley. The whole time he held the sharp tip of his dagger in the middle of my back. Once at the car, he forced me to the ground, on my back. While he held me down with a knee to my chest, he tied my wrists with tape.

I thought about kicking him, but I remembered what he'd done out of anger to Brian. Screaming wouldn't do any good; the alley was empty and all the businesses were closed. I'd wait till we reached PP International. Lots of places to run and hide there. And who knows, maybe someone would find the clues I'd left on my desk in time to save me.

"The tape might leave residue," he explained while he wrapped my wrists. "I'll have to clean your wrists with alcohol later. I was afraid a rope would cause bruising and the sheriff might wonder if you went willingly. Can't have that." He pulled me to my feet and smiled into my face.

The trip to PP International was silent. It was as if Charles had used up all his words in the library.

I hadn't. I had a few questions. Why had he killed Beasley? And how? I thought about using the standard line "You won't get away with this," but he already had. While the police had been trying to tie Brian's murder to the Harvester, Charles Thornton had been living his life, safe in his paranoia. And was Brian his first murder or had there been others?

When we reached PP International, Charles kept my door locked and got out on his side. Moving around the front of the car, he unlocked mine and pulled me out of the car. With his knife pointed at a spot between my shoulder blades, he marched me to one of the abandoned buildings.

As we walked, we were close enough to the sewage lagoon that the smell of hydrogen sulfide burned my nose and made my eyes water. I looked to my left and saw the lagoon. To the right of the lagoon was the old trailer the manager had lived in.

Tilting my head back, I looked at the night sky. It reminded me of the vision I'd had the night I worked with the runes. A full moon shone and the sky was covered with stars. Their reflection floated on the dark surface, as they had in the vision. But the water in the lagoon wasn't clean and cool, like the pool; it was oily and dank. And I didn't see a dark warrior to help me tonight. Tonight I was on my own.

A slight jab in the back quickened my steps.

We approached a building that was open on one side. In the bright moonlight I saw the empty hog crates where the animals had spent their entire lives. What a place to die.

No, I stopped the thought before it had formed. I wasn't going to die. I'd fight with all I had. All I had to do was get away from Charles and his knife.

When we reached the building, Charles shoved me up against the fence separating the stalls. Holding me in place from behind with his body, he reached around and tied my wrists to the fence with more tape. I squirmed against his weight, but he grabbed my hair and yanked my head back. I stopped struggling.

Charles anchored me to the fence. "If you'll excuse me, I have to get things set up," he whispered in my ear before he walked away.

I heard Charles making noise in the building behind me and a sense of urgency shook me from the inside out. *Think. How am I going to get out of this?* I pulled against the tape.

I felt the tape wrapped around the fence loosen. I tugged again and wiggled my wrists. I felt the tape on the fence give. I took a quick look over my shoulder at Charles, still arranging the scene of my hanging. No longer attached to the fence, I worked my wrists back and forth, loosening the tape. When I had enough space, I pulled one hand free. Another quick look over my shoulder and I took off, running for all I was worth.

I ran toward the lagoon. If I reached the other side of the lagoon, I could hide near the old trailer. Maybe even find a phone inside.

My legs pumped and my muscles began to burn. I didn't have much time. Any minute Charles would turn around and find me gone.

"Hey!" Charles yelled.

Guess that minute is now.

I ran harder when I heard footsteps pounding behind me. I'd almost reached the lagoon when Charles tackled me, knocking me down. In the bright moonlight I saw his knife spin over my head and into the lagoon. He flipped me over and gave me a hard right to the jaw. I saw stars, but not the ones in the sky. They floated like tiny lights behind my eyelids. Shaking them away, I opened my eyes to see Charles's face looming above me.

His eyes were wild with rage and his lips were pulled back, exposing his teeth in a bizarre grin. And his hands held my shoulders to the ground.

I bucked and kicked, trying to throw him off, but he was too heavy.

He yelled and screamed at me, but I didn't hear the words through my fear. His face got closer and closer as he shrieked.

Raising my head, I smashed my forehead into his nose. Charles reared back and grabbed his nose in pain, releasing my shoulders. No longer pinned beneath him, I jerked my knee up, making contact with his lower back. The force threw him off-balance, and with a push, I shoved him off me. Rolling the other way, I crawled away, trying to get to my feet.

I managed to stand, but he was on me in an instant. His hands tightened around my throat and he shook me like a dog shaking a rat.

"I'm going to kill you with my bare hands," he shouted, the blood dripping from his nose. "I'm going to throw your wretched body in the sewer where it belongs."

I clawed at his wrists with my hands, fighting his grip.

"Then I'm going after the evil woman who spawned you—the old lady, your beloved grandmother. She'll know the fires of hell before I'm finished with her."

His words finally penetrated my fear-soaked brain. Abby—he planned to kill Abby!

A scream of pure animal rage ripped from my raw throat. And with it, I brought my knee up with a force I didn't know I possessed.

A howl tore from Charles while his hands fell away and he dropped like bag of cement. He rolled on the ground in pain, closer and closer to the edge of the lagoon.

Rubbing my aching throat, I staggered after him.

Standing above him, I looked down at him.

His face, contorted in pain, was smeared with blood from his bleeding nose. His eyes were scrunched shut.

This was the man who'd killed Brian and Fletcher Beasley; who'd scared a harmless old man to death; and had caused misery in the lives of innocent people.

"I'm not the one who belongs in a sewer," I said, placing my foot on his hip. "You are."

Using all the energy I had left, I pushed against his body with my foot and watched, with a grim smile, as he rolled off the edge of the lagoon and into the hog shit.

Thirty-Four

"I wasn't going to let him drown, honest," I explained in a sincere voice. "See." I pointed at the ground. "I have a rope. The rope he planned on using to hang me. But you got here before I had the chance to throw it to him."

The dark warrior had finally shown up, a short time after Charles took his header into the lagoon, and now I was trying to convince him I really hadn't tried to commit murder.

Comacho eyed me skeptically.

Bill was at PP International too. Right now, he refereed a dispute between Alan and another one of the deputies. Their voices carried to where we stood.

"You take him in your car," said the young deputy.

"No. Put him in yours," Alan replied.

"But I cleaned mine out today," the other deputy whined.

"Clean it out again," Alan said.

"Boys. We'll draw straws." I heard Bill's voice say.

The softly muttered *damn* floated on the night breeze. And the voice didn't belong to Alan; it belonged to the other deputy. He'd won the privilege of hauling the manure-covered Charles to the county jail.

"Hey," Bill's voice called out, "be sure and hose him down before you book him. I don't want the jail stinking."

"Yeah," Alan's voice joined in. "You might want to drive back to town with the windows down."

The other deputy muttered while he stuffed Charles in the back of his patrol car.

"Okay, let's go through this again," Comacho said, pulling his hand through his hair.

"Henry, I'd watch that if I were you," Bill said as he walked by.

Comacho turned and gave Bill a puzzled look. "What do you mean?"

"Pulling your hand through your hair. It's a real easy habit to develop when you're around Ophelia too much." Bill pulled his hat off and pointed to his head. "How do you think I went bald?"

I rolled my eyes. Bill was all fun and games, now that I'd caught his killer for him.

Comacho took a deep breath and lifted his hand to his head again. Realizing what he was about to do, he shook his head slightly and dropped his hand. "Okay. Where were we?"

I groaned. "About to go over what happened for the millionth time."

"All right, we'll drop it for now." He looked at me sternly. "But I want to talk to you tomorrow."

"After we get Abby home," I said, crossing my arms and planting my feet.

Comacho looked surprised. "The doctors are releasing her tomorrow?"

"Yes. Except for some weakness in her hand, everything's normal. They wanted to observe her for twenty-four hours, just in case."

"Wow, that's amazing. Especially for a woman her age."

I laughed. "You'd better not let her hear you say that."

"What?"

I laughed again. "Never mind. Are you finished with your questions?"

"Yes." Comacho turned on his heel and started to walk away.

"Wait a second," I said, grabbing his sleeve. "It's my turn now."

"Okay," he said with a shrug. "I figure I owe you that much. What do you want to know?"

"You haven't told me how or why you and Bill came rushing out here. Did you find my clues?"

"You mean the doodle of the witches' hat and the cat?"

"And 'PPI' written upside down. I had to write it upside down in case Charles was watching me," I said proudly. "I thought writing upside down was clever. Wait a second," I said fisting my hand on my hip. "The doodle wasn't a cat, it was a weasel. Get it, Weasely Beasley? You told me it was Beasley's nickname."

"Guess I missed that one," he said grinning.

"What about leaving the book open to the Salem Witch Trials, did you get that one?"

His grin widened. "Nope, missed that one, too."

I must be as oblique as the runes.

I frowned. "Why did you drive out here?"

"Ahh," he said turning his head to look around. "Ahh, I got a call after we left the motel. The police caught the Harvester in Indiana."

"No kidding? How did they catch him?"

"Ahh, it's kind of hard to explain," he said, glancing over his shoulder and back to me.

I winked at him. "Try."

"Okay," he said, giving up. "After you told me about the barn you saw in the...whatever you call them—"

"Vision," I said, supplying the word for him.

"Yeah, one of those. I called a colleague in Indiana, where most of the bodies have been found. Asked him if any of the suspects they'd looked at had a place with a barn. He said one did, but he had an alibi. I suggested they dig deeper. He followed my advice and learned the alibi had lied." He lifted a shoulder. "Once they had that information, they were able to tie up other loose ends and convince a judge to give them a search warrant. They went out to the barn and found enough evidence to hang the guy."

I suspected he was leaving a lot of information out, but I let it pass.

"Catching the Harvester still doesn't explain why you came out here," I said, not willing to let him off the hook.

Comacho squirmed and took a deep breath. "All right. After I found out you were right about the Harvester, I thought, 'Okay, maybe if she was right about the Harvester, maybe she was right about some other stuff.'"

"In other words, you decided to believe me about Beasley?" I crossed my arms on my chest.

"I didn't say that," he quickly denied. "But I thought maybe I should talk to you again. I drove by the library, all the lights were on, it was unlocked, and your car was there." He hesitated. "But you weren't."

"And you found my doodles and figured out where Charles had taken me." I nodded, my head satisfied.

"No, Alan saw you in the car with Charles headed this way."

"I didn't see Alan."

"You weren't supposed to. He was back off the road with his radar on."

"He was running a speed trap?" I said, pouting. I was disappointed my clues hadn't led them here.

"We prefer not to call them that," he said in a serious tone. "I called Bill to tell him what I'd found and he put it out on the radio. Alan heard, called back in what he'd seen, and here we are. Any more questions?"

"How did Charles kill Beasley?"

"Poison. Medical examiner found it during the autopsy. We don't know for sure yet, but we think Thornton slipped some antifreeze in Beasley's coffee. Waited for him to die, brought the body out here, and dumped him."

"And Beasley didn't taste the poison, because of all the sugar," I said to myself.

"What did you say?" Comacho asked.

"Beasley used a lot of sugar in his coffee. I noticed it that day in the hospital cafeteria."

"Oh yeah, the day you threatened him," Comacho said, nodding.

"Please, I'd rather not talk about the argument," I replied, putting a hand on my hip.

"I'm sure you don't want to talk about it," he said and chuckled. "A word of advice, Ophelia—don't threaten people. You can get in trouble doing that."

No kidding. Hey, did he call me Ophelia?

I narrowed my eyes and watched him.

He lifted an eyebrow. "You have more questions?"

Other questions. *Hmm, should I ask him how he got the nickname* Ki-Kay? *Nope, better not.*

"Yes," I said, snapping my fingers. "Not really a question, but would you check on something for me?"

"Maybe. Depends on what it is," he answered, his voice full of suspicion.

"A body, skeleton, was found in Massachusetts. The sheriff thinks it belongs to a woman who disappeared fifteen years ago. Would you check if the woman had any connection with Charles's family?"

"I suppose. You have her name?"

"No, but I can get it and call you."

Comacho rubbed his chin thinking. "Why do you want to know?"

"I think Charles killed her."

"Why?"

"He came after me because he thought I'd caused that student's convulsion. His mother suffered from convulsions. He told me she was bewitched and killed through witchcraft. The woman in Massachusetts was killed by pressing—piling on rocks till the person dies. Pressing was used during the Salem Witch Trials and I thought, maybe . . ." I stopped and lifted a hand. "It's just a hunch."

"A hunch or a *hunch*?" Comacho cocked his head and watched me.

"A hunch. Does that mean you believe I'm psychic?" I asked, surprised.

He cleared his throat and stared at the stars. "I don't know. I've seen some strange stuff in the last few days."

"Henry, you do believe I'm psychic." And for some reason, it made me happy.

"Put it this way," he said, smiling, "I'm willing to consider the possibility."

I grinned at him. "Do you believe I'm a witch too, Henry?"

"Don't press your luck, Jensen," he said with a glare.

* * *

Later that night, I dreamed of Brian again, but not as a twisted corpse lying in a Dumpster.

In my dream it was spring. The trees were covered with buds, and all the flowerbeds around the college were full of tender green shoots forcing their way up, seeking the spring sun.

I saw Brian striding across the campus, his arms full of graded papers. Reaching the steps of one of the buildings, he raced up them two at a time. At the door, he turned and saw me. His face broke into a big grin. Balancing the papers in one arm, he raised his other arm in a big wave. His lips moved, but I was too far away to hear them. With a final smile, he opened the door and disappeared inside.

In my dream I stood for a long time, gazing at the building. I may have been too far away to hear Brian's words, but I read his lips.

His final words were *"Thank you."*

Thirty-Five

The next afternoon while Mother and I sprang Abby from the hospital, Arthur and Darci waited for us at Abby's. Pulling up to the house, Abby saw the banner. WELCOME HOME, ABBY! hung across the porch railing and green and yellow streamers flapped in the light breeze. Arthur and Darci, proud of their handiwork, stood at the end of the walk.

A shy look crossed Arthur's face as he opened the door and helped Abby out. I saw a similar look on Abby's. *Hmm, Abby and Arthur? Septuagenarian romance? Don't even go there, Jensen,* I thought and slammed the lid of the trunk shut.

The inside of the house had been decorated in a similar manner. Streamers, draped in long swags, ran down the length of the hallway. In the dining room, another WELCOME HOME banner had been pinned to Abby's lace curtains. The table held candles and a cake.

At the corner of the table, Edna Walters waited with her hands resting on top of her walker. When Abby entered the room, she hobbled over to her.

"Edna, the cake's lovely," Abby said in a pleasant voice.

Edna preened at the praise. "Least I could do, after all you've done for me and mine over the years," she said, her false teeth clicking. Edna slid a glance at my mother and smiled.

Now that I knew the whole story about Harley and his ex-wife, I was relieved Edna harbored no resentment toward my mother.

After we had settled, Abby in her chair in the living room, the neighbors began to arrive, each one bringing food for Abby. Casseroles, covered dishes, pies, more cakes, soon the kitchen counter was littered with offerings from her friends and neighbors.

Abby wouldn't need to cook for a month.

No one stayed long, but each friend and neighbor wanted to pay their respect to Abby. Standing in the doorway, I watched proudly while she held court. If someday I could be half the woman she was, I would consider my life well spent.

An arm slipped around my waist and I glanced at my mother standing next to me. Her face wore the same expression of pride as mine.

"She's really special, isn't she?" my mother asked with a nod toward Abby.

"Yes, she is," I said, leaning against her. "And so are you."

A look of surprise crossed her face. "Me?" she asked as she placed a hand on her chest. "I don't have the talent you and Mother have."

"No, but you have talents of your own. You kept the doctors in line, you watched over Abby while I was ..." I trailed off, trying to think of the right word to describe what had happened to me the last few days.

"Busy?" Mother said, supplying the word for me.

I grinned. "Yeah, while I was busy." I cocked my head and looked at her. "Good job, Mom."

"Why, thank you," she said, standing tall.

A knock at the door drew our attention. Darci opened the door to Bill, Alan, and Henry Comacho. The three men followed her down the hall, past Mother and me, and into the living room, each man giving us a nod of acknowledgment as they went by.

Comacho looked tired. He wore the same jeans and shirt from last night and had dark circles under his eyes. Had he spent the entire night questioning Charles?

Bill and Alan moved straight to Abby while Comacho hung back. Abby noticed Comacho and reached out to draw him closer.

Clasping her hand, Comacho bent low till his head was even with Abby's. She whispered something in his ear.

I was too far away to hear the words, but whatever they were, Comacho found them amusing. He threw back his head and laughed as Abby smiled up at him. Moving away from Abby, he walked up to me.

"May I talk to you?" he asked.

My eyebrows drew together, puzzled. "Sure."

"Let's go outside," he said as he placed his hand on my elbow to guide me.

I led the way to Abby's wide front porch without speaking. We moved across the porch to the swing, where so many times in my dreams, I'd seen Henry and Grandpa talking. A sense of déjà vu came over me, but I brushed it aside. Sitting on the swing, I motioned Henry to join me.

For a few moments we sat, swinging slowly back and forth, enjoying the quiet.

Henry broke the silence. "We questioned Thornton.

Once he started talking," he said, shaking his head in bewilderment, "we couldn't get him to shut up. The guy is paranoid and all night we had to listen to his theories on witches." He shook his head again. "Kept mentioning Cousin Lucy."

My lip curled in disgust. "Yeah, he talked about her in the library too."

"Anyway, along with spouting opinions on witchcraft, he also confessed to everything—Brian's murder, setting Gus on fire, hurting Abby, and murdering Beasley."

"Why did he kill Beasley?"

"Beasley was determined to get something on you, so he tried his old trick of badgering people till they told him what he wanted to know. On Charles. Only this time, the trick didn't work so well. Charles, in his paranoia, was convinced Beasley had found out about him."

"And he killed him," I said, my voice hushed. "What about the woman in Massachusetts?"

"He didn't say anything about her." Henry stared down at his hands resting on his knees. "But after you gave me her name, I called the sheriff's department. Your hunch was right." He lifted his head and his eyes met mine. "The woman did laundry for the Thornton family."

I felt the sadness settle around my heart while I thought of the woman and how she died. "Charles knew her."

"Yes. And she disappeared two months after his mother died. We'll question Charles again and ask about the woman. The sheriff out there is going to question Charles's relatives concerning his whereabouts when the woman disappeared."

"Relatives?" I said with a scowl. "Cousin Lucy?"

"Not likely. She died about a month after his mother.

The sheriff said both sides of Charles's family have medical histories of heart problems that can cause seizures. Cousin Lucy went into a seizure, had a heart attack, and died. In front of Charles, and—"

I interrupted him. "Confirming what she'd told him about *bewitching*. He blamed witchcraft for the death of his mother and cousin and he went after the woman he thought was a witch."

"That's my guess," he said. "When he saw the girl in the library go into the convulsion while talking to you, the scene set him off."

"Witches were afoot," I said, my tone sarcastic.

"Something like that." Henry gently laid a hand on my knee. "It's not your fault. The guy was pretty far around the bend to start with. If it's true about the woman in Massachusetts, he'd already killed once, before that day in the library. He would have killed again. It was only a matter of time."

I gave him a weak smile as he moved his hand away. "I know you're trying to make me feel better, but...?" I sighed. "It's going to take a while to work through the part I played in Brian's death. And Gus's."

He gave a quick nod. "Remember while you're doing that, if it hadn't been for you, we might not have caught him. More people might've died."

He noticed the shocked look on my face. "What? You don't think I can be understanding?"

I laughed. "I haven't seen too much evidence of it since I met you. You're the Iceman, remember?" I replied, teasing him.

A chagrined expression crossed his face. "Yeah, well, there's more to me than what appears on the surface."

Oh, Enrique Comacho, I'm sure there is, I thought, but kept my thought to myself.

"Hey," I said, nudging him, "what did Abby whisper to you?"

Now it was his turn to laugh. "She said I had a nice aura. It doesn't have any holes in it." He looked perplexed. "Whatever that means."

"It means Abby thinks you're a good person," I answered, my voice low.

"Yeah, well she's okay too." He fidgeted in his seat. "So are you, Jensen," he said, averting his eyes.

Comacho sure needed a lot of work on giving compliments.

A comfortable silence settled as we moved back and forth in the swing. I felt the tension and worry of the past few days ease away from me, leaving a sense of peace.

It didn't last long.

Comacho stopped the swing's motion and turned to me. "There's something I want to ask you. Can you do this all the time? Find things, I mean?"

"Do you mean 'things' or do you mean 'bodies'?" I asked, afraid of what his answer would be.

"Bodies, but not always dead ones," he assured me. "People who are missing? Who, maybe if we find fast enough, we can save?"

He didn't have to spell it out for me. I knew what he was asking. He wanted me to tap into my gift to help them with impossible cases. Could I do it? Did I want to do it?

Before I answered, his next words rushed out at me. "See, I've got a couple of files I'd like you to look at—"

I held up a hand stopping him. "Henry, I don't know. I've worked hard to come to terms with my gift, my heritage. I'm just now starting to understand things about my talent, about myself. And truly, I don't know if I can help you."

He looked embarrassed. "Sure, sure," he said, rising quickly. "It was only a thought. Ahh, if you decide you want to try, you've got my card." His eyes darted to his car and I felt the air around us take on a chill while his ice wall crystalized around him. "I'd better go. I've got a lot of paperwork waiting. See you around, Jensen."

Whipping his sunglasses out of his pocket and adjusting them firmly on his face, he moved down the steps to his car. A moment later he was gone.

A couple of hours later, I found myself standing with Abby in the clearing, where a short time ago I had asked for the strength to face my destiny.

The tall weeds had been dry and brittle that night, but now tender shoots of green sprouted from their base. Overhead the branches were covered with new leaves. A sense of complete peace filled the clearing—and me.

"Ahh, it's good to be outside," Abby said, taking a deep breath.

"Aren't you tired from all your company?"

I had questioned the wisdom of walking to the woods, but Abby was insistent. She needed to reconnect with the earth, she said.

Not looking at me, her eyes stared out over the clearing. "No, not now. This recharges me," she said holding her arms wide.

I didn't want to disturb the quiet moment, but I had some questions for her about the past few days.

Reading my mind, she smiled at me. "What do you want to ask me? You look puzzled."

"I guess I am." I gazed off in the distance. "Have you ever heard of a witch bottle?"

"Yes."

"Charles made one to use against me," I said, frowning.

"And he became ill," she said with finality.

"Yeah, you're right," I said with a snap of my fingers. "The next day, when I called him about the flowers, he said he had food poisoning. How did you know?"

"It wasn't food poisoning." She arched an eyebrow. "Think, Ophelia—what are the properties of a fire agate?"

I squinted my eyes while I thought about her question. "It protects the wearer against harm. And if anyone casts negative energy toward the wearer, the energy bounces back at the one who wished ill." My eyes widened. "Of course. Charles got a dose of what he wished for me." I placed my hand on the talisman. "This talisman thing is kind of a handy thing to wear, isn't it?"

Her face lit up with amusement. "Yes, it is. Why do you think I gave it to you?"

"Any other questions?" she asked.

"No, not right now," I replied and let the silence wrap around us.

And in the silence, I felt the peace, the promise of new life everywhere around us. Looking to the horizon, I watched the sun setting in the west. The sky was aflame with colors of rose, mauve, and yellow. An absurd thought popped into my mind.

Grinning, I looked at Abby. "This scene reminds me of an old movie—the murderer's brought to justice, the mystery's solved. We've reached the happily ever after part." I paused. "You know, the part where the heroines ride off into the sunset. Right?"

I watched her strong profile in the fading light while the sun sank lower on the horizon. A trace of a smile played at the corner of her mouth and her green eyes stared out over the quiet clearing.

Taking Abby's hand in mine, I gave it a squeeze and tried again. "We get to ride off into the sunset. Right? Right?"

Her eyes moved to meet mine and one eyebrow arched.

"Not exactly," she replied.

PERENNIAL DARK ALLEY

Men from Boys: A short story collection featuring some of the true masters of crime fiction, including Dennis Lehane, Lawrence Block, and Michael Connelly.
0-06-076285-3

Fender Benders: From **Bill Fitzhugh** comes the story of three people planning on making a "killing" on Nashville's music row.
0-06-081523-X

Cross Dressing: It'll take nothing short of a miracle to get Dan Steele, counterfeit cleric, out of a sinfully funny jam in this wickedly good tale from **Bill Fitzhugh.**
0-06-081524-8

The Fix: Debut crime novelist **Anthony Lee** tells the story of a young gangster who finds himself caught between honor and necessity.
0-06-059534-5

The Pearl Diver: From **Sujata Massey**, antiques dealer and sometime sleuth Rei Shimura travels to Washington D.C. in search of her missing cousin.
0-06-059790-9

The Blood Price: In this novel by **Jonathan Evans**, international trekker Paul Wood must navigate through the world of international people smugglers.
0-06-078236-6

PERENNIAL
DARK ALLEY
An Imprint of HarperCollinsPublishers
www.harpercollins.com

Visit www.AuthorTracker.com for exclusive information on you favorite HarperCollins authors.

DKA 0106